Harley & Rose

a novel

USA *Today* Bestselling Author
CARMEN JENNER

Harley & Rose Published: Carmen Jenner October 18 2016
carmenjennerauthor@gmail.com
Editing: Lauren McKellar
www.laurenkmckellar.com/hire-an-editor
Cover Design: © By Hang Le
www.byhangle.com
Formatting: Be Designs
www.be-designs.com.au

Just always be waiting for me.

— J.M. Barrie, Peter Pan.

For Ben, who saves me every day.

Chapter One
Rose

Weddings are a time of joy, of celebration and love. What they're not supposed to be is miserable. I'd dreamed of this day since I was five years old, and if you'd asked mini me how I saw it going, spending my time drunk and half-naked while my best friend mourned the death of his relationship in the presidential suite of our hotel was not it.

Granted, I also wouldn't have been dressed in canary yellow. I wouldn't have chosen the frangipanis that currently violated the emo-sanctity of this room with their cloying scent and their happy little yellow faces, and I wouldn't have been sitting beside my best friend as he sobbed into my cleavage after the bitch he intended to marry left him for her Krav Maga instructor five minutes before she was supposed to walk down the aisle.

Okay, so Harley wasn't sobbing, and it wasn't as if I just got my boobs out and said, "Here, let my funbags be your comfort in this hour of need." *Yeesh*. It was all far more innocent than that. Harley was simply resting his glorious face on my boobs as I stroked his mane of tawny hair back from his face.

Completely innocent.

Still, my best friend's wedding wasn't supposed to go like this. I should have been the woman gliding toward him at the altar. I'd be a vision in a blush Vera Wang ball-gown with a draped bodice, a sweetheart neckline, and a tossed tulle skirt. My bouquet would be made up of blush peonies, fat white roses, and a spray of pink astilbe. But best of all, we'd say "I do" in front of our friends and family in a vintage-inspired April afternoon ceremony. There would be an ice cream van on standby for peckish guests, and a four-tiered *Glass Slipper Gourmet* cake with cascading roses, peonies and hydrangeas delicately draped all over it. We would dance to our favorite Jeff Buckley song—Lilac Wine—under a sea of stars and paper lanterns at the San Francisco Conservatory of Flowers.

Obviously, I'd given a lot of thought to our wedding.

Fortunately for the both of us, this canary yellow monstrosity wasn't *our* wedding, and praise be to baby Jesus the Wicked Wench of the West Coast is gone. Unfortunately, Harley isn't happy about this fact.

Somewhere in my champagne addled brain, I'm completely aware that no good can come of having Harley cry into my cleavage two hours after he was so unceremoniously dumped at the altar, but

Drunk Rose doesn't care that he's using my boobs in place of a Kleenex.

"She left. The bitch left me at the altar," he says for the millionth time, and I have to keep from smacking him in the head the way I used to when we were kids. *Of course she left him.* She's a money-grubbing whore who has more Gucci clutches than sense.

"I know, Pan," I soothe.

"You're the only one, you know that, right?"

"I know." The only one who understands him? The only one who is always there and never falters? The only one he still loves after all this time? *Yeah, if wishes were horses I'd be a freaking champion rodeo rider.* It doesn't matter which "only one" he means because all of these are true but the last. I'd be his only one for the rest of my days if he'd let me. If he'd just open his damn eyes.

I trace the lines of his face, the puffiness around his eyes, the bridge of his nose, the smooth angles of his cheekbones and his sharp jaw with its coarse stubble. It's nice to be able to touch him like this again without Bitchy Barbie shooting daggers at me. Besides, it's not like touching is a new thing for us. Harley and I have been together since we were five years old. Well, not *together*—obviously, because he was marrying someone else—but together in the sense that we've been best friends since the first day of kindergarten.

The Hamiltons moved into the Edwardian row house next to ours in Noe Valley, San Francisco, two days before the school year started, and Harley's bedroom was directly opposite mine. The day they moved in, he waved through the open window. I poked out my tongue and drew my blinds closed.

The first day back at school, Bryson Hopper pushed me over in the sandpit. Harley helped me up, and then I pushed *him* over. From that day on, we've been pushing one another's buttons. We've also played at other things that don't involve buttons or any kind of clothing, rather a definite lack of.

He shakes his head. "Fuck. I spent a goddamned fortune on this wedding. The caterer still has to be paid for all the goddamn food that we didn't eat, not to mention the venue, the musicians, and the flowers."

"The flowers were a gift from me and if you so much as think about trying to give me money for them, I will hurt you, Harley."

"They were beautiful; you know?" His head is in my lap now, causing my stomach muscles and other things farther down to tighten and ache. "Your creations always are."

"Well, I may have caved on the bridal party frangipanis, but no way was I going to let her get away with covering every surface of the venue with them. Can you imagine looking back at those pictures in ten years' time?" I ask, exasperated. Harley doesn't say a thing because he knows how I get around brides with the wrong choice of flowers. You want the happiest day of your life to appear timeless and beautiful, not as if you attended some busted-ass Malibu Barbie luau. And if that is your thing, then you need a new thing ... and possibly the help of someone like Dale Tutela. That man is a god with event planning.

"If I had my way entirely it would have been gorgeous," I say breathlessly, dreaming of the wedding I'd been planning for over half my life. I glance down at Harley, whose expression seems so hollow, his bright blue eyes haunted, it breaks my heart into a million pieces. On the flipside, some of the pieces of my shattered heart are jumping for joy. This makes me a horrible friend because I shouldn't be happy right now. I shouldn't be, but I am. My best friend is heartbroken, dumped at the altar, and I'm drunk and exulted. I should point out that he's drunk too, so it's not as if I'm popping champagne bottles and toasting to a life of him being alone, but even so, guilt worms its way through my gut because this started out as the happiest day of his life and the worst of mine, and somehow everything got turned upside-down.

"What am I supposed to do?" Harley whispers.

"There's nothing you can do. Except open another bottle of this fine champagne that the strumpet's parents paid for." I hold up the booze in question and clink it heavily against the open bottle in his own hand that's mostly gone untouched. "Then, you're going to lick your wounds and hop a flight to Hawaii where you can spend the entire week of what was supposed to be your honeymoon sprawled out in that big beautiful bed. You can sleep all day, eat delicious food, drink cocktails, and when you decide to move there permanently you won't even complain when your best friend comes to live in your spare room."

"Come with me."

I inhale sharply. "What? Oh no. No that's a very bad idea."

"Why? How is it any different from the two of us taking the weekend to drive down to Big Sur, or going to the cottage without the parentals?"

"Okay for a start, this isn't Carmel or Big Sur, it's Hawaii." I rest my free hand on his chest. The hurried *thwamp, thwamp, thwamp*, beneath my palm causes my own heart to skip a few beats. "Secondly, it's your honeymoon, Pan. I can't go on your honeymoon with you."

"It's kind of hard to have a honeymoon without a bride."

I pat the side of his face and he leans into my hand. "No one would understand. You've got to do this alone, Harley."

"Fuck everyone else. I don't want to do it alone," Harley snaps. I flinch a little and he exhales loudly. His eyes slide shut, and his voice is tender and miserable when he says, "The last thing I need is to be alone right now."

"You can't take another woman on your honeymoon. It's … bad luck. Besides, I have the shop, and I doubt very much that I'll be able to get my own room at such short notice."

His eyes spring open, and he glares at me. "Why the fuck would you get your own room?"

"Because we cannot sleep together."

"Why?"

My eyes dart around the luxurious suite, looking for something, anything that constitutes as a valid excuse. Once again, my focus settles on my boobs. "I'm self-conscious."

Harley snorts. "About what? Your snoring? That shit's not news, Rose. We've slept together a bunch of times."

"Things are different now—"

"What's different? That you have a killer rack? I've seen it all. It's not like I'm going to freak out because you have girly bits. Been there, tapped that, remember?"

"Yeah, I remember." *Oh god, did I remember*. His deft hands, soft lips, scratchy stubble, the weight of his hips as they pressed into mine, and the deliciously melty slide of our respective boy and girl bits coming together. The way his mouth tips up in the corner in a satisfied smirk right after he comes. I remember it all too well, and that's exactly why this is a bad idea.

"Please?" He begs, and his voice is ragged with emotion. My heart squeezes. "I can't do this alone. Come with me."

Oh I want to. I want to come and come and ... Goddamn him. I'm about to make the biggest mistake of my life, because I never can say no to Harley, and he knows it. He tilts his head and sends me these stupid puppy-dog eyes that have always been my undoing—they've always led me into one disaster after another. It's why I call him Pan. He's the original lost boy, and he's always been so damn good at getting me to follow behind him like a lovesick Wendy with Peter.

"Please?" he whispers, and I'm done for. *Manipulative bastard.*

I shake my head and let out a resigned sigh. "When do we leave?"

Harley looks at his watch. "Fuck, like four hours."

"You owe me," I warn.

"Yeah, I'll owe you. I'll give you anything you want—I'll build you a goddamn monument in Golden Gate Park for being the best friend a man could have, just please, Rose, please don't make me go on my own."

"Fine," I say, grinning. "But I get the window seat." I shove him off my lap and slowly, and very carefully—in other words, drunkenly—get to my feet.

Harley grunts and lays his head back down on the floor. "Where the hell are you going?"

"To pack, dumbass. I got a plane to catch."

"Don't leave," he whines, snaking a hand around my foot. "We'll buy you shit when we get there. All you need are a couple of bikinis."

I shake him off and shoot him a look that says he should quickly shut up. He does, grinning for a moment before it's lost to the shadow of despair that smothers the light from his eyes. "I'll swing by in an hour to pick you up. Don't fall asleep."

"Don't fall asleep," he murmurs. "Got it."

"You have everything you need, right?"

"Everything but my wife." He raises his champagne bottle in a toast. "Cheers to that."

Inwardly, I cringe, but on the outside I just smile and say, "Pan, by the time we're done with this pseudo-moon, you'll have forgotten all about the woman who left you at the altar. I'll make sure of it."

With another warning about him falling asleep, I fix my dress, smooth my hair, and leave the room. I practically bowl over the bell boy who's wheeling a cart with champagne, strawberries, and what looks like a pound of chocolate fudge towards room 317. "Oh, shit. No one cancelled that order, huh?"

"I'm sorry?" Bell boy asks. He has a baby face and strawberry blond hair, and he's cute in that boy-next-door sort of way. Well, maybe not in *my* boy-next-door way, because the boy who lived next door to me was, and still is—thank you, Jesus—a complete fucking knockout.

"You're taking that to 317, right?"

"Yes, Mr. Hamilton asked that it be promptly delivered to the room at eight p.m."

"Yeah, here's the thing," I say. "When Mr. Hamilton ordered that, he was unaware his bride-to-be was a lying, cheating skank who would leave him at the altar. So at the risk of him losing his shit and trashing his hotel room, it's probably best if you just turn around and take that back to the kitchen."

The boy stares at me like I just kicked him in the shin. "But it's already been paid for …"

I pluck the pearly white "congratulations" card off the tray and fish out a pen from my clutch. "I tell you what—why don't you take this to room 313? Her parents are staying just down the hall." I make a lazy hand gesture in the direction of their suite, though for all I know I could have been pointing towards the service elevator because the man-child in the monkey suit is staring down the hall, looking confused. "Maybe they could use a drink after their daughter ran out on her fifty-thousand-dollar wedding."

"I don't think I can do that ..."

"Of course you can." I place the newly edited card back on the tray and remove a couple of bills, shoving them in his shirt pocket. He balks when he reads my scrawled handwriting defacing the pristine card.

Congratulations!
Your daughter's a whore.

"I can't give them that." The man-child shakes his head, and I lower my own to be able to read his name tag. Is it possible to suddenly become dyslexic? Because I think this might be a thing. Bran. That's a weird-ass name, and in a city full of hipsters, you hear a lot of weird-ass names.

"Bran," I slur, and throw an arm around his shoulder as if we're buddies from way back.

"It's Brian, actually."

"Bra-in," I correct and screw my face up, wondering why his parents would choose such a difficult name for their child. "I'll give you all the money in my purse if you take that card and that cart to room 313."

"Ma'am—"

I gasp loudly. The sound echoes down the empty hall. "You did not just call me ma'am. So not cool, dude. I'm young-ish. I'm hip, and I have totally great tits." I grab the boobs in question and jiggle them to prove my point.

He licks his lips in what looks like a nervous gesture, his gaze darting to my cleavage and back to my face as if he's afraid I might slap him for his efforts. "You … you do. You have totally great tits."

"Right?" I agree. "You can't call a woman who has great tits 'ma'am'. It's soul destroying."

"Sorry," he says, but Bran doesn't sound sorry at all.

I pluck a strawberry from the tray and dip it in chocolate, shoving the whole thing in my mouth while making the universal sign with raised brows and a bobbing head for *this shit is good*. "Come on, man. Just take the cart to 312, pleeease?"

"Er … you said 313."

"Exactly." I throw up my hands in exasperated agreeance, stumble around the not-so-bright man-child known as Bran, and wander off down the hall to the elevator, smiling all the while because I'd be lying if I said I wasn't happy my best friend isn't wearing a wedding ring on his finger right now.

Who gets married in February anyway? That might be fine if you live in Canada and are okay with freezing off your lady parts at a white winter wedding, but a San Franciscan wedding? No. Not unless you're hoping your bride will just up and float away on the next big gust of wind. Turns out we didn't need the San Franciscan weather to lose Harley's fiancée, but that didn't matter, because this was never meant to be his wedding day. And he was never meant to walk down the aisle with that trollop by his side.

One day, it will be me watching the way his eyes crinkle at the corners and brim with tears as I walk toward him. One day, it will be my ring he wears and I, his. One day, I'll marry my best friend.

I just need a little time to convince him of that.

Chapter Two
Rose

I turn my key in the lock and stumble through the front door of my shop, Darling Buds. Yes, the name may have been inspired by our shared love of J.M. Barrie's *Peter Pan*, but ten years of playing Wendy Darling to Harley's Peter will do that to a girl, I suppose. Just to annoy the ever-loving crap out of my very best friend, I like to say it came from H.E. Bates' novel, The Darling Buds of May. I think he knows that isn't true.

Darling Buds is a tiny little store with a studio apartment above it on 24th Street. It's sandwiched between a kitschy home décor boutique and an independent bookstore, and located just a half a block down from the smallest Wholefoods you've ever seen. And the best part about living where I work? No daily commute. It's just a few doors down from Harley's apartment too, which is why I'll never move. Unless of course he does.

I've always loved flowers; I've loved to put my hands into the soil and grow things ever since I was a kid. When Harley was running his Tonka trucks through the dirt, I was planting blades of grass and imagining they'd flower into luscious, fat rosebuds, or a beanstalk that led to the sky. Much to my mother's dismay, when it was time to say goodbye at my Grammy's funeral, I was found rearranging the wreaths and the coffin spray— because everybody knows you don't put daffodils in a mixed bouquet, and if they hadn't known, they did now.

I gather my face products, toothbrush and toothpaste, and a few low-maintenance items of makeup, placing them in a travel bag and throwing them on the bed, then I take my suitcase from out of the cupboard and start randomly tossing in articles of clothing. I'm choosing between two pairs of swimsuits when a key slides into the lock downstairs. My parents are the only ones with a key so I don't give too much thought as to what they're doing here and I continue packing.

"Well she must be here; the lights are on," my mother says, presumably to my dad.

"Mom?"

"Oh, Rose, good you're here. She's here, Herb."

"I heard," Dad says matter-of-factly, as my mother's footsteps echo up the stairs. "Alright, bring them in."

I race out to the landing and almost collide with my mother on the staircase overlooking the shop. She's switched out her deep navy Tadashi Shoji cord-embroidered lace cocktail dress for a velour hot pink track suit with Juicy stamped over her ass. For a woman who owns basically every wrap dress that Diane Von Furstenberg ever put out, I'm surprised the two items coexist peacefully in her wardrobe. Embarrassing leisurewear aside, my mother has impeccable taste; she's like the Blythe Danner of SF. My dad, on the other hand? Not so much. He wears argyle sweater vests all year around, unless of course there's a function to attend, and then he swaps argyle for tweed. Today he's in a burgundy velour Adidas tracksuit. *What is happening with my parents right now?* Did someone put LSD in my champagne? My dad is also, I note, having delivery guys bring in all of the arrangements from the wedding. Harley's wedding.

"Ah, what's going on?" I demand while my mother parks herself in front of me on the top stair.

"We thought we'd bring these back. Seems a terrible waste not to resell them."

"They were a gift, Mom," I explain. I don't have time to go into detail about the fact that I can't resell flowers that have already been cut and wreathed, or the centerpieces that will start to droop in a few hours' time.

"Yes, and the wedding was called off. Traditionally, if a wedding doesn't go ahead, people get their gifts back."

"Mom, you can't give back flower arrangements. I can't sell these. They've been at the hotel all day, and they'll start dying off pretty soon."

"Oh relax." She waves me away with a lazy hand gesture. "Rochelle said to bring them back here. They're devastated, by the way. How's Harley holding up?"

"Well, let's see, his fiancée left him at the altar and he's been humiliated in front of two hundred friends, relatives, and strangers. How do you think he is?"

"Poor boy. Still, he dodged a bullet if you ask me. I knew that whore wasn't going to go through with it; I could see she had cold feet from a mile away."

"Mom!" I chastise.

"Well, it's true." She shoos me back up the stairs and because I know my parents, and I know that there's no halting the disaster going on downstairs, I trudge back to my suitcase and continue loading it up with things. I don't know what things, because so far I'm definite on the fact I have toiletries in my bag and possibly one T-shirt—everything else, I'm not sure about.

There's a crash from downstairs. I listen for a beat. I don't hear muffled curses or panicked screams because someone fell through a window, so I carry on packing, but shoot my mother a stern look. "Will you please tell Dad not to break anything?"

"Where are you going?" My mother eyes my case suspiciously. "And why aren't you with Harley?"

"I'm closing the store for a few days. I need a break, and I can't trust anyone to run this place without me, so I'm going—"

"What am I, chopped liver?" she interrupts.

"What do you mean you're closing the store?" My dad booms from below. "Time is money, honey. You think Saks 5th Avenue closes its doors because they need a day off?"

"A flower shop is a little bit different than Saks, Dad. I have a regular clientele of twenty-five; I'm not even in the same universe as Saks."

"Still, there's only one way they got to be so big."

I sigh and rub my temple. "Ugh. I don't … I don't have time for any of this."

"Well what's the rush?" Mom asks, frowning as she looks around my tiny apartment. "Why are you fleeing in the middle of the night like a hardened criminal? Why can't you leave tomorrow?"

"Because our flight leaves three hours from now, and it's going to take me forty-five minutes to get across town."

"Our flight? Just who are you going away with?"

I close my eyes because I know what's

coming.

When I open them again, my mother is looking at me with a horror-stricken expression. "Oh, Rose. You're not?"

"He asked. What was I supposed to do?"

"He asked you if he could put his penis in your vagina when you were five, too, but did you let him? No."

"Please don't talk about my daughter's vagina," Dad rumbles from down below. "Wait, you met a man?"

I drive my fingers into my hair, messing up the carefully coiffed style that a hairdresser had spent close to an hour on. I'm not even completely sober yet, and already I have a hangover. "I'm going away with Harley, Dad."

"Oh, alright then," he mutters, and goes back to instructing the men banging around in my shop.

"She's going on his honeymoon," my mother shouts, as if I'm not standing three feet away. "You cannot do this, Rose. Herb, will you please talk some sense into your daughter?"

"You're making a big deal about nothing." I head back to my chest of drawers to avoid her all-seeing stare. The woman throws more shade than the queens in *RuPaul's Drag Race*. "He's my best friend, and he's heartbroken. He doesn't want to go alone."

"So tell him to take Rochelle."

"Okay, the only thing worse than not going on your honeymoon with your new wife is going with your mother."

"Why doesn't he just cash in the tickets?"

"Because maybe he needs a break from all the questions he's about to face. Mom, I've never said a thing when it came to you butting into my life, but I'm putting my foot down with this. Harley is my friend; I'm going away with him in a friendly capacity. We're just two friends in Hawaii, soaking up the sun, drinking Mai Tais on the beach and trying to forget all about the whore who broke his heart."

The more I try to convince her, the more I convince myself. *We need this.* We both work too hard, and since Alecia shimmied her way between us a year ago, Harley and I have been slowly drifting apart. A vacation in paradise is exactly what we need.

My mother brushes past me and grabs my hand, leading me into the entrance of my kitchen. "And I might even believe that, if I were anyone else. But I know you, Rose Perry, and I know you've been in love with that boy since the first day of kindergarten."

That isn't exactly true. I haven't been in love with Harley all this time—just most of it. I'd had other lovers, and I've had periods when I didn't even like Harley, much less love him. Granted, now isn't one of those times, but she's way off base. Okay, maybe she's not *way* off, just mostly off base.

"Have you thought about what this will do to you?"

"We've been on plenty of vacations. We're adults." I argue, but my protestations sound flimsy, even to me. "He's broken-hearted."

"And what are you?"

"I'm fine," I say, at a much higher decibel than necessary. "And I really do need to go pack."

"So pack. Don't let me stop you."

And I don't, though I sort of wish I did because every swimsuit I put in my bag my mother wrinkles her nose at over the expensive glass of wine she's commandeered from my kitchen. The same one I'd planned on opening and drinking myself into a stupor with after this god-awful wedding.

I take the bottle from the nightstand and swig it right from the lip. I'm going to need all the Dutch courage I can get if I'm going to get through the next few hours of this night without giving my mother's words too much thought.

Chapter Three

Rose

After my mother consumes half the bottle and I practically inhale the cup of coffee my dad makes me on the store's espresso machine that cost twice as much as my rent a month, I leave the shop in a cab, and both my heart and bloodstream have sobered some on the way downtown to pick up Harley. When I try to rouse him—the bastard has in fact fallen asleep—he isn't any more enthusiastic about the trip now than he was an hour ago. Though he has been a little more enthusiastic about the champagne I'd left him with because he'd been out cold with one empty bottle lying on the coffee table and another spilling over the carpet. I pick up his clothes from the floor and toss them into his suitcase. And then I throw him in the shower and go downstairs to get him a coffee and settle the extra on the cleaning bill.

By the time I reach the room with two coffees in tow, Harley is miraculously out of the shower, but the hot water hasn't sobered him at all. He sits in a towel on the edge of the bed, swigging from the champagne bottle that had been leaking all over the floor.

"Okay mister, let's put the booze away, because champagne has never been your friend, and we have a plane to catch." I set my coffee down and replace the bottle in his hand with a steaming paper cup.

He lifts it to his mouth but doesn't drink it. "She left me."

My shoulders fall in defeat. "I know, honey."

"I can't say I blame her, but still, she said forever, you know?"

I sit down on the bed beside him and wrap my arm around his shoulder. Beads of water from his skin soak through my sleeves, but I just hold him tighter. "Then she wasn't right for you. I know it hurts now; it's going to hurt for a while longer yet—"

"Who is?"

"What?"

He straightens, causing my arm to slip from his wet skin, and looks me dead in the eye when he says, "Who is right for me?"

Me. I'm right for you. I'm the woman you should have been marrying.

I glance down at the coffee I'm nursing. "I don't know, but I'm sure she's out there somewhere."

Harley hands me his paper cup and stands. He adjusts his towel, walks over to his suitcase, and stares at his belongings, but he doesn't make a move to put on any of the clothes. "Maybe this isn't such a good idea."

No, no, no. This is a great idea. The best ever idea.

"Come on. You need this. *I* need this. Let's just go and have fun. You remember fun, right? We used to have a lot of it before we started paying taxes and having brunch with our accountants, and before fiancées came along."

"Fiancée," he corrects. "It's not like you were getting married and left at the altar."

Ouch.

"Right, well, before she came along we used to have fun. Let's get back to that. We'll drink Mai Tais on the beach, we'll tan until we resemble lobsters, and then we'll just laze around the pool all day and pretend this whole wedding thing didn't exist."

"Yeah," he says with a small decisive nod. "Fuck Alecia."

"Thatta boy. Now get dressed. Or we're going to be late."

After we've checked out and organized for the cases of champagne to be delivered to Harley's apartment, we hail a cab, clear security and make it to our gate with thirty minutes to spare. Once we've boarded, Harley settles himself in his seat, flips the armrest up between us, and is out like a light in a matter of minutes. I spend the next two hours of the flight stricken with guilt and ruminating over the fact that I had a chance to talk him out of this and I passed it up for purely selfish reasons. I'm a horrible best friend. I'm the very worst of the worst.

I toss and turn in my chair, trying to get comfortable. I pick up a book and read a little but it's one of those violent yet oddly satisfying motorcycle club stories with a convoluted plot, and I don't have the patience for that now, so I close the book and stroke the tattooed back of the model on the cover. I try to get a little shut-eye, but I'm more worried about Harley slipping into a coma than the bags I'm going to have under my eyes tomorrow, so I stay awake and watch him sleep. On a creeper level of stalkerish things one can do to earn the title of psychopath when it comes to the object of one's desire, I'm guessing I'm about at an eight. Though I'm wondering if the fact that I convinced him to take me on his honeymoon means I hit an even ten before we left the city. Either way, I watch Harley sleep until I eventually drift off too, and I find myself being gently shaken awake by a hand on my shoulder. "Rose, wake up."

I open my eyes and snuggle into his warmth, rubbing my hand against his solid stomach. Harley must have been working out harder than usual. He's always been in great shape, but this feels … different. Like he did when he played varsity football. Harley's hand grasps my fist and squeezes tightly. He groans and whispers in my ear, "Fuck, Rose."

And I realize that it's not his stomach at all that I'm stroking but his crotch instead, and what's worse still is that his own hand is wedged between my thighs. He's not touching me as inappropriately as I'm touching him, of course, but it seems that while we slept our bodies conspired against us and decided to assume our old sleeping positions.

Because vacationing in paradise wasn't torture enough for my sad little penis starved vagina.

I yank free from his grasp and glare until he removes his own hand from between my thighs, what he used to refer to as "his spot". "I am so sorry."

He just gives a chuckle and straightens in his chair. "Don't worry about it; it's not like we haven't done it before, right?"

He's right. We've woken like this several times in the past when he's fallen asleep at my place or me at his. It's always awkward, and every time it happened I've been terrified he'll read more into my embarrassment than I want him to see.

I laugh nervously and say, "Yeah, happens all the time."

"Remember that one time—"

"Yeah, Harley, I remember," I interrupt, because no matter which incident he's about to refer to, all of our trips down memory lane hurt.

"Right," Harley says, and just like that the humor of this situation is gone, replaced instead by the bitterness of rejection and the sting of missed opportunity. It's a never-ending cycle with us, and one he should know better than to dig up.

Chapter Four

Rose

We check into our hotel around noon and find our way up to the suite. Harley hands me the key and I slip it in the door, opening it wide. I don't make it two steps before I'm dropping my bags and running for the balcony. I shriek like a little kid entering the gates at Disney when I throw open the door and take in the view. Nothing but resorts, crystal clear aquamarine water, and pristine white beach for miles, all the way to the big, beautiful Diamond Head Volcano.

"Holy shit! Get over here and look at this view, Pan." I turn and lean against the balcony railing, craning my head back. I close my eyes as the sun kisses my face and the excited squeals of children filter up to us from the resort pools below.

"It's really something," he agrees. His expression is somber as he sits down on the huge king-size mattress, and I feel my own heart fall when I realize how insensitive I'm being. Roses are strewn all over the white comforter and a bottle of champagne sits in an ice bucket beside the bed. I'm not here on vacation with the man I'm in love with, I'm here as his best friend, the woman charged with lifting his spirits—or buying him spirits—since I'm the one who's supposed to get him drunk and help him forget all about making the worst decision of his life.

"Shit, I'm sorry. I'm not helping here at all, am I?" I throw my purse on the bed beside him and pick up the bottle, popping the cork on the champagne. I reach for one of the long-stemmed glasses before realizing I should just hand him the whole thing. So I do. He accepts it, his fingers brushing my own and his gaze locking on mine. Kamikaze butterflies whirl and crash inside my stomach as I stare down at him. The moment stretches on, our hands briefly touching, our eyes saying everything while our mouths remain tightly closed.

The hotel phone rings, the spell is broken, and I disappear into the bathroom, locking myself away in order to catch my breath. This isn't what he needs right now. He needs time, he needs a friend, and he needs liquor—lots and lots of liquor. When I'm done giving myself the third degree, I exit the bathroom and make a beeline for my purse.

"We need alcohol," I say, as if I've been madly gathering supplies for the apocalypse and forgot the most important thing. "I'm going to go in search of booze. Lots of booze."

"Okay." Harley nods. "I'm just gonna take a shower and get some sleep."

"Oh. Well, I could stay with you if you want?" I ask, hopefully.

He kisses the top of my head when he passes on his way to the bathroom. "I'm good. You go."

"Are you sure? I don't mind."

"Rose," he says, and I know he's reaching the end of his patience with me because that's what it means when he says my name and it sounds like a curse.

"Okay, I guess I'll be sipping cocktails by the pool if you change your mind."

"I'll see you later." And just like that he's gone, disappeared into the bathroom and running the shower.

I strip off my clothes, figuring I've only got a few minutes because Harley doesn't waste water. I rummage through my bag and find one of the few bathing suits that my mother approved of. It's a black 50s-style Marilyn Monroe halter suit, with the ruched front panel that hides all my flaws. It's not like I have a paunch or anything, but as I mentioned earlier, I ain't getting any younger, and gravity is a fucking bitch who needs to die a very slow and very painful death at the hand of botched surgery.

I wiggle into my suit, throw on a cover-up and grab a towel, and then I make my way out of the room and down to the pool area. There are bodies everywhere, tons of kids with bright neon pool donuts, their parents tanning by the poolside. I head straight for the bar, order a Blue Hawaii, and ask them to keep 'em coming. And then I stretch out on a lounger and sun myself as if heat stroke and skin cancer aren't possibilities.

After I've drained dry my third cocktail, some douchebag blocks my sun. I open my eyes, prepared to ask the person to move on, politely of course, but then I get dripped on and since I can't tell if it's water or sweat—or God forbid some other type of bodily fluid—I feel bolder than I ordinarily would about expressing my annoyance.

"Hey, asshole," I say, sliding my sunglasses onto my head. My mouth drops open.

"Rose, I thought that was you," says a very familiar voice.

I know who this is without looking at his face, and the reason I haven't looked at his face yet is because I'm stuck. My eyes are literally glued to the bulge outlined against his wet swim trunks. It really doesn't help when my gaze trails a little higher and I'm greeted with a very nice six-pack. Roaming just a little bit higher now, I see two perfectly defined pecs, tanned with lovely bitable oval-shaped nipples. I have a thing about nipples. Too small, and it's a major turn off. Too big, and I'm wondering whether or not you'll be the one to breastfeed my children when I eventually have them. But this guy? He has the Holy Grail of nipples, not too large, not too small, not all shriveled up, even though he clearly just slid out of the pool, and certainly not ones that prove his age.

I know his age, or thereabouts, as he's a regular of mine. Just like I know he's happily married, because I'm the girl who gets to arrange his lucky, lucky wife the huge bouquet of lilies every week.

"Oh god, Mr. Carter. I am so sorry," I say, sitting up and folding my legs under me.

"It's fine." Warm brown eyes study me as he smiles. Mr. Carter looks like he just stepped off the set of a Hugo Boss commercial. He's always dressed impeccably in a tailored suit, his dark hair graying at the temples. He might be closer to fifty than thirty, but the man is fine, and seeing him ditch the suit for a pair of swim trunks? Yowza. When I tell Izzy—my employee of one year, and the closest thing I have to a girlfriend—about this, she will lose her shit. "I came and dripped water all over you; I was an asshole."

A nervous laugh bubbles up out of my throat. "I'm … I'm really sorry."

"Relax, Rose, and how many times must I tell you to call me Dermot?"

"Dermot, right. Sorry. Again." I shift on my recliner, itching to reach for my cover-up because while I know he's happily married, and while I might be a good fifteen years younger than him, I still become skittish around this silver fox. Seeing the fantastic body beneath the suit doesn't help with my own self-consciousness, and I make a mental note to buy a thigh master when I get home and use it. A lot.

From dawn 'til dusk, work keeps me busy. There are buckets of water to be refreshed and bunches of flowers to be sorted, and with all those trips in and out of the van, it's not like I'm sitting on my ass all day letting it get bigger, but there's nothing like a tropical vacation when you've been working on your winter fat stores by benching a pint of Ben & Jerry's a day to really boost your self-esteem.

"So what are you doing here?" I ask at the same time as he says, "What brings you to Waikiki?"

"I'm here with a friend." I tuck my hair behind my ear and shield my eyes in order to see him better.

Dermot crouches down beside my lounger. "And where is she?"

I give a nervous laugh and pray he hasn't seen the bright red spots of color that flare on my cheeks. "He's up in the room."

Dermot's brows shoot up, but he schools his features and politely says, "Is he a *friend* friend?"

While I know it's none of his business, I find myself answering anyway. "My best friend, actually."

"Kind of a romantic destination for friends, isn't it?"

"Actually we're on his honeymoon."

He laughs, and then his eyes grow wide when he realizes I'm not kidding. "I'm going to need you to repeat that for me."

"I know, it seems totally skeezy, but it's really not. His fiancée left him at the altar, and he's really sad right now so…"

"So you just thought you'd tag along on his honeymoon and torment him some more?"

"I'm hardly tormenting him," I protest but he interrupts.

"Trust me, if he's seen you in that suit, then he's definitely tormented."

Now it may be the sun beating down upon us, the three drinks that I've had, or the fact that the alcohol barely had time to leave my bloodstream before I began pumping it in again, but that actually makes me a little swoony. I know it's a line from a married man, but it's a man, a very handsome man, and it's been a lifetime since anyone complimented me like this. So this bitch is gonna swoon like a whore in church at the second coming of Christ, and no one can say shit about it.

"It's nothing like that."

"Whatever you say, Miss Perry," he says, the barest hint of a smile forming on his lips. He runs his hand along the wet, rigid indents of his abs and my eyes slowly follow the movement. "Well, it's good to see you, but I should get washed up and ready for dinner."

And I'm going upstairs to take a really cold shower. "Enjoy," I tell him.

"Let's do drinks while we're here, yes? You'll bring your *friend* friend who in no way wants to fuck you."

I gasp at the abruptness of his words. Don't get me wrong—I swear like a damn sailor, but it's so unexpected from Dermot, so base and primal that my head is automatically filled with visions of him shoving me onto my hands and knees in his hotel suite and taking me from behind. *Jesus.* I squeeze my thighs together to ward away the ache between my legs.

"I'll let the missus know and she can finally meet the woman who creates such beautiful bouquets for her every week."

"Sure, sounds great." I plaster on a fake smile. I can't think of anything worse than meeting his lovely wife when I've just fantasized about her husband coming inside me. *Who the hell does that*?

With a nod, Dermot leaves and I hold my breath as I watch him go, right up until he disappears into the lobby of our building.

Somewhat guiltily, I cast my gaze up to our balcony. Harley stands there watching me, and though I can't be one hundred percent sure from this many stories away, he looks pissed. I give him a nervous wave and he turns and stalks back into the room. Okay. Clearly he's not feeling any better after a shower and a nap. I want to go to him, but I know he needs time so I slide my sunglasses back into place and close my eyes.

When I've had entirely too much sun, and the noise from the other vacationers makes me stabby, I gather my things, head to the bar and grab a couple of takeaway frozen margaritas, and ride the elevators back upstairs. The curtains are drawn, the AC is blasting cool air around the room, and Harley is lying on the bed completely naked.

Holy shit. I can't see anything other than his firm ass, long, muscled torso, and brown curls that are spread out around him as he lies face-down on the pillow, but it's enough. He hasn't even bothered to pull the sheet up, and as I stand there gaping at him, I gulp back half of my margarita in one go.

My gaze slides down his length and back up, and I jump when I realize he's staring at me. I also lose a little of my frozen margarita. "What are you doing?" he whispers.

"Er … I …" I decide words are no longer my friend and I drown out any other pathetic excuse I might have had by swallowing down the rest of my margarita and consuming half of his. I set my empty cup on the counter above the bar fridge and offer him the half-drunk margarita.

"I brought you booze," I say cheerfully, when I've recovered my composure. He sits up in order to take the drink from my hand, and he's not the only thing sitting up because his cock is awake, hard, and practically waving at me. "Oh." I shield my eyes. I may or may not have peeked through my splayed fingers though. "You're um ..." I point towards his groin with the other hand. "You're ... er ... you're—"

"Jesus, Rose. It's okay; you can say I've got wood. You should know better than anyone that it doesn't bite."

"Why are you naked?"

"I was sleeping. You know I can't sleep with clothes on."

"Yes, but I'm here."

"And you've seen it before." He shrugs. "You two were getting close on the plane a few hours ago—are you really freaking out about my junk now?"

"I'm not freaking out."

"You sure?" He grins, and I have to fight the urge to throw something at his head. "'Cause it kind of looks like you're freaking out."

"I am not freaking out. I see penis all the time."

"Really?" He stands up, and I find an awful lot of interest in my phone sitting on the counter because I can see in my peripheral that it's coming closer. "When was the last time you touched one?"

"Not long ago," I snap. "Would you put some clothes on please?"

"Jesus, you're uptight."

"I'm not uptight." We're touching now, his body leaning into mine, his erection hot as it presses against the fabric of my cover-up, and I find I didn't even need to leave the room in order to get my suit wet.

"You know you can touch it if you want?" Harley whispers. "Be like old times?"

"I don't want to touch it," I say. *Oh, but I do*. I want to touch it so bad that my hand practically twitches. "Put some fucking clothes on, Harley."

"You know you've always been cute when you're flustered." He presses a kiss to my temple.

I swat him away. "Shut up."

Harley snags the set of shorts he had on earlier from the pile of clothes on the floor and slides them on. "We're gonna need more booze."

Yes, we are.

Chapter Five
Rose

Age thirteen

"Hey," Harley says, walking through the back door instead of scaling the fence that separates our yards the way he normally would. I ignore him as my hands dig into the rich soil, sifting it through my fingers as if the small clumps of earth were grains of sand. Running out. Time is always running out. "Your mom told me about your grandma."

"Did she tell you I wanted to be alone?"

"Do the parentals ever tell us anything useful?"

I shrug. "My mom told me about the birds and the bees once; it's how I learned that bees were tiny little flower rapists, and I made it my mission to swat the bastards every time I saw one."

"I knew you hated bees for a reason." He laughs, sitting down beside me in the soft grass and picking up a seed pod. "What are we planting?"

"Paperwhites, Grams always loved those."

"I remember."

Harley uses his hands to smooth away the

top layer of soil and teases the roots before laying it in the shallow bed he created. I love that he knows how to do this without being told because he's watched me plant bulbs from the narcissus family for years, and he paid attention, even when I thought he wasn't. Sometimes I think he enjoys gardening as much as I do, though he'd never admit it. I pick up a bulb, disrupt the roots and place it in the soil beside his.

We work in silence until all the bulbs are planted and I sit back with tears in my eyes because in thirty days we'll have flowers that my Grams would have loved, only she won't be here to see them. "Do you think we know when we're about to die?"

"Jesus, Rose," he says softly. A beat later, he stands up with his hands on his hips and in his best Peter Pan accent—which is always perfect because we've watched that movie more times than we've jumped off my parents' balcony onto the trampoline below—he says, "I'll never die."

"Yes, you will. One day we'll all die." I pick up the watering can and shower the bulbs so the roots have a better chance of growing. "I just hope I go first."

"Why?" Harley glances down at me with an eyebrow cocked and a troubled expression.

I set the can on the grass and brush my hands off on my clothes. I don't bother going inside to wash them, because I've always loved the feel of soil caking in the whorls and loops of my fingerprints. "Because I wouldn't want to be here if you weren't."

"Then we'll die together," he proclaims, pulling me to my feet and climbing up onto the trampoline, forcing me to go with him or lose an arm in the process. He turns us to face the empty backyard and shouts, "To die will be—"

"An awfully big adventure," we both finish, as he falls onto the trampoline and I fall right alongside him.

Harley pulls me into the crook of his arm and kisses the top of my head. "I'm sorry about your grandma, Wendy."

I shove at his chest for calling me that stupid name, but just as I'm reminding myself to be as indifferent as Peter and as courageous as Tiger Lily, I burst into tears. Harley holds me close. I like the feel of his arms around me.

Through wet lashes I stare up at him, and he does the most surprising thing ever—he kisses me. At first it's nothing more than the gentle press of his lips against mine, but within seconds it changes into more. His tongue pushes into my mouth and slides against my own, coaxing as I lay there paralyzed with fear. For years I've dreamed about this moment. I've dreamed that he'd kiss me, and that it would feel like fireworks exploding. But now that the moment is here, I'm frozen.

He places his hand on my cheek and rubs his thumb back and forth. I like the way this feels, this tender touch, so new, so different. Sparks form low in my belly, shooting off in every direction until I feel it—the fireworks every Hollywood movie ever promised me. I take his face in my hands and force his lips back to mine, but a gasp ruins it all.

I scramble to one end of the trampoline. Harley scrambles to the other and my mom laughs her light, tinkling laugh. "Don't stop on account of me, darlings."

Mortified, I bury my face in my hands and feel Harley's weight shift off of the trampoline. Dirt is smeared on his cheeks from my fingertips, and it makes me smile because they look like a brand. "That's okay, Evelyn. I have to go practice drills anyway. I'm trying out for the team on Monday."

"You are?" I'm not sure why, but there's a hard edge to my voice when I ask this question. Harley used to play in the pee wee league in elementary school, but he hurt his knee at nine years old and Rochelle forced him to give it up. He hasn't talked about it since, though I know he must miss it. I guess it's not really a surprise that he'd go back now that he's older, it's just that he usually talks to me about these things.

"Yeah. You'll come watch, right?"

I nod, but don't say another word. I don't

want him to go back to playing football. It's a dangerous sport at the best of times, not to mention for younger players who take multiple hits to the head. I don't say any of this, because as Harley watches my reaction, I know he doesn't like what he sees, which I guess is why he hasn't told me before now.

"I'll see you later?"

"Yeah, later," I agree, and watch him turn and walk up the steps toward my mom.

Mom grasps Harley's shoulder, stopping him before he can walk by. "Oh, honey, you have a little something there on your cheek."

She's talking about my muddy fingerprints on his face. To my abject horror, Mom licks her fingertips and starts cleaning his face with her spit. "Mom, no!"

"Oh hush! Harley's practically a son to me."

Oh my god, she did not just say that.

He smiles as he looks back at me, but it doesn't reach his eyes. Harley jumps the fence instead of walking through the gate like a normal person, and immediately afterward my mom squeals and throws herself on the trampoline beside me. Harley likely hasn't even cleared the yard yet and Mom is humiliating me even more by kicking her feet in the air and announcing loudly to the world that her daughter just had her first kiss.

I want to bury myself in the soil alongside

Grammy's paperwhites until I've grown too old for the awkwardness of first kisses, embarrassing moms, and boys next door who steal your breath with a single look.

Okay, so maybe I'll never be too old for that last one.

Chapter Six
Rose

"Wake up, Wifey," Harley shouts. Crawling up the bed, he straddles my hips. I groan and close my eyes, and not just because the light pouring in from the open curtain makes permanent eye damage a real possibility, but also because he's squashing my tiny bladder.

"Get off," I grumble.

"Well, I thought we'd save that for tonight, but okay..." he peters off and begins unfastening the button on his pants.

"You're disgusting." I shove at his chest and buck my hips in an effort to unseat him but this only brings him closer, until his arms form two strong barricades on either side of my head. He leans in, and I wedge my arm between us and bury my eyes in the crook of my elbow. Not that it isn't nice to see him in a better mood—the man has been mercurial since we arrived, standoffish and snappish one day, emotionally drained and almost needy the next. I've tried my best to be what he needs, but I honestly don't have a clue what that is. I don't think he knew either. Still, better mood or not, I had a little too much wine with dinner and I can't deal with the practical joker right now. "Go away, Pan."

Mercifully, he climbs off of me, and my bladder practically does a song and dance with relief, and then the sheet is ripped away and I'm hit with a blast of frigid air from the AC.

"Jesus," Harley mutters. I uncover my eyes to find him staring down at me. I wear a fitted Wonder Woman tank with matching star-spangled panties. I would have been wearing pajama pants too, if I hadn't been gesticulating wildly with my wine glass last night as we sat out on the balcony, but considering Harley slept completely naked, I didn't think he'd have an issue with me going pantless.

"What?"

"It's as if my eleven-year-old fantasies have all come true."

I roll my eyes. "Shut up. Your eleven-year-old fantasies all involved Tammy Druitt."

"The ones I was vocal about, maybe," he says. I shoot him a disbelieving look and he grins. "I couldn't exactly tell my best friend I was jacking off into my hand while I imagined her mouth around my dick."

"You didn't have a problem telling me that when we were eighteen," I tease, attempting to cover myself with the sheet again. Harley pulls it free from my grasp and tosses it out of reach, then he grips my ankle and yanks me down the bed. I squeal and kick to no avail and he hovers over me again, this time leaning too close as he pins me with his gaze.

"Because I couldn't fucking help myself. It wasn't a choice. I had to fuck you, possess you, and make sure the whole world knew you were mine. I gotta tell you, Rose, you waking up in my bed like this—it's something I could get used to again."

Wow. I don't know which Harley I am dealing with right now, but it is largely different from the man I've seen in recent weeks, and I'm buying whatever he's selling. And the panties he seems so fond of are pretty much ruined because that little alpha male speech has ensured they'll stay wet for hours to come.

"Now get up. I'm going to go grab us coffee and you're going to put this on." He throws a paper bag on the bed and I side-eye it dubiously.

"What is that?"

"I thought of you when I saw it."

I frown suspiciously but sit up, clapping my hands anyway because I've always loved Harley's presents. I break the seal on the bag and rifle through the aquamarine tissue paper, but pretty soon I'm glaring down at the contents. "A white bikini?"

He grins. "What? You don't like it?"

I pull out the tiny scraps of fabric that I'm somehow supposed to pour my body into and my frown deepens. As far as swimsuits go, it's cute: a white eyelet ruffle bandeau top with a pair of plain bottoms. Okay, so the thing is actually really pretty, but I don't wear bikinis, and I especially didn't wear white bikinis. "I'm not wearing this."

He shrugs. "Fine, don't wear it, but you won't get your other surprise."

I give him the stink eye. *Goddamn him.* He knows I can't resist the promise of a good surprise. And his surprises are always good. Except for the time he showed up this past Thanksgiving with Alecia in tow and a big shiny rock on her finger. That was not a happy surprise for anyone. Oddly enough, it didn't even seem like he was happy about it.

"Stupid, dumb jerk," I mutter, grabbing the bikini off the bed and heading for the bathroom. His chuckle follows me long after I've slammed the door closed.

After I've peed, brushed my teeth and showered, I stand in front of the mirror, glaring at the offending bikini. I toy with the ruffle and smile to myself because he saw this and thought of me, and even though the idea of trying to stuff myself into it practically has me breaking out in hives, I know there's no way around it.

Harley bangs on the door. "Rose, what's the hold up?"

"Shut up, ass face," I say, scowling in his

direction.

"You haven't even put it on yet, have you?" He chuckles, leaning against the frosted glass panel. "I'm giving you five seconds, babe."

I know he isn't kidding with this, either, so I let the towel fall to the floor and I yank on the bikini. I'm just snapping the bottoms into place when he bangs again.

"Time's up."

"I can't wear this," I say as he opens the door. My body is turned toward him, but only because half of my ass is hanging out of the cheeky-cut swimwear. Harley doesn't need me to turn around in order to see how much skin they expose. The huge mirror over the vanity is doing a fine job of showing it to him. He takes a slow sip from the paper coffee cup in his hand.

"Well?" I demand, snatching the cup from his grasp and gulping down a huge mouthful. It burns my tongue and throat and brings tears to my eyes that are in no way related to the fact that he hasn't said anything yet.

"You wanna know what I think?" He takes a step toward me and reflexively I take one back, only I have nowhere to go because my ass hits the bathroom vanity, and I swallow hard and nod. Harley's arm snakes around my waist, his fingers sliding down to the fabric of my bikini bottoms and across my exposed flesh. My body thrums. I hold my breath and he leans in close to whisper in my ear, "I think it's lucky you're not my wife, because you'd be walking with a limp for the rest of our honeymoon."

When it comes to surprises, Harley is the winner for forever and always. This whole honeymoon has been planned to the nth degree and our time has been divided evenly between sightseeing and exploring our cocktail options with a day of relaxation in between. I try not to think about what activities he had planned for his wife on those days that we stayed at the resort, preferring to focus instead on the amazing things we've done so far. Our second night on the island we got leied at the starlight luau with Hula kahiko performers, saw fire twirling, entered conch-blowing competitions—not as dirty as it sounds—and ate at a traditional Hawaiian buffet. It was ridiculously touristy, and I loved every second, but I had a feeling nothing we'd done so far would compare with today's surprise.

After he left me in the bathroom drooling like an idiot, I threw on a floral blue and white print dress and tossed my sunscreen into my purse, and we set off, me with the coffee he bought me and Harley carrying my Liberty London tote bag that is full to bursting with clothes. I don't ask why we might need a change of clothing because he often does things like this to throw me off the scent of a surprise, but when we jump into a cab and pull into the Honolulu Harbor a half hour later, I glare at him, demanding answers. I also hope like hell he's packed a change of underwear because the idea of sailing scares the crap out of me.

We make our way down the dock, passing an even mixture of small and large sailboats and what look like speedboats all gently bobbing in the water. A man in a baseball cap, white polo shirt and a pair of tan shorts walks toward us with his hand extended. "You must be Mr. and Mrs. Hamilton?"

Harley shakes the man's hand vigorously and nods. "I'm Harley. This is my wife, Rose."

I do a double take, glancing at Harley as if he's just lost his mind, but I guess it makes sense to say we're married rather than explain our situation to a complete stranger, so I let it slide and shake the man's hand too.

"I'm Ken. I'll be your captain today." He points to a teenage boy standing on the deck of the boat beside us. He's cute in that awkward way that boys who are just growing into their adult bodies are. For a brief second, as he smiles and offers me a hand, I glimpse his future as a playboy captain of the Hawaiian Islands. "That's my boy, Chip."

I have to say the name ruins that image in a heartbeat, and now because the only words I know associated with life on the water are ahoy and mateys, I'm craving chocolate chip cookies. I shake his hand, and he pulls me onto the boat saying, "Watch your step."

I know this must have cost Harley a pretty penny because the yacht is huge. I know next to nothing about sailing—can you call it sailing when there are no actual sails in sight? I'm anxious about where we're headed, and it does me good to feel Harley's presence at my back. One hand rests at my spine while the other extends to shake Chip's hand, but aside from this small gesture, Harley doesn't take his hands off me. He must feel the anxiety rolling off me in waves.

We're led to a backwards-facing seat by the rear of the boat and Chip takes my tote bag from Harley, telling us he'll put it in the master suite. He offers to take my purse too, but I choose to keep it with me in case I need to make a quick getaway once the engine starts up. Before long, Chip is back with a tray in his hands, and bless the sweet kid, he's offering us mimosas.

I take a glass from the tray and Chip makes himself scarce as I guzzle half of it in one go. Harley raises a brow at me. "Nervous, love?"

"This is quite the surprise, Pan."

"You haven't even seen the best part yet." He grins, clinking his glass against mine.

The next words out of my mouth were going to be, "I've changed my mind and am no longer so keen on surprises," when Ken interrupts by telling us we should be underway in another ten minutes, and that our destination will be reached in a few hours or so, depending on the trade winds.

Askance, I glance at Harley. "Hours?"

"What? You have somewhere else to be?"

I take a deep breath, inhaling the briny air and tilting my face up to the sun. His sturdy shoulder supports me. No. As long as he doesn't move from my side, I have nowhere else to be.

Moments later, Ken starts the engine, which is actually a lot quieter than I'd expected, and we pull out from the dock. I feel Harley's eyes on me, the outside of his thigh flush with mine, and neither one of us moves to put space between us. In fact, he does the opposite by sliding an arm across the seat behind me, and I lean my head against him. So many days and nights we've touched like this—it's so incidental, and yet it means so much. At least to me. Before long, my anxiety is forgotten as we both take in the landmarks of the Oahu coast as we sail smoothly by.

We stop in a cove, and a light lunch is brought to us at the front of the deck. There's wine, brie and crackers, olives and hummus, and a bunch of delicious Hawaiian foods to pick over.

After we eat, I take a deep breath in and turn to Harley. I've had a little too much wine already, no surprise there, so I likely shouldn't be saying anything that's running unchecked through my mind. Still, I can't resist, because I can't think of a better place than paradise to tell someone how much you love them.

"I …" I exhale slowly and chicken out. I lose my nerve, and thank god, because I can't tell him I'm in love with him five days after Alecia left him. I can't do that to him. He might flirt, tease and play pretend, but that's all it is—pretend. Besides, I'm sure he already knows how I feel, and laying that on him isn't fair. "Never mind."

Harley gives me a puzzled look. "What?"

I may not be able to tell him I love him, but letting him know what this time with him means to me isn't wrong, is it? "I have something to say."

"Do you, love?" He smiles wryly.

I nod. "I know some part of you is taking all

this in and wishing Alecia was here with you right now, and for that I'm truly sorry." He shakes his head, as if to say he doesn't want to talk about it, and I reach out and grab his hand, forcing him to look at me. "I hate that your heart is broken, but as long as I live, I'll never forget this day or what being here with you means to me."

My eyes glisten with tears, and for a moment I'm embarrassed because I shouldn't have said anything. He might see too much.

He doesn't say a word, just reaches out and smooths his thumb over my cheek, but his mood has shifted dramatically as he looks out over the beautiful cove.

And with that said, I get up and walk to the back of the boat where Ken and his son are eating their lunch. "We can swim here, right?"

"Of course," Ken says. "We'll set sail again in around fifteen minutes, so ..."

Before he can finish the sentence, I'm down the stairs and stepping onto the deck platform at the rear of the boat. I glance out at the sparkling waters of the North Pacific and strip off my dress.

"Jesus," Harley says.

"Holy shit," Chip mutters, and I know every pair of eyes on that boat are on me. There's a brief second where I feel guilty that I'm giving Ken's underage son an eyeful, but I dive into the cool, crystalline water and forget all about them. It isn't long before Harley dive bombs me. When he comes up, he pulls me to him and I squeal and thrash, but his arm is tight around my waist, his back to my front, and he all but growls in my ear, "Have you made it your sole mission in life to torture me, love?"

I quit struggling and whisper, "You bought the swimsuit."

"Yeah, I'm starting to think that was a mistake."

I break free of his hold and swim away, only to be caught by the arm and dragged back toward him, and a water fight, the likes of which we haven't seen since we were kids at the beach in Carmel, ensues. All the tension of the last few minutes vanishes, rushed away by the tepid island breeze.

We play for another few minutes, Harley dunking me under the surface, me jumping on his back like a wet spider monkey. As I prepare to swim off, he snags me around the waist and draws me to him. For a beat he glances at my lips, I stare at his, and heat surges between us as if the water somehow just reached boiling point. I breathe, he breathes, and I turn my head, because I won't be his rebound. The spell is broken. Stripped away by fate, fear, or common sense. I'm not sure which, but it doesn't matter, because this is dangerous ground for us.

Ken leans over the couch, reminding us of our tight schedule. Harley releases me, and gliding out of the water, he lifts himself up onto the deck in a way that seems so effortless. I swim slowly to the boat, wanting to draw out the moment because the sight of him standing, wet head to toe, his hair free of the man bun for once and slicked back as beads and rivulets of water cascade down his body is something else. He offers a hand up and I take it because I know my ascension from the ocean will be about as graceful as a baby elephant attempting to escape a bathtub. His fingers lace with mine while his other grips my forearm, and within seconds I'm catapulted up in the air and my wet body slams hard against his. His hands immediately go to my ass, because he's always been a complete pervert, and I swat him away as I climb the stairs to the deck. When I reach the top I look back and find his gaze glued to my body. I roll my eyes and return to the front deck, stretching out on a towel in the sun as the engine starts up again and Harley lies down beside me.

We spend the next few hours tanning on the deck, sleeping, and pointing out all the amazing sites we see. When we're rocking to and fro at open sea on the Pacific, I'm torn between grinning like a fool and screaming like a little girl. I grip the railing tight because the sea spray blasting my face and the salt caking my hands, and the rocking of our boat as we slice through the waves is the most terrifying and exhilarating thing I've ever experienced.

When we finally hit smoother waters just off the coast of Kauai, I breathe easier, and my stomach isn't quite so upset either. Early afternoon sunlight glistens on the ocean, making everything gleam as if it were set alight. We dock at Nawiliwili port and it takes a few minutes for the heaviness to settle back into my legs now that we're on land. I notice Harley doesn't bring my tote and just when I'm about to go back for it he tells me not to worry. I know he grasps how important that bag is because it was a Christmas present from him last year, so that means we're heading back to the boat at some point today. Right now, my stomach isn't sure how it feels about that.

We take a cab to yet another place I've never heard of and we pull up to a hangar at what looks like a tiny airport. The sign on the building says, "Hawaiian Helicopter Tours" and my jaw drops as I stare at the bright blue helicopter waiting on the tarmac.

"No," I say in disbelief. Pan's smile confirms my excitement and I give him a hard shove in the chest. "Get the fuck out, seriously?"

"Seriously," he shouts over the noise of the rotating motors. I'm so excited, I'm shaking. I've always wanted to ride in a helicopter, I mean, who wouldn't? But the fact that we get to do it over the

Garden Isle? I'm at a complete loss for words. It's no surprise that I'm hurrying through the motions of climbing inside and attempting to listen to what the pilot has to tell us about our tour. I cannot stop smiling. *How is this my life right now?*

"Happy?" Harley asks, his smooth voice coming through the headphones and causing goosebumps to break out over my skin as if he were whispering in my ear. He looks like a goofball with his huge headphones on, his hair a wiry mess from the salt of the Pacific, and I know I look the same.

"You have no idea," I say.

"I have some." He smooths a large hand along his thigh, that again is flush with mine, but he doesn't keep it there or return it to his lap. Instead, he runs his long fingers over my knee, brushing the fabric of my dress out of the way so his hot palm lays against my leg, skin to skin. He rests it there, and I try to ignore the way everything in my body thrums for more of his touch.

Our pilot tells us we're all set and the helicopter jerks a little as we lift up in the air. My stomach drops. I reach for Harley's hand, the one that's softly tracing patterns on my thigh, and I grasp it tightly as the pilot tells us we're flying over the small town of Lihue. We glide through Hanapepe Valley, and on to the "Jurassic Park Falls." From there it seems like it's one glorious waterfall after the other, all untouched and hidden away where man can't destroy it. The sharp, pleated hills of the Na Pali Coast steal my breath, and I wish we could just land so I could sink my feet into the sand and stare up at those knife-blade folds in the Earth and be dwarfed by their beauty and the magic of it all. We fly past the Bali Hai Cliffs, and the pristine waters of Hanalei Bay, and over some resort that I frown at for ruining the illusion that this place exists untouched, the way nature intended. A short time later we come up on Mt Waialeale, and into the center of a freaking volcano crater, and as Harley and I gaze with eyes as round as saucers at the five-thousand-foot walls surrounding us, I see God. I see how insignificant we all are, and I understand that these hills and these trees and these mountains around us were here long before we ever were, and they'll be here long after.

Never in a million years did I think I'd get this close to heaven, but it's here, all around us, if we'd only open our eyes.

When we make it back to the airport I'm so overwhelmed with everything I've just seen and experienced that I break down the second I step off the helicopter and I walk at a clip to get away from the rotors and the noise. Harley catches up to me and yanks me back. I don't know how he can tell— How does he ever know anything I'm thinking?— but he wraps me up in his arms while I cry silently against his chest.

"I … that …" I stutter. "That was …"

He leans in and presses his lips to mine. It isn't a passionate kiss; it isn't romantic; it's just as if he were pressing his lips to my forehead. It's just a Harley and Rose thing, so when I pull away because it's too much and I'm on a complete sensory overload, he knows the reason why. We might not talk freely about our past or how we feel for one another now, but deep down he knows and he has an idea what something like this means to me. But it's more than just sharing a once-in-a-lifetime experience with my best friend—it's everything. It's the majesty of these islands, the magic of him, and the fact that if things had gone differently that day it would be his wife here with him and not me. That's the thought that keeps pestering me like a mosquito relentlessly buzzing at my ear: five days ago he was marrying another woman, and now he's not.

The ride back to the boat is a blur, and when we board and set sail the tepid breeze has all but died away and the sea spray hits my face like ice. I sit down at the front of the yacht as Harley talks briefly with Ken and his son, and then he comes and sits behind me. His strong arms and thighs wrap around my own as I lean back into the warmth of him. It's perfect, pure torture, and I can't think of anywhere else I'd rather be.

Later, after several more wines and hours

upon hours of gazing up at the sea of stars, I go downstairs to shower the salt from my body before bed. Harley and I explored the salon, state bedroom and VIP master suite earlier, and I am impressed. I could live comfortably with Harley in this space for several days before I thought about strangling him. In fact, I've come to the conclusion that the living space on this boat is bigger than that of my apartment. The bedroom we'll be sleeping in is certainly big enough for the two of us, and Harley doesn't even have to duck all that much because of the six-foot ceilings. The shower is a little cramped and drying myself in the spatial equivalent of a vertical shoebox is proving difficult, so I wrap myself in a towel and hurry into the bedroom, colliding straight into Harley's back as the boat rocks over the waves. My arms wrap tightly around his sides in order to steady myself and keep from falling.

"Ooh, naked girl," Harley mutters, prying my hands from his forearm and holding me upright as he turns toward me. "If I'd known you were so wet for me, I'd have come down sooner."

"Funny, asshole." I poke out my tongue and shake off his hold, turning to the tote bag on the bed. After rifling through several times and emptying the contents onto the duvet in a plume of red rose petals, I realize that I have no clothes. There's a sweater for each of us, a T-shirt, pair of boxers and chinos for Harley, and a single pair of lacey panties for me. *I'm going to kill him.* I turn and find him appraising my sunburnt skin.

"Any ideas as to why my clothes never made it into the tote bag you packed this morning?"

He feigns indifference, but there's a grin creeping in around the corners of his mouth, so I pick up the bag and hit him with it. "Ow, ow, don't hurt me. How was I supposed to know what you needed?"

"Oh I don't know, Harley, maybe ask?" I abandon my assault and turn to the bed, studying the items of clothing that he did manage to pack. "I can't help but notice that you managed to bring enough for you."

He shrugs. "I knew what I'd need."

"I'm not sleeping naked next to you," I snap. I don't mention that either one of us could take the bed in the other room, mostly because although I know we'll be sailing all night, I'm sure Ken and Chip need somewhere to rest at some point and though they've been complete professionals this whole time, they're still strangers to me. I don't think Harley has even thought of this being an option, and if he has, he's not saying as much.

"Fine, take my shirt," he says, picking it up and tossing it to me from the rumpled pile I just made on the bed.

"Turn around."

"Rose," he protests. "I've seen it all before."

"Just do it."

He turns around and studies the mattress, toying with the rose petals strewn across it. I slip into his shirt, which is miles too big for me, and pull on the lacy panties that he didn't forget to pack, and then I climb onto the bed, brushing off rose petals in my annoyance. "What is it with everyone and their goddamn rose petals? It's not romantic when you have to remove flora and fauna from the bed before you lie down on it."

"Says the woman who makes a living off selling romance through flora and fauna." Harley chuckles, stepping away from the bed. He sheds his clothes on the way to the bathroom. I try not to look as he disappears into the shower. I'm still trying not to look five minutes later when he comes out completely naked, flicks off the lights, and climbs in beside me. And I don't say a word when his big body slides up behind mine and he rolls me over to face him—I'm too busy holding my breath as he shoves his hand into the space between my thighs. Waking up like this is one thing, but tempting fate with it intentionally causes my heart to squeeze painfully because it's so damn familiar. I'm sure he can feel how wet I am with his fingers wedged up against my lady parts, but he doesn't comment on this either, so I slide my hand across his belly and snuggle in close, allowing the rocking motion of the boat to lull me to sleep.

Chapter Seven

Rose

Age seventeen

"Hey," Harley says, crossing the drive and taking my porch steps two at a time. He sits down beside me, crushing the tulle skirt of my dress. Earlier when I'd put it on, and swished about my room in yards of ice blue fabric and silver beading, I'd felt like Cinderella, only Prince Charming must not have got the memo, because he was currently late.

"No Alex yet?" Harley asks casually, as if he were just asking the time, or if he could borrow a pencil. I ignore the fact that my eyes are pricking because I have no intention of ruining this makeup.

"Riley said she's running late too. Maybe we should just go together and meet them there." Harley started dating Riley a little earlier in the year. She's cheerleader pretty, popular, and a complete bitch. Naturally, he fell head over heels like an idiot.

"He'll be here." I say, and Harley nods. I'm not even sure I believe it though. Alex is a stoner with shaggy black hair, startling sea green eyes, and his own car. He also gave no fucks, and that's what I like about him. Mostly, that's what I like about him. Tonight? Not so much.

I glance at the two clear boxes in Harley's hand. "Why do you have two corsages?"

He shrugs and chews his bottom lip. "I didn't know if he'd get you one, and my mom says it's a rite of passage, so …"

It's then, that despite all my efforts against it, I do cry.

"Shit, Rose, I'm sorry. I didn't mean—"

"Will you put it on?" I wipe away the tears with the tips of my freshly manicured fingers and hope like hell I don't have panda eyes.

"'Course." He sets down the other box, and I stare for a brief second at the corsage inside. Riley's. It's a yellow rose with some baby's breath and dark green waxy leaves. It's hideous, much like the girl it belongs to.

"Rose," Harley says, pulling me from my reverie. He holds the corsage in his hands and I smile sadly and offer him my arm. Once the bracelet is on, he traces the inside of my wrist with his fingertips.

"It's beautiful," I whisper.

"Rose," Harley says, but he chews his lip before saying anything more. His eyes search mine, and it looks as if there's some kind of internal debate going on inside his mind when he blurts out,

"Don't sleep with him."

"Harley—"

"Just hear me out, I know it's not fair of me to ask you this but—"

"You're right, it's not." I pull my hand free of his and glare.

"He's not the guy for you. Okay?" He's gulping down huge lungsful of air. "He doesn't deserve you."

I inhale sharply too, not because what he says is a huge surprise—Alex has been a pretty sucky boyfriend—but because Harley is so strung out about this. Harley doesn't do strung out.

"Please?" he says breathlessly. "Rose, I'm begging you not to do this."

"God." I throw my hands up in exasperation and stand. "You can't say things like that Harley. You're with Riley!"

"I know." For a beat he says nothing, I say nothing, and then his phone rings in his pocket and he pulls it out and looks at the display. "Shit."

"You should get that."

He doesn't, and it rings a few more times before the message must go to voicemail. There's not even a five-second pause before it rings again.

"You should go before the ice princess has a meltdown."

He frowns but he stays rooted firmly on my front porch. Harley always had to push the limits. If there was a night sky above him, he'd find a way to shove it back and let the sun through. If someone told him no, he'd work on that someone until they not only said yes, but had believed that yes was their idea in the first place.

I was smart enough to realize that he was attempting to do that very same thing with me. I just didn't know why he cared. "Will you just go already?"

"He isn't for you, Wendy," he says softly, rising to his feet.

"And who is, you?" I demand. He doesn't have an answer for me, which is telling given that Harley always knows just what to say at just the right time.

I turn and walk into the house, slamming the door behind me.

It takes Mom twenty minutes to fix my face after I get done crying. I don't tell her what he'd said or why I was so upset when Harley left—she is my mom, after all, and would likely have kittens if I said I was contemplating sex for the first time with my stoner boyfriend. She doesn't press me for information and I don't supply it, but I'm sure she knows it has something to do with Harley.

When Alex finally does arrive, he's an hour and a half late and he doesn't get out of the car, just honks his horn at me from the drive. Mom gets her panties in a twist about us not taking pictures, but I decide I don't want them immortalizing what a colossal screw-up this night has been so far. I just want to get through it, cash in my damn V-card, and move on with my life.

When I climb in his black, beat-up Javelin SST coupe, he smells like booze and cigarettes. Ordinarily, that might make me feel wildly grown-up, as if I were spontaneous and crazy and liked living that way. Tonight, it just annoys me.

Alex's gaze rolls over me from head to toe, and he raises his eyebrows and says, "Nice dress. Can't wait to get you out of it."

I have to resist the urge to bop him in the nose. There's no apology for his being late, and Harley had been right—there was no corsage either, other than the one my best friend had given me. When we make it to prom there's no sign of Harley and the ice princess, and as soon as we walk in it seems as if Alex is ducking outside for a smoke.

I head to the bathroom and enter a stall. I feel like crying, only I can't muster a single tear. It is what it is. High school sucks, life as a crazy cat lady will suck even more, and then I'll die. The end.

Moments later, as I'm trying not to pee on my dress, a gaggle of females enters the bathroom and presumably they fluff their hair and touch up their lipstick. I can't see on account of the door in front of me, but none of the stall doors close.

"And then I had to pay the hotel on my

mother's credit card," one of the girls complains, and I recognize the voice as Riley's. That means the other airheaded murmurs of disapproval belong to those in her brood of bitches, Callie and Lisa.

"You're joking?"

"I mean, what kind of man doesn't book the hotel for prom night? Honestly, sometimes boys are so clueless. He's lucky he's hot, or else I would have dumped him when I first found out that he was really friends with that freak Rose."

"OMG, did you see her date?" Callie's ditzy high-pitched voice bounces around the room. "He's totally gorg, but he looks like a homeless person. Like, put on a tux already and brush your hair."

"They're both so weird. And why is Harley even friends with her? Did they like, sleep together?" Lisa asks, and I'm guessing Riley is the one who gasps.

"Uh, no! She's a total stalker; she follows him around like a lost puppy. Harley said she just won't get a clue."

That isn't true. *Is it?* Harley would never say that about me. Harley is the only person on earth who gets me, and I him. Besides, I'm not the one buying him corsages and begging him not to sleep with his girlfriend. Riley is lying through her whore teeth, and this bitch is going down.

I pull back the door and prepare to storm over and yank her hair out by the roots, but Riley and her little brigade of bitches are already exiting the bathroom, not a single one of them looking back before they get lost to the wild lights and tragic music of prom.

I glance at my reflection, at my flushed pink cheeks and my sad eyes, and I frown because I'm pretty sure prom's supposed to be way more fun than this. I sigh, wash my hands and dry them carefully, and decide to go home. I don't even bother looking for Alex—what's the point? But he finds me anyway, as I stalk on my too-high heels towards the school gates. He pushes off from the wall and follows me, grabbing my arm and pulling me to him.

"Hey, what's the hurry, baby?"

"Don't call me baby."

"Jesus, did you just get your rag or something?" He tosses his cigarette to the ground and doesn't bother to extinguish it properly. Of course he doesn't. What does Alex care if my very overpriced dress suddenly catches alight? He'd probably do it deliberately just to get me naked.

Earlier tonight, I might have jumped at the chance to get naked with him. That's the thing about teenage girls— unless they're religious zealots whose fathers buy them promise rings— eww, gross—no seventeen-almost-eighteen-year-old girl wants to hang onto her virginity. Especially not when her boyfriend looks like Alex Dean. It doesn't take a genius to figure out that I've been saving my virginity for someone else, someone who I'll look back on ten, twenty, forty years from now, and know that I'd made the right choice. I've been saving my virginity for my best friend, and that, ladies and gentlemen, is why I'm destined to die a virgin.

Alex wraps an arm around my waist and pulls me close. "You ready to get outta here and finally show me that sweet pussy of yours?"

I stomp on the cigarette butt and glare at him. "I'm ready to get out of here, but I won't be showing you my sweet pussy." I swear to god it takes everything I have not to giggle like a little girl when I repeat those last words back to him.

"What the fuck, babe?" He moves closer, crowding my space. Alex rubs up against me, and for a moment I want to be sick because the truth is he may be hot, he may be way, way hotter than me, but Harley was right—he's not worthy of me. I'm not punching above my weight—he is.

"Get off me."

"You know what? Fuck this. I could walk into that gymnasium and have any one of those bitches eating my cock before we've even left the carpark."

"You're right, you could," I whisper against his ear and step back. "Just not this one."

Alex shoves away from me, his shoe kicking

mine in the process. I lose my balance and teeter on my heels. It wasn't intentional, I know that much. I also know he won't reach out to break my fall either, but that's okay because someone else does. Harley sets me to rights and shoves Alex hard as he's walking away. "What the fuck, man? You hitting girls now too? Hitting on them wasn't enough?"

"Take a fucking hike, pretty boy. This doesn't concern you."

"The hell it doesn't," Harley says, getting up in his face. "You touch her again and I'll break your fucking neck."

"Harley," I warn. I've never seen this side of him before, and I'm equal parts awed and afraid.

"Fuck this. Her pussy ain't even worth—"

Harley's fist connects with Alex's face. The sound is terrible—a dull thudding crunch. It makes my stomach turn and strikes fear into my heart when Harley doesn't just stop at one punch, and Alex doesn't go down. He takes the blows Harley dishes out, and then comes back swinging with a dirty uppercut to Harley's jaw.

"Stop it!" Neither one listens to me, and when I'm about to throw myself into the fray in order to break them up, I'm pulled back by huge arms lifting me in the air as I kick my feet. "Put me down."

"I got you, Rose. You're okay," a low voice

whispers in my ear and sets me on the ground again, but his strong arms don't let go. I turn around and find Kordell Green, a huge defensive linebacker with midnight skin and dark chocolate eyes smiling down at me. "I got you, and my boy got this."

I whirl around in time to see Harley throw another punch that has Alex reeling back, but Alex is a scrappy fighter. He grew up in the Tenderloin, and this isn't his first fistfight. I know Harley's gotten into a few fights when he's been out with the guys, but Alex is used to fighting, and Harley isn't.

In a matter of seconds, Alex comes back swinging and his left hook hits Harley right in the temple. I scream. Harley staggers back but doesn't fall, which is so obviously not what Alex wanted, so he lays into him again, but Harley's no lightweight. They hit the ground scrapping, shoving at one another with fists and splayed palms. All his football training must pay off because Harley winds up on top and throws a punch to Alex's head that knocks him out cold. Harley rears up and just sits there astride Alex, breathing for a moment.

"See? Our boy had it under control," Kordell says. Out of all Harley's team mates, I like him the most. He has to be more than three hundred pounds, but he's a gentle giant, unless he's on the field.

A crowd has gathered around us, and I'm quite sure the teachers won't be far behind, but Harley looks at me, exhausted and bleeding, his eye swelling, and I cover my mouth so my squeaking cry won't be heard. He slowly staggers to his feet and stumbles toward me. My hands automatically fly from my mouth to his neck as my eyes roam over his face. "Are you okay?"

He nods, a smile splitting his cut lip open farther. Harley's teammates all seem to pour out of the gym at once, and I'm wedged in by their heavily muscled bodies as they congratulate him on a job well done. That doesn't sit right with me, and though he's been a complete douche all night, I'm worried about Alex, who's still lying prone on the pavement. I glance at Kordell, who isn't getting caught up in the testosterone.

"Thanks for having my back, man," Harley says, and Kordell just nods as if this was a given, which I suppose it is. The team are family, they look out for each other, but that pack mentality also means things can get out of hand fast.

"You better get out of here before Coach catches wind of this," Kordell warns. Harley nods and slips his warm hand into mine, interlocking long fingers with my own, and I'm tugged through the crowd of rowdy football players.

"Watson, gimme your keys," Harley shouts, and the ginger-haired wide receiver fishes in his pocket, pulls out a set of keys, and lobs them toward us. Harley catches them in mid-air, and for the first time I notice how busted up his hand is. "I'm taking you home."

"You don't have to do that."

As if on cue, the ice princess screeches her harpy cry from behind the crowd, and her and the pussy posse push through the wall of footballers blocking their path. "Oh my god! Are you serious, Harley? You got into a fight on prom? Over her?" she asks in distaste, glaring at me. "She's not even your date."

"No, but she should have been," he whispers, so low I think I've misheard. When his eyes meet mine, I know I heard everything with one hundred per cent clarity. "She's my friend. Her boyfriend was being a fucking tool and needed to have his ass handed to him."

"And you just had to be the one to do it." She sneers, and then mocks me in a low baritone. "Poor Rose. She's so lonely; she's so sad; she's so pathetic. If I don't take care of her, who will?" It's a terrible impersonation of Harley, but it has the desired effect because it cuts right to the core, just the way she intended. Harley *had* always taken care of me. *Is that what he really thinks?*

His fingers disengage from my own and he takes a step towards her. "Quit being a bitch, Riley. I'm taking Rose home. I'll come back for you."

"You leave with her and I won't be here for you to come back to," Ice Princess snaps, and turns on her heel.

Harley snatches up my hand again and leads me through the school gates to Watson's truck. He's still taking care of me, as if I were a feeble child, incapable of functioning on my own, and Riley's words twist in my gut like a knife. He rests his hand on my ass and helps me climb up, then he attempts to buckle my seat belt, but I slap his hands away in order to do it myself. Harley's brow furrows. He shuts the door, walking over to the driver's side, and climbs in, turns the key, and quickly shuts off the music. Harley puts his foot to the floor and proceeds to drive like a maniac all the way through the city.

We don't say a word when we pull up to my house. I just unbuckle my belt and turn to undo my door when his hand comes to rest on my knee. I feel the weight of it, the warmth of it through my layers of tulle.

I glance up at him. "You want to come inside and have my dad take a look at that?" I ask, referring to his split lip. My dad is a pediatric surgeon at Benioff's Children's Hospital in Oakland. He could patch Harley up in a few minutes.

"Nah. Chicks dig scars, right?"

"Right." I half-smile back, but all the humor left me hours ago. In fact, there hasn't been a single humorous thing about this night—well, except for my stupidity in thinking Alex should be my first.

"Well, thanks for beating the shit out of Alex for me."

"You don't have to thank me. I've been wanting to beat that shithead's face in since the second the two of you hooked up."

I nod, because this isn't news to me, but I still haven't figured out why. Why does he care if I sleep with Alex? Was it over between him and Riley now? "Sorry for ruining prom. I bet Riley's not too happy with either one of us right now."

"Riley can wait. She's not important."

My brows crease with surprise, and a little bit of annoyance. If she's not important, why the hell did he take her to prom? Before I can read too much into that, Harley leans into my personal space, so close we breathe the same breath. We've done this a hundred times over since we were thirteen, but we've never crossed that line again.

"What are you doing?" I whisper.

"He's wrong about you, you know?"

"What?" I ask, but my question is cut short by his lips as they come crashing down on mine. His tongue pushes into my mouth and a surprised moan escapes me, but it's swallowed by his. Harley's hands cup my face, and mine slide to the back of his head. I kiss him back, warm and wet and full of need, and then fireworks explode behind my eyelids, the way they did the first time we kissed. The way it should have been all that time with Alex.

Too soon, he breaks the kiss and leans his forehead against mine. "Rose," he whispers breathlessly.

"Yeah?" I sigh, just as winded. I wish he'd shut up and go back to kissing me, but Harley pulls back, and his face turns white as a sheet.

"Shit."

My heart sinks because I can only imagine what that means. He hadn't meant to do that, and I … *had*.

My thoughts are interrupted by a knock on my window, and I jump about twenty feet in the air when I see my father standing on the other side of that thin pane of glass. For a moment I'm tempted to tell Harley to floor it, but then I'd be in even more trouble. We both would.

My dad makes the international symbol for 'roll down your window,' and I gulp because not only does he look as dumbfounded as I do right now, but he also looks mad. Really, really mad.

"Oh shit, he is pissed," Harley says.

"Yup." I roll down the window.

"What the hell are you two doing out here?"

"Harley drove me home."

"Yes, I can see that." Dad scowls. "I mean what are you two doing out here, in this car, necking like a bunch of—"

"Ew, Dad, necking," I say. "Really?"

This obviously doesn't win me any points

with him because his scowl deepens.

"Sorry, sir," Harley says, and the part of me that isn't terrified of my father carving Harley up into little pieces with his bone saw is ecstatic because my best friend kissed me and those lips were as warm and pillowy-soft as I remembered, and oh my god, now is really not the time to be staring at Harley like I want another taste.

"Sir now, is it?" Dad says. Harley has never called him 'sir' a day in his life. Dad's an open book, and a gentleman through and through. Usually, the minute anyone calls my dad sir or Doctor Perry, all slights were forgiven. That's not happening here though. "What happened to your face?"

"Alex happened," I say, reaching for the door handle, but since my dad is leaning his body against the car, it appears I'm trapped and going exactly nowhere.

"And he did this because you were kissing my daughter?"

"Harley beat the crap out of him because Alex was being a douche. Jeez, Dad." I yank on the handle again, panicking a little despite my teen angst because I know my worst fear is about to happen, and then as if she were summoned, my mother opens the front door of our house and shouts, "Herb, who is it?"

"It's Rose," Dad says, and then he glares at

Harley. "And her very good friend Harley. You'd better come inside, and I'll fix that cut."

"Dad, he's fine."

"No. I have to get back—"

"They're home already?" my mother yells all of this from the front porch because she's in her pajamas and couldn't possibly be seen in the street in her sleepwear, but standing on the porch is apparently fine. "Well, what are they doing sitting out there in the dark? And whose car is that?"

"He's just coming inside to have me take a look at his face."

"What happened to his face?"

"I'm sorry," I say, though I know that he knows how they get.

"Apparently Harley beat the crap out of Rose's boyfriend," Dad deadpans, never once taking his death glare off of us.

"Alex? Well good, that little dipshit deserved it. Who does he think he is, showing up late to pick up my daughter for prom? Did you see her face? She was devastated."

"Mom!" I shout, and then I give up because just when I think it couldn't get worse, everything snowballs from there. My dad sends Harley another death glare and to make matters even worse, Rochelle and Dean come wandering out of their front door and across our drive to see what all the commotion is about. This bolsters my own mother's courage and she comes tottering down the stairs in her fluffy kitten-heeled slippers, her satin robe billowing behind her.

"Harley, what happened to your face?" Rochelle asks.

Mom answers for him, "He beat up Rose's date."

Harley flops his head back on the seat and exhales loudly. I know just how he feels. "He was being an asshole."

"Language," Rochelle warns.

"He was being an A-hole, Mom."

"Well, what did he do?"

"It doesn't matter."

"Son, this could be a potential law suit waiting to happen." This comes from Harley's dad, Dean. "Now if I'm going to get a call from this boy's father in the morning, or worse, a warrant for your arrest, I'm going to need all of the details."

"Jesus Christ," Harley mutters under his breath, and Rochelle chastises him again. "He was pressuring her for sex, okay?"

Dean mutters a curse. My dad's face turns outright murderous. The moms gasp simultaneously, as if they themselves had never once been teenage girls. My heart settles heavy inside my chest and my stomach sinks with their reactions. I feel like a fool. Why am I not more outraged on my own behalf, and why do we live in a society where boys are pressuring girls for sex at all? Why are girls only valuable to boys if they put out? And why was I so willing to give away my virginity to some asshole who could have replaced me with any one of those girls in that gym and not given a single shit?

"Thank goodness Harley saved the day by driving Rose home and making out with her in the front seat of a borrowed car," Dad seethes, and I know that it's going to take some time for him to get over the fact that he caught me kissing the one boy he thought he could trust with his daughter.

"Making out?" Mom and Rochelle say at the same time, and both of them look far too happy. Heat licks at my cheeks, and I could just die because I had no intention of telling my parents about the situation with Alex, and I certainly wasn't planning on telling them about Harley and me. I also know that now Mom and Rochelle will never give up on making sure this becomes a thing. I'm surprised they haven't already sent out wedding invitations.

"Okay, well fun as this was, I'm going to bed." I turn from the window, and our parents' expectant faces, and smile at Harley. "Thanks for driving me."

He doesn't reply, just tilts his chin in my direction as I open the door, practically barging my dad out of the way, who's still giving Harley the stink eye. I hop down from the truck and breeze past my parents. Though I know Dad is eager to get his hands on Harley and make him pay just a little with rubbing alcohol and possibly a few stitches, Harley tells his folks that he's fine and he roars off into the night.

Inside my room, Mom hovers like a gnat as she helps me unzip my dress. She asks me several times about Alex, and whether or not I'm okay, and how far I let him take it, and the relief is written all over her face when I tell her that Harley stepped in before Alex had caused any damage. I think she knew I wasn't all that interested in Alex to begin with, so she knows I'm not brokenhearted. She tries several times to glean details about my kiss with Harley, but I choose to keep those to myself. I feel as if I talk about it, somehow it makes it less special, so much to her disappointment, I keep my mouth tightly shut.

After taking the pins from my hair and removing my makeup, I sit on my bed and read as I wait for Harley to return home and sneak in my open window, but he doesn't. At least not before I fall asleep, and the next morning, when I finally work up the courage to climb in through his window, I find his bed empty and untouched. He didn't sleep here at all last night. My heart sinks as I realize where he was. He spent the night with Riley, in a hotel room charged to her mother's card. And

I'm a fool for thinking that kiss meant anything to him just because it meant everything to me.

Chapter Eight

Rose

I sip my Mai Tai and look out over the ocean as the sun sets. The waitress Brittany gives me the side eye again because I'm taking up precious space at one of the couple's tables without ordering anything more than a few cocktails. Harley was supposed to be joining me for dinner, but after the magic of Kauai yesterday it was as if he'd done a complete one-eighty by the time I came back from acquiring our morning coffees. I don't know whether it was bad news from home, or whether Alecia had tried to contact him, but he threw his phone against the wall and stormed into the bathroom as I was coming through the hotel suite door.

I'd bombarded him with questions, but he wasn't talking. He wasn't doing much of anything but lying around the room drinking. Ordinarily, I'd have been all for that, but I knew when my best friend needed space, so I kissed his cheek and left him to his misery. That was hours ago, and I've been back to the room twice since, but he was nowhere to be found. I texted him, reminding him of our dinner reservation, but as I'm sitting alone at our table, avoiding the glares from the not-so-sweet-tempered Brittany, who keeps dropping by every two seconds to ask if I'm ready to order, I know that wherever he is, he's not coming.

Coming here was a bad idea, and just as I'm preparing to signal the ever-watchful Brittany for the check, I hear a familiar voice from behind.

"One moment," Dermot tells Brittany as she prepares to lead him past my table. I stand up to greet him, and he pulls me in for an awkward cheek kiss/hug. This is new for us. Dermot is a client, and though I've always known that he's a colossal flirt, we've never disrupted our distributor/consumer relationship with touching of any kind. "Alone again?"

"Looks like," I say with a tight smile.

"You know I'm beginning to think you're making up this runaway bridegroom."

I really like Dermot. My checkbook and my accountant both really like Dermot and his regular contribution to my business, and yes, even though my heart is hung up on my unattainable best friend, my lady parts really, really appreciate Dermot—on a purely aesthetic level, of course. However, that was an extraordinarily douchie thing to say.

Like I would honeymoon in Hawaii, by myself.

"You know I'm beginning to think you're making up a wife in order to cover the fact that you're gay. What's that they say about the successful, good-looking men in SF? They're either married or gay."

"Oh Rose, I am definitely not gay," he murmurs, his gaze rolling over me from head to toe and though I was just teasing, I'm inclined to believe him.

Feeling parched, and a little shaken up, I raise my glass in a toast. "You are married though."

"You got me." He grins and indicates to the unoccupied seat at my table. "May I?"

"Of course," I say, and shoot Brittany—who's been watching our exchange this entire time with her eyes bugging out—a look. She turns her attention to Dermot, laying the cloth napkin in his lap for him and asking if he'd like something to drink. He thanks her and orders a Jameson, while I order another Mai Tai, and Brittany then sets down menus for us both and bounces away to fill our order with her ponytail swinging.

"So where is this mysterious best friend?"

"I'm not really sure."

"Aren't you supposed to be keeping tabs on him, making him feel not so alone?"

"That was the plan, though it's not working out so well today." I try to keep the hurt from my voice, but I know Dermot hears it because when I glance up from my chipped fingernail polish, he's studying me closely. His deep brown eyes penetrate mine, and they seem to search for more than I'm willing to give. "So what about Mrs. Carter?"

"Hard day at the spa. She wanted to order in."

"Shouldn't you be ordering in with her?"

"If you knew Mrs. Carter, you'd be asking why I bother going back to the suite at all," he says, not looking at me but at the ocean. "I keep wondering why we do this—celebrate anniversaries when we can't stand to be alone together for a single night." He straightens his collar and glances at the bar. Clearly this is a man in need of a serious drink. "My apologies. You've been stood up by your best friend, who still in no way wants to fuck you, and my wife would rather fuck her gynecologist than her husband, so where does that leave us, sweet Rose?"

Poor Dermot. I guess we're both chasing after people who don't want to be caught. The only difference is Mrs. Carter said 'I do'. Man, she sounds like a complete bitch.

"Miserable in paradise, and paying for overpriced drinks." I laugh, because really if I didn't laugh, I'd cry.

"Touché."

Brittany finally comes back with our drinks, batting her lashes coquettishly at Dermot. He pays her no mind; it seems Mr. Carter only has eyes for his Jameson, and … me? "Well, I've grown awfully fond of overpriced drinks."

He raises his glass to mine in a toast. "To unrequited love, then."

I stop with the drink halfway to my mouth. "I didn't say I was in love with him."

"You didn't have to."

Touché, indeed.

Dermot is a man who likes to take charge. I learned this when he took the liberty of ordering dinner for me. I also gave him hell about it, and so ensued a drinking challenge like no other. I ordered him one hideously fruity cocktail after another, and he in turn ordered me every type of whiskey the restaurant served. This was a lot of alcohol. I drank, probably more than most women my age, and a lot more than was good for me, but this was something else.

Bossy or not, I had a good time with Dermot. He's charming and funny, and it doesn't hurt that he's easy on the eyes. Under different circumstances—namely him not being married and me not being in love with my best friend—Dermot Carter is the sort of man I could fall hard for. He's a gentleman, sweet, successful, and so charismatic that he has me snared completely in his web. There's an undercurrent of danger with him too, as if those big brown eyes know your every move before you make it and you aren't sure if you'll love or hate the punishment he doles out if you put a foot wrong. *I'm betting I'd love it.* Not that this is something I'll ever get to experience, but a girl can fantasize, and no one ever got hurt from my fantasies, except for perhaps my vibrator, which is why I bought a new top-of-the line Lelo Olga in sterling silver. *No more melted rubber for me.*

It's late when we finally get up to leave, and I've had far more than I can handle. I stumble a little as I stand and give Brittany a fake-ass smile. Dermot rests his hand at the small of my back as he ushers me out of the restaurant. It feels nice, and I'm glad he has no qualms about touching his florist.

When it comes to walking through the dimly lit bar just off the restaurant, I decide this looks like a fantastic place to curl up on one of the couches and drift off to sleep, and I find myself gravitating towards them but Dermot gently steers me away and closer to the stairs. I don't know how he's any better off; he drank just as much as I did, though I suppose he has to have at least 40lbs on me. *Still, no fair.*

When we come to the marble staircase,

Dermot takes my elbow, and that kind of automatic chivalrous gesture causes my vagina to go on red alert. Seriously, if I was wearing a shorter skirt, I bet you could see a flashing red light coming from my whoo-ha with a little siren wailing about how we'd found a keeper. I take another step and almost fall off my sensible little kitten heels.

Dermot's fingers sink into my flesh as he steadies me, and our eyes lock. And this may just be the copious amounts of rocket-fuel in my system but … goddamn, he's pretty. Not in a Harley, rough-and-ready-to-take-you-anywhere kind of way, but in the handsome, successful CEO I-have-my-shit-completely-together way, which is hot. Really, really …

The ground goes out from under me as I take my next step and falter. My shoe flies off, and lands with a plop in one of the various ponds surrounding the resort. I'm flying, freefalling to the ground as Dermot tries to catch me, only I bring him down with me. On top of me. My head smacks off the pavement and spins as my gaze slowly comes back into focus. Dermot's warm breath and strong aftershave engulf me. I let out a whimpering laugh. "Ow."

"Are you okay?" he asks, chuckling. It's then that I realize he's drunk, too. *Ha!* My fruity drinks did get to him. He's just way better at hiding it than I am.

"Uh-huh," I say while shaking my head. Dermot grins, and his gaze drops to my mouth. My hands have somehow entangled themselves in Dermot's luscious salt-and-pepper hair. I play with the strands at the nape of his neck, he leans in and … "Oh god! You're married!"

"I am," he agrees, as if this is a fact he's only just remembered. Pushing up on his elbows, he lifts his weight off of me at the same time that I attempt to wiggle free, but this only serves in thrusting our bodies closer together. He's hard. Not just like semi-hard, but *hard* hard. Like steel, or diamonds. Just how hard are diamonds? I mean obviously they're hard, but can you really compare them to flesh, no matter how impressive the boner?

Dermot wets his lips, those full, beautiful lips, and stares down at me with regret. As if I'm the last morsel of chocolate cake and someone got there before him.

Oh this is bad. This is really, really bad.

"You're married," I say again, though this time my voice is a whisper, and god help me it's chock full of disappointment. I am a horrible person. There is no coming back from this moment. There's only forward into a life of taking my clothes off for money, prostitution, and possible B-grade porn. I wonder if I could work with Danny Mountain? No, no, no. He's married too. *I'm so going to hell.*

"Yes, you're quite right," he says, but he doesn't lift his weight off of me. Instead, he glances down to where our bodies are joined at the hip. "Er … I may have a small problem."

"I'm not sure I'd call that small." And I wouldn't, because the man feels huge pressed against me.

"You're awfully good for my ego, Rose, but you're terrible for my self-control." He kisses my cheek and stands. And though I try to tell myself not to look, it's all I can do. My eyes zero in on the bulge in his pants. My mother taught me to show appreciation for pretty things when you see them. Somehow I don't think she was talking about my client's junk—though she does get a little swoony when Dermot comes in for his morning coffee.

The man in question offers his hand, and I take it and let him pull me up. *Well, this is awkward.*

"I should get back." I point to the Rainbow Tower above us. If I glanced up I'd no doubt be able to see our room, but my head is far too swimmy for that, so I just stare awkwardly at Dermot. *I hope he doesn't decide to go to another florist now.*

"Yes, you should." His eyes stay locked on mine. "I would offer to walk you up, but I'm not sure that would go over too well with your roommate."

"Probably not." I smile and remove the one shoe I have on. I can't take the risk of stumbling again because who knows? This time I might just fall onto some random penis. "So … thanks for dinner, and the trip."

He grins, and it has a chemical reaction with my insides. "You're so welcome. If only we'd seen more."

"Good one." I begin walking backwards and only narrowly miss falling into the koi pond. I really need to be far, far away from handsome men … and fish … apparently, because I'm sure at least one of them got hit in its big bulbous head by my wayward heel. "Well good night."

"Good night, Rose."

I hurriedly disappear before I can make even more of an ass of myself, or you know, dry-hump my client on his wedding anniversary in the middle of an expensive resort.

Chapter Nine
Rose

Clutching my one shoe tightly to my chest, I slide the key in the lock and quietly enter the suite. The bathroom light is on, and the bed is rumpled but empty. Harley sits out on the balcony in the dark with a bottle of whiskey on the small table beside him, his legs propped up on the empty chair. I don't think he heard me come in, because there's a plate glass door between us. I watch him for a bit as he swirls the remaining whiskey in his glass, and then he sets it down on the table untouched. He bows his head. It's hard to see clearly from here, but his shoulders tremble slightly as he buries his face in his hands. That's all it takes for me to be across the room. I pull open the door and I'm hit with the scent of ocean and alcohol. Harley doesn't turn—he just takes a ragged breath as I wrap my arms around him from behind. And then his shoulders tremor uncontrollably as I hold him. Before long, he's howling.

I've never seen him this way and I'm ashamed to say that it breaks something inside of me, because I love him. Drunken interludes with charming CEOs aside, I love him, and witnessing him fall apart over a woman who doesn't deserve him? Well, it hurts like a motherfucker.

When it becomes apparent he still isn't going to talk, I grab his hand and lead him back inside the room. I shove him down on the mattress, expecting to go to the bathroom and change out of this stupid dress, but I don't get that far because Harley tugs on my hand with his vise grip and I fall onto the bed beside him.

He doesn't say a word, just turns my body over as easily as he might move a ragdoll and pulls me close. Laying his head on my boobs, his whiskey-warm breath mingles with my own as I stroke his hair. It's strange to see him so vulnerable, this huge man that dwarfs me, my Harley who's always been so solid, so strong. Guilt slices through me. I should have been here; I should have pushed for answers; I should have forced him to talk to me. Instead, I had dinner with a married man, a man I almost kissed.

Before long, Harley's breathing slows and becomes deeper and then, when I know he's asleep, I softly trace the lines of his beautiful face. *How long have I wanted this?* How long have I dreamed of touching him the way I have this week, of cuddling in bed, of stolen glances, and the clever way he teases me that simultaneously makes me want to both hurt him and kiss him all at once? I've wanted him for so long, but all of those touches mean nothing right now because even though his arms are wrapped tightly around me, I don't have him. Someone else does. And right now, she's the luckiest bitch alive because I would give anything to have him feel that way about me again, and I'd give anything for him to look at me the way Dermot looked at me tonight.

Chapter Ten
Rose

Age seventeen

I spend the morning crying. It's stupid, I know, but I can't help it. That kiss had meant everything, hearing him say that Riley wasn't important had meant everything, and still the douchenozzle spent prom night with her … in a hotel. Having sex.

Bored and alone, I drown my sorrows in chocolate and indulge in a *Buffy* marathon—the second season where Buffy sleeps with Angel and he loses his soul, thank you very much. *Stupid sex.* If Angel had kept it in his pants, we wouldn't have had to sit through a soul destroying season finale with his bumpy vampire face. I stuff a handful of candy in my mouth and throw another at Angel's handsomely annoying face.

"Stupid, sexy jerk!" I shout at the TV, just as Harley climbs in my window and flops down on the bed beside me. I move over an inch and he takes another, and then he shoves his big meaty hand—which is covered in bruises and broken skin—into my M&M's.

"Hey," he says, stuffing a handful of candy in his mouth.

Hey? Hey? Really? He beats up my boyfriend, kisses me on prom night and then goes back to the ice princess to spend the night with her, and all I get is a freaking *hey*? "Hey yourself."

"Okay, you're mad."

I glare at him.

"Where's your dad?" Harley glances at the door. "He's not going to beat the shit out of me, is he?"

"I don't know. He's golfing, or saving children or something." He leans over and nuzzles my neck with his nose. I jerk away. "What are you doing?"

"Come on, get up."

"No. I'm watching," I say, because it's true. Out of all seven seasons of *Buffy*, this episode is still my favorite—even with Angel being a sexy, evil douche. I'm also pretty sure I have chocolate on my face and mega death breath from hell, so I don't plan on going anywhere right now.

"You're not watching, you're wallowing, and you've seen this episode already." He shuts off the TV and the room grows dark.

Dusk falls, the sun sets over the city in one of its beautiful burnt orange sunsets, and for once there's no fog to mask it.

"I do not wallow," I tell him matter-of-factly, stuffing more candy into my mouth in order to hide my death breath.

"We gonna talk about this? Or are you just gonna keep stuffing chocolate in your face so you don't have to speak to me?"

Goddamn him.

"I taught you that trick, remember?" Harley grins, and then he pulls me into him so my body is flush with his as he traces his fingers up my arm and back down again. I close my eyes, because even though I'm hurt and heartbroken, I never felt butterflies explode inside my belly when Alex touched me. Not even when he slipped a hand inside my panties and attempted to get me off. I'd felt nervous, and uncertain, sure, but I didn't feel as if my breath depended on his next caress.

"Wendy?" Harley prompts, and my eyes snap open. I attempt to wriggle free. It doesn't work.

"Don't call me that. We're not kids anymore," I hiss. He just grins.

"I'll never grow up, and you shouldn't either. Now come on." He slides off the bed and rises, grabbing my forearms and pulling me to my feet as the bowl of candy falls to the floor and M&M's spill out across my room.

"I really don't want to go anywhere, Harley."

He brings my hand to his lips, kissing it

softly and hiding that impish grin against my flesh. "What if I told you it would be an awfully big adventure?"

"Then I'd ask you to stop fucking quoting Peter Pan. What are you, six?"

He frowns and then appears to study my body for the first time. "You can't wear this outfit."

"What's wrong with this?" I ask, looking down at my bold, printed tights and oversized T-shirt.

"You look like a hobo." He stalks across the room to my chest of drawers, pulling out a pair of jeans and a black Goonies T-shirt that I wore to death as a kid and should have thrown out before now. It's threadbare and fits so snugly that I don't have to wear a bra with it so … winning.

I scowl, because even though I love this shirt, it's not as comfortable as my hobo outfit, and I meant what I said—I really don't want to go anywhere. With a resigned sigh, I walk into the closet in order to change, because I know he won't turn away. When I'm done, I exit and twist my hair into a braid over my shoulder, and then I grab a cardigan because no matter what time of year it is, SF weather can be a temperamental bitch, and it's a pretty good way to hide my over-excited nipples in this top.

I follow him and shake my head as he climbs through the window and onto the wooden plank wedged across the space between our sills. "You know my dad's not home; you can walk through the front door."

"Where's the fun in that?"

"Oh I don't know; it must be nice to be regular kids who use the freaking stairs."

"Are you coming or not?" He extends his arm out to me, and I sigh because we both know I will. I'd follow him anywhere, and he knows it as well as I do.

Harley isn't exactly forthcoming with where we're going. I ask, of course, but he just gives me that infuriating grin and ignores my questions by turning up the radio in his truck. I'm still mad at him, so I angle my body toward my door and pretend he isn't there, which is kind of difficult to do with his off-key singing.

Ten minutes later, as we turn south onto Highway 1, I know exactly where we are heading. I just don't know why.

"We're going to the cottage?"

When Harley and I were eight and seven-and-three-quarters respectively, our families vacationed together in Carmel-by-the-Sea, a small beach town on California's Monterey Peninsula. Our parents fell in love with the place that summer and decided they'd buy a beach cottage together for summers away from the city. At 1577-square feet, the single-story cottage is small, and when they made the investment, I don't think they all planned to stay there at once, but that's how it's always worked out—one family doesn't stay in Carmel without the other, and we've certainly never been there without the parentals.

Harley shrugs. "I thought we could play hooky and hang out there, like old times."

"Right," I say with a nod, and I feel stupid because why would we do anything but hang out … like old times? "Only our parents were with us then. And I didn't tell my mom where I was going; I don't have any clothes."

"So? Wear mine."

I make a face and tuck my hair behind my ear. I know he won't go back for any of my things and I didn't bring any money, which means I'm stuck wearing this outfit or clothing that's miles too big for me.

I've always loved Harley's spontaneity. I've often wished a little of it would rub off on me, and he's great with surprises, but as a very organized planner bordering on OCD, it's a struggle sometimes not to strangle him. "Gimme your phone. I need to call my mom."

He grins at me across the cab. "I didn't bring it."

I whack his arm, probably not the best course of action because Harley's as bad a driver as he is a planner, and he swerves into the lane beside us, ticking off some random commuter. "What? Why?"

"I don't know. I forgot it. We can find a phone when we get there."

"Yeah, okay," I say, and we spend the rest of the two-hour drive listening to the classics like Soundgarden's *Superunknown* and The Red Hot Chili Peppers' *Californiacation*, which are only the best road-trip albums in the history of ever. I have a very uneasy feeling, and I don't know what it is. I've never felt this way with Harley before, but he's acting weird … weirder, than usual, and it's unsettling.

We stop at a gas station, and I grab snacks and stretch my legs while Harley fills the tank. I attempt to use their pay phone, but it's broken and the cashier turns a murderous glare on me when I ask to borrow his, so I take my things and go. When we finally drive through town it's close to nine p.m, and before we've even pulled up to the cottage and opened the privacy gate, I can see something's amiss. The parentals hire a gardener to come through once every two weeks to maintain the grounds that aren't much bigger than the house, but they're spectacular, and part of the reason I love this place so much. With sculpted hedges, moss-covered stones, and wisteria, it looks like a real-life fairy garden. The light flickering through the brier privacy fence draws me like a moth to flame and I'm out of the car and opening the gate before he even has a chance to switch the engine off.

I blink several times, unable to grasp what I'm seeing. Someone has strung up paper lanterns and twinkle lights, and a hundred mason jars filled with candles illuminate the path to the front door. I am speechless. I literally have no words. Harley's presence is at my back now and I turn to look at him, wondering why he's not as awed as I am at the sight, but he's wearing one of his Pan smiles, so I know this is all him.

"What is this?" I glance down at his hands. He's holding a clear garment bag, and tucked safely inside is my prom dress. "Why is my dress here?"

"Because I'm an idiot."

"Well, yeah but, what does that have to do with my prom dress? Are we burning it? Because I gotta say I wouldn't be sad, but my mom might kill us both."

"We're not burning your dress. You're going to go put it on."

"Why?" I turn back to the garden, unable to take my eyes off the beauty of it for very long.

"You had a shitty prom," he says, brushing the wisps of hair that have fallen free of my braid from off my shoulder. He presses a kiss to my neck, and a shiver runs through me from head to toe. "I thought maybe we could make it better."

"But ... you went back to Riley ..."

"Yeah, to break up with her."

I turn my head and stare at him in disbelief. "On prom night?"

He grimaces. "I'm kind of a sucky boyfriend, huh?"

"Kinda." I can't pretend this news doesn't thrill me though. In fact, I'm practically beaming because maybe now he can be my sucky boyfriend, only without the suck. "Then where were you last night?"

"With Kordell, devising a plan."

"So you've been here all day?"

His arms wrap around my waist, and I inhale and hold my breath, afraid to let it go for the fear that I'm dreaming or that I've lost my mind or that I'm not really here and am in fact completely freaking crazy. His lips brush my ear and my head swims. Nope, definitely here, and definitely not crazy. "Well, some of us didn't lie around in bed all day pouting."

"I wasn't pouting."

"Yes you were," he whispers, and bites down on my earlobe. My arms automatically slip around the back of his neck. "I didn't do all of this, though. The moms helped."

"They know we're here?" My whole body tremors as he kisses that sweet spot beneath my ear, and my breath comes a little faster. "Oh man, my dad is going to kill you."

"You don't think I'd leave all those candles burning, do you? I texted them before I climbed in your window. We passed them two streets back, but you were doing that thing you do where you pretend you're Chris Cornell while belting out 'Black Hole Sun.'" The arm around my waist snakes up under the hem of my T-shirt, but he doesn't take it too far, and for that I'm grateful because he went to a lot of effort to create this night for me, and though I want to just lead him inside and let him touch me everywhere, I'm nervous and frightened as a colt, and I may need a little time to ease into the newness of his hands and mouth on my body. "And your dad thinks you're staying at a girlfriend's house, so at the risk of keeping all of my appendages, I'd like it to stay that way."

I turn in his arms. His eyes are lit up like torches from the candles and twinkle lights, and I can't help but smile sheepishly with the way he looks at me. I lower my gaze to his chest and my hands that are splayed against it over his thundering heartbeat. "I don't know what to say."

"Say you'll go to prom with me."

I shake my head in disbelief. "Yes. I'll go to prom with you."

With one arm, he pulls me in and kisses my lips. Just like last night, it doesn't take long for me to get carried away, and I grip the back of his neck as if it were a lifeline. Harley groans and pulls away. "God, I want you so fucking much," he says, cupping my face with his hand. And I can feel just how true that statement is. It scares me. He thrusts the dress towards me and inhales a deep breath. "Here, put this on before I ruin everything."

In a daze, I take it from him, and he places his hands on my shoulders and turns me to face the cottage. The front door is closed but through the window I can see a fire slowly burning in the stone fireplace and more candles lining the kitchen counter and dining table.

I find my way in the near dark to one of the bedrooms and slip on my dress. The bodice is tight with a zipper in the back that I can't reach, so I hurry back outside with my hair in its loose braid and my feet bare against the cool stone path. Harley fastens my zipper with agonizingly slow movements, and I know it's just so he can touch the bare skin of my back. It's the same reason I don't tell him to hurry up, because the anticipation is beautiful and torturous.

I twirl slowly for him, feeling a little self-conscious in the dress with my ratty hair and bare feet, but it's clear Harley doesn't see these imperfections because he pulls me close and whispers, "You're so goddamn beautiful."

And so is prom. Under a sky bursting with stars, we dance slowly to the sound of the waves crashing on the shore nearby, and later, as he leads me inside and we curl up on a soft blanket by the fireplace, I let him lead me somewhere else I've never been.

And even though it hurts like hell, it is magic, and it is fireworks, and when I close my eyes a supernova sets the whole world alight.

Chapter Eleven

Rose

"Ah shit," Harley says glancing down at his phone after it dings. He drops it all the time when he's landscaping in the city and mercifully, the heavy-duty case acts like a tank, so aside from a few scratches, it works fine despite him throwing it at the wall yesterday. We haven't talked about last night. I didn't ask him what caused him to go AWOL, and he didn't ask where I was or why I'd stumbled in blind drunk, but maybe he was too distracted to notice. Instead, we'd woken and had breakfast at one of the restaurants downstairs and then we'd lain around on the beach for several hours drinking daiquiris—virgin, thank you very much, because neither one of us were willing to face alcohol today. I am going to have to go on the ultimate cleansing diet after this vacation because my liver is not a happy camper right now.

"What's the matter?" I dry my freshly washed hair vigorously with the towel. Today is our last day on the island, and as much as I'll miss the view and the scent of briny ocean and baking hot sand, my hair won't miss it.

"I forgot about the couples massage I

booked." Harley stares at his phone, avoiding my gaze.

"Oh," I say quietly. "That."

Like I could forget him asking me if I thought a romantic couples massage was a good idea. Okay, so I actually had forgotten, but I blame too much sand, sun, and Blue Hawaiis. We had been hanging out at his apartment back in SF and he'd asked me about it. With tears pricking my eyes and bile burning like acid in the pit of my stomach, I told him to spare no expense and book the couples massage. *What did I care?* I'd be two thousand and three hundred miles away in SF, making love to a bottle of Bombay Sapphire and getting my freak on with my Lelo Olga, who'd oddly earned the nickname George Clooney, because I have a thing for silver foxes.

"We could go," he says.

I glare at him. "To a couples massage?"

Harley shrugs. Apparently this isn't a big deal for him. "Why not?"

"Because of all the romantic, honeymoony-type things, I'm pretty sure that would constitute as an activity we should avoid."

"It's just a massage," he argues. "It's not like they're going to leave the room so we can fuck."

"Right." *Oh god, but the way he says fuck still makes my insides turn liquid and melty.* "I'm pretty sure that only happens in pornos anyway."

Harley raises a brow and smirks at me. "And here I thought the only thing you watched was *My Wedding Affair*. Do me a favor and call me next time you're sitting down to watch porn. I'll bring the popcorn."

I roll my eyes, but the thought of Harley watching porn with me on my couch is insanely hot. "Anyway, it's still a bad idea."

"No, it's a brilliant idea. Let's do it."

"What? No. No, it's not; it's a terrible idea."

Harley glances up at me through thick, dark lashes and a serious expression. "Please, Rose? For me?"

I'm going to kill him. I follow that manipulative bastard into the day spa with my arms folded across my chest. We're greeted by a sweet Hawaiian woman who confirms Harley's reservation and proceeds to lei us before leading us toward a private room as she explains how they have the very best honeymoon treatment on the island. Once again, he doesn't bother to correct the woman when she calls me his bride.

It isn't that I don't like it, or that I don't want to be on the receiving end of a Hawaiian Honeymoon couples massage with Harley by my side—it's just that I don't want it like this. I don't want to play pretend. I want the dress, the cake, the one hundred and fifty-two guests, and an entire room full of flowers. I want the whole damn thing, and I want that with him. Hell, I'd throw all of my years of planning out the window just to have his ring on my finger, but I have none of that—just the pathetic inclination to meet my best friend's every wild whim, and the inability to say no to him. *Oh, and let's not forget the mad crush I've had since I was five years old.*

As we approach a door at the end of the hall, Harley pries open my hand, threads his fingers with mine, and whispers, "You ready?"

"No," I deadpan. I'm pulled inside the room anyway to excited murmurs of welcomes and congratulations from our masseuses. I glare at Harley, but he just winks at me and kisses the back of my hand before I can snatch it away. *Well, at least he's not wallowing anymore.*

The women introduce themselves as Margaretta and Kailani, and they tell us to remove our clothing once they leave the room but Harley, ever the asshole, decides to just drop trou right there in front of everyone, much to the amusement and chagrin of the women. I might have had the sense to make fun of him or be embarrassed too, if I wasn't busy staring at his junk for the second time in a week. I swear to god it's like attempting not to look at a solar eclipse—you know it's there, this wondrous sight that doesn't really come around all that much, and because of this, you look, even though you're fully aware you might lose an eye. That's what Harley's penis is, a solar eclipse, and judging by the way it grows under my stare, I wouldn't be all that surprised if I did lose an eye. *But ... but ... it's just so pretty.*

"Rose."

"Huh?"

"You're staring, love."

"Oh," I nod and snap out of my stupor, noticing for the first time that Harley and I are alone in the room. I frown as I step off Cloud Nine and take a seat in the waiting room of Reality. "Where did everyone go?"

"Seriously? My dick still has the power to render you speechless?" he asks.

"Well, only because you're hard right now," I protest, taking a step back from him until my ass meets the table.

He moves forward again until there's the barest hint of space between us without him touching me. "I'm hard because you're staring at it."

I swallow, wet my lips, and try not to reach

out and stroke the pretty with my fingertips. "Shut up, asshole. It's been a really long time."

"How long?" he asks, but his tone has gone from teasing to serious.

There's a knock at the door, saving me from answering that question. Harley grabs a towel from off the table and wraps it around his waist, then he leans into me and pulls my body flush with his. I let out a squeak. I can't bring myself to meet the woman's face as she pokes her head inside the door and asks if we're ready for her because my best friend is standing in front of me with a raging hard-on, and I'm beet red and trying like hell not to beg him to bend me over and fuck me on the massage table the second she leaves.

"You're not ready," Margaretta says a little disapprovingly.

Harley shakes his head, turning his gaze back to mine when he says, "My wife's a little shy about her body."

I frown. "No I'm not."

"Why?" the woman says. "You're so pretty and skinny."

"She's beautiful, right?" Harley asks the woman, but he looks at me as he says it, and he brushes my thick sandy blonde hair off my shoulder.

I am far from skinny, but I'm okay with that, and this isn't so much an issue with my body as it is

an issue with undressing in front of Harley. I've
never been nervous about him seeing me in the past,
but this is different. I am older now; gravity isn't as
kind as it once was, and things have filled out a
little since my teens and early twenties. I'm not
ashamed of my body; I'm just not sure I want
Harley's eyes roaming over me while I'm
undressing. It's dangerous ground, and he might
have been flirting with danger this entire trip, but I
see that for what it is. He needs to feel something
other than alone. I want him, but I want more from
him than a quickie on vacation.

"Now, hurry, hurry, get undressed,"
Margaretta urges and closes the door again. I'm left
standing in Harley's embrace, his naked body
pressed tightly to mine and his lips pressed against
my temple. I allow myself to lean into him for just a
fraction of a second. For a beat, it's as if we're back
in time and nothing has changed. His other arm
wraps tightly around my shoulders, and he squeezes
me so hard I can't breathe, and then he moves away,
giving me his back as he climbs onto the table and
rests his head on his hands. I turn around to remove
my clothes. I fold them and set them on the chair.
And then wrap the towel around my body. I can't
look at him as I climb up onto my own massage
bed. because everything is too raw, too familiar,
and too much like the last time we stood hip to hip
in his childhood bedroom in SF, embracing one

another.

Another soft knock sounds at the door and Kailani and Margaretta enter. They explain the treatments we'll both be receiving: Hawaiian Lomi Lomi massages, body scrubs, and a paraffin wax treatment for relieving pain and aiding with softening the skin. It all sounds like heaven, but I quickly learn that heaven is not as it was advertised in the brochure because I feel as if I'm being beaten to a bloody pulp. Margaretta does not muck around, and after thirty minutes of scrubbing my body with what feels like sandpaper, tenderizing my muscles with her elbows and knees and slapping some hot wax on my back, rolling me in a plastic film like a burrito and leaving me to cook, I think I pass out from the pain.

I wake to feather-light touches on my shoulder and blink in confusion. Harley stands beside me wrapped only in a towel, his body glistening with oil, his fingertips tracing circles over my slick flesh. "Hey," he says. "You've been out for twenty minutes."

I groan and attempt to push up on my

elbows, but my body aches all over. "I have?"

He continues his ministrations, gliding his fingers across my shoulder and down my spine all the way to the small of my back. Pushing the towel aside, he grabs a handful of my ass and squeezes. Shivers follow in his wake. I'm paralyzed by his touch, desperate for more, and terrified of it all at once. A thrill runs through me, but I shove it down. *No, no, no.* This is not allowed to happen now. Not seven days after his fiancée left him at the altar. Not when the heartbreak is still fresh, and I see the despair every morning I roll over and meet his gaze. *I will not be his rebound girl.*

"Harley," I whisper, as he lowers his head and presses a kiss into the soft crease where my ass meets my thigh. His tongue darts out and trails across my slick flesh, and I moan and throw my head back.

I won't let him do this to me again. I won't ... oh god, that feels good.

I swallow hard, and my whole body stiffens with anticipation as his tongue grazes the soft flesh of my outer labia. And then everything comes to a screaming halt as the image of him standing at that altar, waiting for a woman who wasn't me smashes its way into my mind. His eyes had met mine across the packed church when Alecia's head bridesmaid had whispered in his ear that his fiancée was no longer coming. He'd taken a deep breath, turned back to the gathered guests and said, as nonchalantly as someone might tell you they had a salad for lunch, "Sorry to bring you all out here today, but it appears my bride is nowhere to be found."

The room had been filled with stunned gasps and murmurs, and with one more glance in my direction, Harley had walked back down the aisle and left. I'd found him at the hotel suite thirty minutes later with the champagne he'd confiscated from the hotel ballroom.

Now, deft hands that know every inch of my body grip my hips and pull me closer, but I struggle out of his grasp and slide off the table. Of course, I don't account for the fact that I'm covered head-to-toe in oil and completely naked, so I go down hard on the parquetry floor.

"Ow, shit!"

Harley peers at me over the table, and I want so badly to go to him and have him finish what he started with those hands and lips and tongue. I also want to just melt right into the floor. "Rose, what the hell are you doing?"

"No." I hold out my hand to ward him away. "Don't come any closer."

"What?"

"You got dumped at the altar six days ago. Now I know she was a bitch, but you were preparing to marry this woman. You gave her your word and your ring, and she ran off with someone else, and now you're here with me, preparing to rip my heart out all over again."

"Rose—"

"Shut up and listen. I can't do this with you again after everything, after all the years we've worked to get back to being us. I can't let you destroy that because you decide you want a pity fuck."

Harley's gaze turns from molten to ice in seconds. "But you can kiss that client of yours? Isn't that ironic, that you make up the arrangements to send to his wife every week, and yet you still have no problem dry humping him by the pool?"

"You saw us?"

"Yeah, I saw. I saw him trying to shove his tongue down your fucking throat, so how is this any different?"

"Are you shitting me right now?" I throw my hands up in exasperation. "He's my client, a married one at that. Yes, it was wrong of us to drink too much at dinner and flirt as if we were both free to do so, but that's as far as it went. We both stopped that shit before it even started, and that is largely different than you and I—"

"Why?"

"Because you broke my fucking heart, Harley. Again. You proposed to another woman and it destroyed me." I suck in a deep breath and cover my mouth, but the words are out, and I can tell by the haunted look in his eyes that the damage is done.

"I didn't ... I didn't kn—"

"You didn't know? Is that it?" I swipe at my tears and make a choked sound in the back of my throat. "God, I know you are not this stupid."

"I thought you were over it."

"Over it?" I laugh but there's no humor in the sound. "I wish I could put you aside as easily as you seem to be able to dismiss me, but I can't, because I've been loving you so long I don't know how to stop."

I wrap the towel around my body and grab my clothes from the armchair. Harley reaches out a hand to stop me. "Please don't touch me."

"Rose, I'm not letting you walk like this. I fucked up."

"Yeah, you did," I whisper, yanking open the door. On the other side, Margaretta stands with her hand raised to knock but clutches her chest as if I just gave her a heart attack.

"Is there somewhere I can change?"

She points in the direction of the amenities across the hall. I stalk by and push open the door, ignoring Harley's pleas.

I'm at least twenty minutes in the bathroom. I cry for a good stretch of time, splash my face with water, rinse and repeat. I don't know how I'll face him now. I don't know how to undo the things I've said. I can't. Instead, I decide to hit the bar by the pool, because going back to our room means having to talk to him, and I am too damn angry with the both of us to hold a conversation and behave like an adult right now.

Dermot left this morning, so I know there's no chance of running into him again. Down here I'm as alone as I've ever been back in SF, only this time I have a view of paradise to make up for it and a chatty bartender named Mick, a handsome black man with gleaming white teeth and an infectious smile.

Mick will be my new best friend, I decide, when I'm three sheets to the wind and the Hawaiian sun has set. The tepid breeze glides off the ocean, and after what I think is my fifth cocktail and a handful of peanuts, I finally start to relax. Until some asshat sits down beside me. I close my eyes and breathe in the scent of him. It's some kind of beautiful torture being this close. *Always has been.*

"What can I get you?" Mick asks, and Harley opens his mouth, but I beat him to it.

"He isn't here for the drink." I swirl my umbrella in my almost empty glass. "He's just here to tell me it's time to leave."

"Have you been looking after my girl the whole time …" Harley pauses, reading the nametag pinned to my new friend's shirt. "Mick?"

"I'm not your girl." I slide my forearm across the sticky bar and lay my head down.

"The hell you aren't," he says, quietly. "Like it or not, you've always been my girl, Rose."

"Rose?" Mick says, side-eyeing me suspiciously. "You told me your name was Alecia."

"Oops," I deadpan.

Harley frowns. "How many has she had?"

"Six."

"Jesus." He pulls out his wallet and throws some cash on the bar for a tip. I charged all my drinks to the room, on account of not having a single thing on me but a bikini and a sundress. "Come on. I'm taking you back to the suite."

"No you're not. Mick, another drink, good sir."

"Sorry, sweet girl, but I have to cut you off."

"Oh come on." I throw my hands up in exasperation. "Why? Because my fake husband says so? I thought you and I were friends, Mick."

"He's not your friend, he's a bartender who's being nice to you because big tips keep him fed for the week," Harley says coolly. "Or they would, if you'd paid them."

"Did you just say tits?" I slur, and maybe my two besties are right—maybe I have had too much.

"I'm taking you back to the room." Harley gets up off his seat and reaches for my arms, but I pull away from his grasp.

"No. I'm hangin' out with Rick. He's going to teach me how to surf."

"Mick," Harley overemphasizes my new best buddy's name, as if he's trying to prove some point. *God, he's such a, dumb, handsome jerk.* "He isn't teaching you how to do anything because you're coming back to the room with me, and we're gonna talk this shit through."

I narrow my eyes on him. "You're a really shitty fake husband, you know that, right?"

"I know, and you're still nagging me as though you've had my ring on your finger for years."

I gasp in shock. *Oh no he didn't.* Before I can get my wits about me, Harley pulls me off the stool and throws me over his shoulder in a fireman's carry.

"Put me down," I scream, reaching out to the bartender in the hopes he'll come to my rescue. "Dick, save me."

The man just waves and gives me that ridiculously sweet smile as Harley carries me away, slung over his shoulder. He grunts as my fists strike his back, but he turns us and heads toward the exit. I bob against his body the entire way to the elevator, and then, when we're alone inside a giant, moving metal box, my stomach twists and I murmur, "Put me down. I'm gonna be sick."

"Nice try, love."

"Harley I'm ..." My stomach heaves as I puke all down his back and over the floor. He stiffens beneath me and then gently sets me on my feet as the elevator pings and the doors slide open.

"Feel better now?" he asks sarcastically, and I glare at him. Harley takes my hand and leads me out of the elevator, but he's walking funny on account of my puke covering his shirt and jeans.

I'm mortified, but I don't apologize because really, he brought this on himself. If he'd just left me at the bar with my new friend ... "What was his name?" I say, as he stops outside our door and slides the plastic card thingy into our lock.

Harley ignores me in favor of pulling me into the apartment. I make a beeline for the bed, but I don't get very far before he jerks me into the bathroom and I lean over the toilet, puking up my guts and watching all that perfectly good alcohol go to waste. He takes the band from his own hair and ties mine back, and then, as I lean against the cool tiles of the tub, he runs a shower and steps inside, fully clothed. After peeling off his sodden clothes, he leans over, wraps an arm around my waist, and pulls me in with him.

"Get off me," I complain.

Harley attempts to remove my dress, but I swat at him. I'm too tired to keep fending him off though, and he keeps at it until my defenses are whittled away to nothing and I eventually raise my arms for him. He doesn't try to rid me of my bikini, he just tugs me back against his body and we're engulfed by the warm spray. Seconds pass as he holds me in his arms. "I didn't do it to hurt you."

"And yet it did anyway," I murmur.

"Rose, I hate feeling like this," he says against my ear. "I hate knowing that no matter what I do, I'm going to break your heart."

"It wouldn't be the first time, and it won't be the last." There's no anger in my words, no bitterness now, just truth, and to my surprise he nods as if he agrees with that. "That's what love does—it breaks you down until there's nothing left. We're no different."

"I don't believe that."

"Of course you don't," I whisper. "Because you never really had someone you love rip your heart out."

"That's not true. You walked away from me once, remember?"

"And you fell in love with someone else," I say and then I quote J.M. Barrie, because I think if I speak a language he knows, then he'll finally understand, "Absence makes the heart grow fonder … or forgetful."

"That doesn't mean I stopped loving you."

"That's exactly what it means." I take a step back and climb out of the tub as Harley watches me, then I strip off my wet swimwear, yank a towel from the railing and wrap it around my body. I leave the room, avoiding his gaze the entire time. I don't even finish drying myself completely before I climb beneath the covers. I should go through my suitcase and find clothing to sleep in. I should pack, but I don't care about any of it.

I miss my city with the fog and fire sunsets, the scent of dumplings and pork buns wafting from The Golden Dragon. I miss fresh-cut flowers, and the bakery across the street whose chef brings me the "cupcake of the day" right before closing. I miss how uncomplicated we were when he was marrying someone else.

I ignore the fact that Harley will be sleeping a few inches from my naked body, and I drift off to sleep without shedding another tear. All of what I told him was true—some people are just meant to break your heart, as if it were their sole mission here on earth to teach you not to fall in love with the wrong person.

Some people will break your heart over and over again, because some of us never learn.

Chapter Twelve

Rose

Age eighteen

Head down against the May wind, I make my way from class toward the football field. We'd run late today with the yearbook because it was the last day to finalize the layout before printing, and I hadn't had a chance to meet Harley earlier, so he'd texted to say he was on the field.

The last month of school was winding down, and since Harley and I had officially become a thing, I'd spent a fair amount of time with the football team. I actually liked them, so watching them come together as a team for the last few months of their lives had been kind of special. But football was done with, my eighteenth birthday had come and gone in the blink of an eye, and I felt no different. I was older, one step further away from childhood, and no matter where I go from here, I'll never get these moments back. So while high school wasn't exactly my favorite place in the world, I didn't mind it all that much with him by my side.

Until it comes to scenes like the one I am

witnessing play out before me. Harley stands on the bleachers with Kordell, Watson, and a group of girls all huddled around closely. Jaycee Grainier—a slutty sophomore who has made no attempt to hide her interest in Harley—has five long, pink talons resting on his forearm as she laughs at something he's said. I don't consider myself a jealous person, but as she thrusts her chest forward and moves closer to him, all the while keeping her hand firmly fixed on his forearm, I see red and I stalk toward them.

I don't direct my anger at her, though. Instead, my gaze of hell-hath-no-fury is turned right at Harley.

He pulls away from Talons and meets me halfway scooping me up into a hug, placing huge, hard kisses against my cheek and neck. His hair is damp, he smells of boy sweat, and green field, and his jersey sticks to him as if he's just played a game. I try to hold onto my anger, I really do, because though she was the one putting her grubby paws all over him, he was allowing her, but I can never stay mad at him for long.

"Put me down." I squirm in his arms.

"Kiss me."

"No, everyone's watching."

"Oooh shut down," Watson says, and Harley sends me one of those delicious mischievous smiles. I sigh and press my lips to his in a chaste kiss, but he parts them with his tongue thrust deep inside my mouth. I let out a whimper and quickly lose myself to the sensation. His hands slide from my hips to my ass, and I pull away with a shriek before we can make an even bigger spectacle of ourselves.

"Okay, mister. What gives? You only get this excited after you win."

He smiles against my lips. "Not true. I get this excited every time you strip down to your panties for me too."

I blush and bat him away. Then I look closer at Watson and Kordell and see the sweat on their brow and jerseys too. "Did you guys play this afternoon?"

"Did we play? Rose, that was the fuckin' shit," Watson says, making overly expressive hand gestures. We walk toward the student carpark. Talons stays with us, though her friends quickly make themselves scarce. "Your boy here was on fire. Man, never thought I'd see Nick Raban actually cheer for a player he's got his eye on. I read somewhere scouts aren't supposed to do that. Supposed to act all mean and shit."

I snap my head in Harley's direction. "Scouts?"

"Err, yeah." He takes my hand and kisses it before lacing his fingers with mine. "Just some guy looking for late recruits."

"Some guy?" Kordell says with a deep

chuckle. "Brother, you can't be callin' Nick Raban 'some guy.'"

"Wait," I say, the pieces finally slipping into place. I stop dead in my tracks, and the slutty sophomore bumps into me. I turn and glare at her before narrowing my gaze on Harley. "Isn't he the scout for Louisiana State?"

He shrugs. "It's nothing. He liked how I played is all."

"Yeah, liked it so much he decided to come all this way in the off-season to see you play in person," Kordell says.

"How long have you known about this?" I demand as Harley pulls me along toward his truck.

"Not long."

"Harley, those guys don't just come out randomly to high schools all over the country, especially not this time of year. Not unless they're brought here for a reason."

"Come on, let's go home," Harley says.

I pull my hand out of his grasp. "I don't wanna go home."

"Uh-oh," Talons chimes in, and I swear to god I'm about to beat this bitch down in a big way.

"Don't you have a BJ or two to give out behind the men's washroom?" I snap, and even I'm shocked by how harsh that was. Her mouth gapes open, and I cringe on the inside because I don't know what's got into me. *Oh wait, yes I do.*

"Alright then, that's our cue to leave you two lovebirds alone," Watson says, taking Jaycee under his wing and steering her away from me. *Probably wise.* "Come on, darlin'. I'll give you a ride."

Kordell pats Harley on the back in what looks like commiseration and says, "I'll see you tomorrow, brother."

Then we're alone. I soften my tone, because I know I'm being unreasonable. This is a big thing, a huge thing. This is unheard of, and he'd been so happy before I ruined it all. "How long have you known he was coming?"

"A couple weeks." Harley kicks at a pebble on the lot, watching it skitter across the pavement. "Coach sent him my tape. That's why he's been riding me so hard."

"A couple weeks like before we got together, or a couple weeks like when you told me at the cottage that you were taking a year off of study so you could stay in SF?"

"I didn't know he was coming for sure until last week."

I frown. "Why wouldn't you tell me?"

He sighs and heads for his truck. "Because I knew you'd react just like this."

That stops me in my tracks. I can't ignore the hammering of my heart, or the lump that has formed in my throat at the mere thought of him being miles away, but I am being selfish. Really damn selfish. This is Harley, and playing pro football is his dream. It's a dream he thought was unattainable, despite all the work he's put into being the best.

"I'm an ass." I move into him, wrapping my arms around his neck and playing with the wisps of hair there. He slides his hands around my waist and leans his forehead against mine, and though I feel like crying inside, I smile up at him. "I'm so happy for you."

"Are you?" he asks, not with sarcasm or malicious intent, but as if he genuinely wants to know, so I nod and kiss his lips.

"You have to tell me everything. What did he say? Do you think you have a chance?"

"I don't know." He shrugs. "I don't really want to think about it."

I laugh, because surely he's joking. "Harley, Nick Raban from LSU came to watch you play. How are you not dying with excitement right now?"

"I'm just not."

"Why? What possible reason do you have not to be happy about this?"

"Because it means leaving you behind," he snaps.

And there it is, the truth we'll never get over. The truth that could destroy us. I've been accepted to Berkley—a UC Berkley extension—one of the greatest business schools in the country, and the best part is, I don't have to leave the city to attend because I'll be studying at the SF campus. I've also been offered an internship with SF's most coveted floral designer, Sara Lau. I've wanted that spot for an entire year, and I beat several other hopefuls for it. I can't give that up to move halfway across the country.

"We don't even know if it's going to happen." Harley takes hold of my hand and walks me to the passenger side of his truck. He opens the door, and I climb in. "Let's just wait and see, okay?"

"Wait and see. Sure," I agree, but fear twists in my belly like a worm on a hook. I don't need to wait and see, because it isn't a question of if he'll get a full-ride scholarship to play varsity now that Nick Raban has been to watch him—it's a question of which college he'll say yes to. He's that good. "Do your parents know?"

"No," he says, starting up the vehicle and pulling out of the lot. "I didn't want the pressure; you know how Dad gets on game night. If I'd told him about this, I'd have never left the field for weeks."

"Well, you have to tell him now. They're going to be so excited. This is it, Harley—you're standing on the precipice, and all of your dreams are about to come true."

"They already did, love. This thing with LSU is just a fantasy. Only the best of the best get chosen, and I'm just … me."

"Oh please. If you only knew what you were—"

"I'd have a much bigger head." He grabs my hand and runs tiny kisses from my wrist to the tips of my fingers, and then he settles our interlocked hands on his knee while he drives. "Enough talk of football—I'd much rather talk about what I'm going to do to you when I sneak in your bedroom window tonight." I blush from the tips of my toes to the roots of my hair as I meet his mischievous gaze. He grins. "Or we could just drive somewhere now and get busy in my truck."

I roll my eyes and elbow him in the stomach. He feigns hurt, but I know my little elbows hardly make a dint in that wall of muscle.

"Don't tell my parents about LSU," he blurts out fifteen minutes later as he turns from Noe Street onto 29th. "I don't want to get their hopes up. No more talk."

"No more talk," I agree, though my thoughts have other ideas. When we pull in the drive, Rochelle comes racing out of the house, shrieking with joy. I glance at Dean, who's beaming at us through the windshield, and my heart sinks. They know. Coach Reinhart must have called them.

Harley climbs out of the truck and they both

sweep him up in a huge hug. I slowly exit the car and cross the pavement to my house.

"I'll see you later, Harley," I say, but I don't think he hears me over Rochelle's shrieking. My parents aren't home yet, which I'm thankful for because I don't think I could deal with Mom's questions right now when I don't have the answers to any of them, so I trudge upstairs to my room and lock myself away, flopping down on the bed and throwing myself into school work.

An hour later, there's a ping against the open window, and a wadded up piece of paper lands on my floor. I tuck my pencil behind my ear, stand up and walk over to it, unfolding the page and reading the text written in bold black Sharpie.

Wendy,
Forgive me?
Pan.

I smile sadly down at the note. *There's nothing to forgive.* When I glance up, Harley stands at the window dressed in a blue button-down that's rolled at the sleeves and stretched tightly against his broad chest. Growing up, he'd always been taller than me, but between puberty and football he's filled out everywhere. Gone is the tall and slightly gangly boy I knew, who might've blown away in a strong SF wind. Instead, at eighteen he is a man, an athlete at his physical peak with plenty of hard-won muscle, an exquisitely chiseled face, and his hair a messy mop of tawny curls atop his head. Sometimes it's difficult to remember that the boy next door was ever a boy at all.

I brace my hands against the sill and lean out, appraising him appreciatively. "Fancy."

"Dinner at The Dragon. You wanna come?"

"Nah, I've got schoolwork to do," I say, and smile half-heartedly. "Besides, your parents have been waiting for this moment since you started your illustrious football career as a pee wee; you should give them that."

He frowns, rubbing a hand across the back of his neck. "Yeah. I guess."

"Enjoy it, Harley," I encourage, though it breaks my heart to do so. "How often can you say all your dreams have just come true?"

"Every day you let me between those gorgeous thighs of yours." He gives me one of those impish grins, and fear beats a stake through my heart because I wonder if one day soon he'll look at other girls like that. *What if we can't make it work when we're two thousand miles apart?*

"Get out of here," I say, throwing my pencil at him. It bounces off of his chest and falls into the small gap between our houses. I can't count how many pencils I've lost this way; I half expected them to pile up over the years so that all I had to do when I needed a HB was reach out the window.

Rochelle calls him from downstairs, and he

turns toward his door shouting, "Just a second."

He turns his attention back to me and leans across the gap with pursed lips. I lean out too until my lips meet his in a strained and heady kiss. Falling from this height has always been a fear of mine.

"I'll come over later, and we'll watch a movie."

"Okay," I say, and give him a stern look when his mother calls him for a second time. "Go."

"I love you, Rose Perry," he crows like a madman. I roll my eyes and step back from the window. "Rose, say it."

"Go." I make a shooing gesture with my hands. "Before your mom has kittens."

"Not until you say it." He fiddles with his phone, and I think he can't be all that serious about it because I only have half of his attention.

"Fine," I say impatiently. "I love you too."

"Say it properly."

I throw my hands up, exasperated. "Oh my god, you're annoying."

"Say it."

"I love you too, Harley."

"I love you too, Harley," his phone echoes back to us.

I give him a death glare because he knows I can't stand the sound of my own voice when it's been recorded. "I'm deleting that the second I get my hands on it."

He shoves the phone down his pants. I fold my arms across my chest and walk away from the window, back to my studies.

"You love me. I have it on record," he singsongs. Seconds later, Rochelle calls him again, and he shouts, "I'm coming!"

"Would you go already?"

"In a hurry to get rid of me, huh?" He smiles sadly, and it's then that I know, he's already made up his mind. LSU, Alabama, Ohio State—it doesn't matter which school he accepts. Coach Reinhart would have sent his tapes to them all. Harley will be leaving SF for good, because there's no way he won't move onto being one of the NFL's most coveted players.

In the morning, I don't wake to kisses on my face and neck like I usually do. Instead, I'm freezing my boobs off as a cool SF breeze sneaks in my open window. My covers are gone, likely kicked off in the middle of the night, and since I didn't have a body cuddled up behind me on my narrow single bed, I seem to have woken with a sniffle. I get up to slam the window closed when something catches my eye—his window. Or more specifically, his drawn blinds. He never draws the blinds. Never.

I head down to breakfast in such a foul mood that even my dad looks afraid as he peers over the edges of his Saturday morning paper while sitting at the table. "Bad sleep?"

I just look at him. It's childish, I know. But goddamn it, it's my right as a teen, and I hardly ever play the teen card, preferring instead to speak my mind no matter the consequences. Mom and Dad share a dithering look across the table and I squawk something about them not understanding what it's like to be a girl genius with infuriatingly basic parents. Even though my mom is kind of a lush now, before leaving her career to be a stay-at-home mom, she curated one of SF's most successful art galleries, and my dad didn't become the head of pediatric surgery at Oakland based on his looks. So naturally, they both burst into peals of laughter as I stomp back up the stairs and throw myself into my room, slamming the door shut behind me.

Harley sits on my bed, nursing his head in his hands as he glances across at me with the same confused expression my parents wore only seconds ago.

"Hey," he says, patting the mattress beside him.

I'm too wired, and too angry to sit down

right now, so I pace. "Hey yourself."

"You're angry with me," he says, and it isn't a question.

"I'm not angry. I just have things to do."

"On a Saturday? I'm an asshole, I know … Could you stop pacing? You're giving me a headache." I stand still, my arms folded against my chest and my glare practically burning a hole through his irritatingly pretty face. "Okay, I'm not sure that's any better, but you are damn cute when you're mad."

"Shut up."

"I'm sorry I didn't come over. Coach happened to be at The Dragon last night, along with Nick Raban; he invited me and my parents to join him. I swear to god, you'd have puked with the way they talked about me. Anyway, after dinner I ran into Watson and Ben, and they dragged me out to a party to celebrate."

"Whose party?" I demand.

He swallows hard and glances at the window as if he's looking for an emergency exit. "Riley's."

My whole body just deflates, and not in any way that means I'm relieved. "You went to a party at your ex-girlfriend's house without me?"

"Come on, Rose, it wasn't like that."

"What was it like, then?"

He rakes a hand through his hair in a

frustrated gesture. "It just happened."

"Oh, you're really making this so much better."

He shakes his head, his expression just as irritated as I'm sure mine is. "That's not what I meant. Nothing happened."

"You know what? I have … things, so if you could just go—"

"Rose," he says softly.

"What?"

He takes a step toward me, and I take one back. We repeat this dance another three times until I leap over the bed in an attempt to get away, and he scoops me up and throws me down on the soft mattress. "It was just a party."

"Yeah, and she's just your ex. Your hot, long-legged, perfecter-than-thou ex."

"Are you trying to talk me out of dating her or back in? I'm confused." He smirks, and a part of me wants to punch him in his pretty face.

"I hate you."

"No you don't. I have it on tape."

"Screw you."

"Okay," he whispers in my ear, and then kisses my neck.

I know I shouldn't think this way, but I already feel as if he's slipping away. Nick Raban coming all this way to meet with him is possibly the greatest thing that will ever happen to Harley, and

I'm so proud. I'm happy for him, but I'm also dying. *We're* dying. Little by little, we're coming closer to the end. A part of me wants to scream and shout that we had plans, that he's breaking all of the promises we made one another in these last few heady weeks, and that everything we dreamed of is going up in smoke because of some stupid football game.

I know that's not fair, though. I know if the situation was reversed, Harley would be nothing but supportive of me, even if it killed him, even if it broke his heart, and so I push down those feelings. I tamp down the frustration and the fear and the anger and I smile, even though my heart is breaking.

I let him push my shirt up my body until his fingers brush my nipples and cause gooseflesh to break out all over me, and I kiss him long and slow and sweet. Louisiana is two thousand miles away and I'll need as many memories as I can get to keep me warm at night when he's not here to jump in through my window.

I let him make love to me with my parents downstairs and my door unlocked because to hell with the consequences. I love him, and the weight in my bones tells me that what we have, what we've made here, has an expiration date, and though that thought breaks my heart, I grab hold of the time we do have, and I don't let go. I know he can sense my unease, because I feel his, too. I have no doubt that he loves me, and moving across the country doesn't necessarily mean the end for us, but I know he feels the big, scary indecision of it all just as heavily as I do.

After my parents have left, Dad to golf and Mom to her book club meeting, Harley and I spend the day hiding out in my room watching old movies. Our kisses are slow and tempered, and our hands frenetic in our exploration of one another. It's a perfect day, but I have no doubt it will be one of the last.

Chapter Thirteen

Rose

I am hungover. Being hungover while dealing with airport security is never fun, and even though we don't have to wait in those ridiculously long international lines, I still need it like a hole in the head. I'm fidgety and cranky and still not talking to Harley.

Maybe that is childish, but I don't know how else to handle the situation. I don't have a single thing to say to him. I love him. After last night he knows that now with one hundred percent certainty, but on some level he had to have known that I loved him back then, and still he chose to marry someone else. I don't blame him for not being in love with me; I blame him for thinking we could have meaningless vacation sex without me losing my head. I blame him for making me want to forget my morals and forge ahead with it anyway, even though it would destroy me in the long run. And I blame him for putting me in a position where I had to say no to him even though I wanted it so badly, because if I didn't there would be nothing left of us to salvage by the time he was finished.

The security officer waves me through the gate and I collect my phone, kindle, and purse from the conveyor belt. We make our way through the airport, then Harley grabs our suitcases from the turnstile and we climb into his truck. I feel the Zen slowly start creeping in as we drive through Glen Park, and the late afternoon fog blankets the city.

Harley seems to be slowing down the closer we get to my apartment, and when he pulls up to the curb, he turns to me. "So listen, thanks for coming on my honeymoon with me."

And all Zen is gone, replaced instead by rage and hurt, injustice, and a lot of stabby feelings. "Sure, no problem." I reach for the handle of my door, but Harley's hand grasps mine and I turn to glare at him.

"Rose, I know I screwed up, on more than one occasion, but we need to talk this through. I'll give you some time to cool off, and tomorrow night I'll come over and—"

"No." I pull my arm free, tired of the liberties he constantly takes with me.

A hard crease forms between his brows and I can tell he's trying not to lose patience. "What do you mean no?"

"I need some space. I need to clear my head and figure out what's best for me, and I can't do that with you around, so ... no. I'll call you when I'm *over it*." I say those last two words with as much venom as I can muster towards this man. If I were capable of it, I'd dig the knife deeper, but I've never wanted to hurt him a day in my life.

Choke the life out of him, maybe ...

I climb out of the truck and head for the back where my suitcase lays next to his. Harley stays in the car a moment longer, as if he's collecting his breath, and then he jumps out and rounds the truck to face me. I grasp the handle of the case and attempt to lift it upwards, but he puts his hand flat against it and slams it back down.

"Wait a goddamn minute, Rose. I'm not letting you walk away from me again, you got it? You're mad; I get that. I hurt you and I'm sorry, but I won't let you push me away. Tomorrow night, you and I are doing this whether you like it or not."

"No, we're not." I take a step back, because my blood is boiling and I don't trust myself not to punch him in his perfect face.

"The hell we're not." He snatches up my arm and pulls me close, until I feel his hot breath on my face as he sneers, "I'm not letting you fuck this up by walking away."

"*Me* fuck this up?" I shout, tearing my arm free and shoving his broad chest. "Me? Fuck you. I am not the one who moved on to the first piece of ass I found."

"Jesus." Harley's tone is seething when he says, "Twelve years on and you're still slinging that in my face, huh?"

"Don't you dare pretend you're not at fault here. I may have walked away in Louisiana, but you're the one who let us die, so don't tell me I'm the one who fucked us up."

I don't even bother with my case this time. I know it will only give him an excuse to spit more vitriol in my face. If I stay here arguing with him on the street, I'm going to lose it completely—I'll break down and give in because it's what I always do, it's what I've always done with him and at some point it needs to stop.

So I walk away. I fumble in my purse for my keys and open the shop, and I slam the door in his face.

Of course, Harley never could let me have the last word, and infuriatingly, as I'm climbing the spiral stairs to my apartment, he opens the door and steps inside.

"I don't want to fight with you, but I need you to know you aren't the only one that lost something," he says, and his voice is so ragged with emotion and hurt that I stop walking and just listen with my back to him. "I've never stopped loving you, Rose, not for a single day."

I laugh incredulously, a bitter, broken sound. "Then you have one hell of a way of showing it."

I walk up the stairs, half expecting him to come after me, but he doesn't, and I'm relieved. I can't keep doing this with him. I can't just move on or get over it. He made me a promise when he left for college and some part of me always thought that he'd fulfil it. It's stupid, really, because how can you trust the promises made by children in love? You can't. That man broke every promise he ever made me, and I should have known better because a leopard doesn't change his spots.

Chapter Fourteen

Rose

Age eighteen

I sit on Harley's front step. The taut muscles in his back constrict beneath his T-shirt as he loads the last of his belongings into the bed of his truck. Our parents crowd around the car, talking amongst themselves—mostly I think our dads are talking football and my mom is consoling Rochelle, who feels as if she's losing her baby.

Harley comes and sits by my side. It's early morning, but hot already, and sweat glistens on his brow and soaks his shirt. He bumps his shoulder against mine, and I take a deep breath, inhaling the citrus-spiced scent of his cologne. He holds out his hand and I lace my fingers with his, all the while swallowing back my tears. I don't want to cry today. It feels as if I've been crying nonstop for weeks. I'm bitter and heart-sore, drowning in my loneliness before he's even left, and I don't want his last memory of me tainted with ugly tears and desperation.

I think he senses all of this, because he

squeezes my hand. I can't look at him; if I do, I'll lose it all together.

"Rose, look at me."

"I don't want to," I say, my voice thick with emotion.

He tilts my chin up until I meet his gaze. "Come on. Let me see that beautiful face." His breath is ragged, in much the same way it was last night when we lay in his bed for the last time and he said his only regret in the past five years was waiting so long to kiss me again. There had been tears in his eyes then, and they glisten now as he cups my cheek. "I love you, Rose Perry."

And that does it—all my self-control flies right out the window and fat ugly tears spill over and slide down my face. "I love you too." I can barely get the words out, I'm sobbing so hard.

"I know. I have it on tape, remember?" He swipes the salt from my cheek and presses his lips to my wet eyelids. "I'm going to be back before you know it. Four years isn't that long, and you'll be finished college and the internship, and then we'll talk about where we go from there."

"It's a lifetime."

"I'll be back at Thanksgiving, and we'll talk every day until then. It'll be like I'm still climbing in your window annoying the shit outta you."

"No, it will feel exactly like you're gone."

"Yeah, you're right, it's gonna suck." He

pulls me to my feet and leads me down the stairs. Sliding an arm around my waist, Harley hugs my mom and shakes Dad's hand, all the while keeping one arm around me, as if he's afraid I'll vanish if he removes it. I step out of his embrace and allow Rochelle and Dean to say proper goodbyes to their son, and then he wraps his arm around my shoulder and pulls me into him. I hold on while we both cry, and then he clears his throat and whispers brokenly, "I'm going to miss you so fucking much."

With one last kiss on my forehead, he turns away and climbs into the truck. The roar of the engine makes it somehow more final, and I sob uncontrollably as he backs out of the drive.

He doesn't make it five yards before the truck slams to a stop, its red taillights hovering, taunting me in the early SF morning. He isn't moving, but I'm on autopilot. One step, two steps, my feet swallow the ground between us, and then he's out of the truck, catching me up in his big arms as I wrap myself around him and smash my lips down on his, kissing him in a way that the parentals probably wished they weren't privy to.

When our kisses return to gentle sorrowful pecks I pull back and whisper, "I love you, Pan."

"Wendy, my Wendy," he says breathlessly. "You wait for me. You wait for me or I'm going to come back and gut the asshole who takes my place."

"No one ever could take your place," I tell him. He nods, setting me on my feet and smoothing the hair back from my forehead.

"Rose, when I get home, I'm going to put a ring on that finger." He cups my face with both hands, searching my gaze like a desperate man seeking salvation. "So you had better wait for me. Promise you'll wait?"

I nod and smile through my tears. "Forever if I have to."

"Forever is an awfully long time."

"Yes, it is," I agree.

Chapter Fifteen
Rose

It has been an entire week since that godawful fight with Harley, and I haven't seen or heard from him since, which I guess isn't all that surprising, seeing as I'm the one who said I needed space. Business at the shop has been booming, but despite what I told him about needing time to figure out who I am without him, I haven't done much figuring at all. I miss him like a junkie misses a fix. My world is incomplete without him in it, as if all color has been stripped away. It's for the best, though, because it always ends the same way with us—with Harley breaking my heart.

The phone rings, and I glance at Izzy and Ginger—the new girl we're trialing this week. Both are tied up with customers so I set the roses down on the counter and wipe one hand on my apron before picking up the handset. "Darling Buds, how may I help you?"

"Rose, darling, it's me," my mother says in my ear.

"Mom, right now is a bad time. We're rushed off our feet; thanks for coming in today to help with that like you said you would," I say caustically.

"I'll be there later. I'm out running errands and decided to stop in at that Zuni place over on Market Street—have you been there?"

Considering restaurants popped up in this city and disappeared just a few months later all the time, I would not have been surprised if I didn't know what she was talking about. But I did. I'd heard talk of Zuni's before, and it was almost impossible to get a reservation there. At least every time I tried, that was the case. "No, Mom, I haven't been there."

"Well, come meet me now. We'll have lunch."

I don't hide the surprise from my voice. "You're having lunch there? I can't get away right now. I have work, and it's Ginger's first week, remember?"

"What good is having your own business when you can't leave whatever time you want?" Mom complains. "You know who does run his own business and make time for lunch with his mother? Harley."

My jaw clenches. "Well, why don't you call him?"

"Don't be like that, darling. I just think you're working too hard."

"You have to work hard in order to run a successful business, Mom," I say impatiently.

"Besides, I took time off a week ago, in Hawaii."

"Yes, and we all know how that turned out," she mutters.

I don't have girlfriends I can talk to about these things. I work too hard for high-maintenance friendships and once you're in a position where you get to select the staff around you, the hierarchy of friendly work relationships shift, and it becomes harder to make friends and keep them when you barely have time to scratch yourself. I don't have anyone to talk to, and when I came back from Harley's honeymoon I'd really, *really* needed someone to talk to. So in a moment of weakness, I'd called my mother. I'd told her all about Hawaii and my fight with Harley, and it had actually been therapeutic. Though it is a decision I'm beginning to regret on account of her bringing it up every five minutes.

"Please, Rose, I'm not going to live forever, you know? There will come a day when I am dead and you'll wish you had taken me up on that offer for lunch."

I sigh. Trust my mother to guilt me into doing her bidding. "It's all the way across town, Mom."

"Then you better hurry," she says and hangs up.

I slam the phone down on its cradle, scaring an elderly lady buying a bunch of daisies and a few potted plants. Ginger squeals like a frightened piglet and holds her hand against her heart. I shoot them both an apologetic glance. "Sorry. Mothers …"

The elderly woman gives me a tight smile, and I can tell she's judging me from behind her ridiculously large frames. I smile tightly back and head over to Izzy, whose customer just left. "Can you hold down the fort for a while? My mother is guilting me into having lunch with her."

"Sure," Izzy says, straightening a vase on the shelf. "Ginger and I will make sure the strippers are gone by the time you get back."

"No strippers," I say, sounding oddly like my mother. I shudder and remove my apron, wondering if perhaps I should change my outfit before heading out. I have on a pair of black wide-leg pants and a boat-neck black and yellow top with thick stripes. I'm not sure about the top—I always feel a little like a bumble bee in it, no matter what I pair it with—but I decide to forgo changing because then I'd likely be upstairs for hours. It's best to get this over with, like ripping off a Band-Aid, because I just know my mother has some ulterior motive. She never invites me to lunch. I grab my purse from under the counter and head for the door.

"Fine, no strippers, but maybe I'll go through the accounts and see if a certain Silver Fox would like to come into the store to pick up his arrangement this week." Izzy winks.

I haven't mentioned Dermot to Izzy at all, but I know she gets a vibe about us because she makes an effort to tease me as soon as the door has closed behind him. Though he hasn't been in since our return from Hawaii, which makes me think he found another barista to make his morning coffee. Even though I'd never intended to wind up blind drunk and in a compromising position with the man, I feel responsible for his absence. Dermot is paid up until the end of the year with his arrangements, but yesterday, when I made up Mrs. Carter's bouquet to send to the house, I was struck with guilt, remorse, and an unhealthy amount of disappointment.

"I like you, Izzy, but please don't make me hurt you," I say. And I do like her. Izzy is young, in her early twenties, with a couple of tattoos and pale lavender hair. She has several facial piercings, and ordinarily that's not my thing, but she manages to make it work for her. Crazy hair and piercings aside, she's a hard worker, and I'd be lost without her.

With a wink back at the girls, I open the door and step out onto the pavement to hail a cab. Thirty minutes later I walk inside the restaurant and find my mother at a window table in the corner. She has company. "Darling, you're here."

"And you're not alone," I say sternly, and then turn my glare on Harley. "Did you put her up to this?"

He meets my glare and raises me a glower, then he shrugs. "I knew you wouldn't see me otherwise."

"You're unbelievable." I shake my head.

"Rose, sit down," Mom implores, glancing around the packed restaurant at the other patrons watching us. "You're making a scene."

I breathe deeply and sit opposite Harley. My mother stands and kisses me on the cheek. "Well, now that you're both here, I must go and help the girls at the shop. You two have a nice lunch, and take as long as you need. I'll close up the store today."

"Mom."

She gives a tinkling wave and wafts away on a breeze of sugar and spice and Chanel No. 5. "Bye, darlings."

I count to ten in my head, but I still want to hurt them both for tricking me into this. I grab my mother's untouched wine—rare for her—and guzzle half the glass in one mouthful, then I signal the waiter for another. "I thought I said I needed time."

"I gave you time; I gave you a whole goddamn week," he says, nursing his beer and playing with the condensation on the outside of the glass. "I'm not giving you any more than that. Now we can do this here or we can do it at my place, where there's bound to be a lot more yelling. Personally, I'd prefer to do it here because I heard this place has the best chicken in town."

I don't know why, but this makes me smile. Maybe it's because we're both so alike. Maybe it's because I love that he thinks about the great food this city has to offer as much as I do. Or maybe it's because I just missed my friend.

"There she is." Harley smiles, and mine falters. He sighs and loses the grin altogether. "Rose, I don't want to do this anymore."

"Do what?"

"Avoid one another like this. I miss you. Life is shit right now, you know? It's really fucking shit, and I need my best friend." He reaches out and places his large hand over mine on the table. "I'll get down on my knees and beg. I'll sacrifice a lamb, pledge allegiance to any goddamn deity you choose, I just—I need you. Okay? In whatever form that takes." He lowers his voice and leans closer. "I can't keep doing this. I can't keep staring at your number in my phone and not call it. I know what I did was wrong, or the way I went about it at least, but please don't shut me out."

My heart, my heart is bleeding, rattling against its bone cage and begging to be given over to the care of his hands, but my head? My head knows that my heart is a damn fool. "I'm sorry it's been hard for you, but I think I need a clean break."

"No, no, Rose, come on. This is us you're talking about. We don't take breaks. We're not friends who need a little time away, we're family, and right now I need you," he says, sounding desperate.

"And what about what I need?" I ask quietly. "Does that not matter to you at all?"

"Ah shit." He rakes a hand through his hair. "Yeah, it matters."

He glances out the window at the traffic going by, but it's as if he's not seeing any of it. His eyes are haunted. He clutches my hand on the table, only now he's squeezing hard enough to bruise, and I don't even think he's aware of it.

I place my free hand on top of his. Harley's eyes snap to mine. He loosens his hold. "Hey, what's going on with you?"

"Nothing." He picks up his beer and drains it dry. His voice is hoarse when he says, "I can't lose you, Rose."

It's in this moment that I realize my head is a damn fool too, because try as I might, I can't stay angry at him. I want to. I want to scream and lash out with my fists and bitter words. I want to slice the knife in both of us deeper and beg him to tell me why. Why he waited. Why he asked another woman to marry him, and why he said those words the other day because there's no way they could be true. If he hasn't stopped loving me in all this time how could he agree to marry Alecia?

I don't ask any of this. I don't lash out, and I

don't drive the knife deeper. I just curse my stupid, lonely heart for being unable to help itself.

"Don't lead me on, Harley. I deserve better than that," I say, with tears pricking my eyes. It's going to cost me something to let him in again, but it would hurt me more to shut him out entirely. "And don't break my heart again."

Relief washes over his face, so beautiful and overwhelming that it's as if I just saved him from a firing squad. He snatches up my hand and presses a series of rough kisses over it from wrists to fingertips.

"I won't," he says on a ragged breath. "I swear I'll never hit on you again."

I frown, because that wasn't exactly what I meant, but a part of me knows that's the only way I can have him in my life. As a friend. Anything else leads to me being heartbroken again. He'll be my best friend, and I'll go back to worshiping Harley Hamilton from afar the way I always have.

It's better this way for both of us, even if it feels as if my chest has been flayed open, my ribs pulled apart, and my heart smashed into a bleeding, broken pulp. It's better this way. Even if my fool heart disagrees.

Chapter Sixteen

Rose

Harley and I are complicated. We've always been complicated. From the day we met it's been our thing, or maybe it has always been simple and we've been the ones to twist it, turn it on its head and convolute what the rest of the world has already seen. All I know is that there isn't a Rose without Harley or a Harley without Rose. So I guess it's no surprise that everything just sort of returned to normal after our forced lunch date with SF's best chicken. *And it really was the best chicken in the city.*

Our lives might've returned to normal, but I still feel as if Harley is holding something back from me. Maybe it's the initial awkwardness of all that we'd confessed to one another when we returned from vacation, or perhaps he was treading carefully, when I was bounding on ahead. Either way, I could see him making an effort to treat me carefully. But this too came with complications. Friends or lovers, we're so much more than either of these labels we put on ourselves—we always had been.

So when my phone rings on a Friday night, I know who it is without viewing the caller ID. I'm in the middle of my favorite episode of *My Wedding Affair*, painting my fingers and toes, which is something I don't get to do often enough. I have a wedding this coming Sunday and though I know no one is looking in my direction while I set up a couple's big day, I still like to look my best. *I am a direct representation of my brand, after all.* I clamp the polish between my first and second toes and answer my phone, careful not to mess up my fingernails.

"Hey, what are you doing right now?"

I pause the button on my TiVo. "Um … paperwork. Why?"

He laughs. "Admit it—you're spending this Friday night alone, watching re-runs of *My Wedding Affair*, aren't you?"

"No," I snap, and hit the mute button, then I unpause the show because I've seen this particular episode enough to know what Dale Tutela is complaining about.

"What is your deal with that show?"

"It's only the best program on television about weddings, Harley," I say impatiently, as if he should already know this. And he should, because I've told him at least a hundred times. "You know how much I like weddings."

"Yeah, I know." I hear the smile in his

voice, which makes me smile too because though he may not understand it, he still gets it. "So listen, you're staying in, right?"

"Why are you calling me? You don't call me—you just come over and annoy the hell out of me until you fall asleep on my couch and I kick you out when the snoring gets too loud."

There's a knock at my front door, and I stiffen and then say, "You're at my door right now, aren't you?" *Crap. Now I'm going to have to ruin my paintjob.* "I'm not walking downstairs to let you in; I'm in my pajamas."

"Which ones?"

I glance down at the embarrassingly gorgeous pink PJs with *Bride to Bee* inscribed on the back and a little bumble bee over the front breast pocket. I bought them a year ago from a designer outlet. I had no intention of actually wearing them, at least not until the night before my wedding, but doing laundry in this city is expensive, not to mention time consuming, and a few months ago when I ran out of clean sleepwear the day before wash day, I pulled them out of a drawer and they just never made it back in. They live under my pillow, or in my hamper until wash day. You'd think I'd be more ashamed of that fact, but they really are comfortable pajamas.

"You're wearing your Bride to Bees, aren't you?"

"Maybe," I say slowly, as if that's a loaded question.

"Well it's not like I haven't seen them before, but my hands are full, so I'm gonna need you to come downstairs and help me with the bags."

I pause my show and toss the remote on the couch beside me, trudging down the stairs only to find him waiting at the door to my shop with a ... camera crew? I freeze, my eyes going wide as dinner plates. I mouth the words, *"What the hell?"*

Harley waves, and I could slap him. The camera is pointed directly at me and the little red light flashes. In a daze, I head to the door and flip the lock back, standing behind it as if the plate-glass window could shield my body from view. "Harley? What's going on?"

"Rose Perry?" A thin man with a slate gray suit and purple tie pushes his way inside my shop, followed by a boom operator and cameraman who nearly knocks over a small stand of potted lavender by the door.

"Please be careful," I say, with no small amount of trepidation coloring my voice because the man holding the boom gets it tangled in a string of twinkle lights.

"Rose, you've been selected to appear on the show *My Wedding Affair*," Slate Gray Suit says, and I just blink at him in response because surely I didn't hear that right. "Harley here sent in your application, and Dale Tutela loved your designs."

"What?" I stare at the crew and then back at Harley. "What is he talking about?"

Harley grins like a madman. It's one of those Pan grins, and I know he isn't messing around with me and I'm not being *Punk'd* because he's a terrible liar. "I heard they were on the lookout for a floral designer here in SF, so I just downloaded the form and forged your signature."

"Oh my god," I say breathlessly.

"You're gonna be on the show, Rose."

"Get out!" I launch myself at Harley who catches me up in a bear hug. I wrap my legs around his waist, and then I kiss him. I don't even think about it—it's as natural as breathing. There's no tongue, no open wet mouths, but instead just a series of gentle pecks on the lips. My breath catches in the back of my throat. His Adam's apple bobs. His eyes are molten and so blue, like chips of polished aquamarine. I lean in to kiss him again, but I pause to gauge his reaction before my lips meet his.

"Oooh, the sexual tension in this room," Gray Suit says. The spell shatters to a million pieces, and Harley and I are left standing in broken glass. "Did you get that, Graham?"

"Yeah, I got it," Graham says.

"You can just edit out my voice later, right?"

"Uh-huh," Graham says, hefting the camera

from off his shoulder and pressing a button. The red light stops blinking.

Harley releases his hands from my ass, and I gently slide down his body, wincing when my feet land hard on the ground in much the same way my heart just came crashing back down to earth.

"I can't believe you did this." I stare awkwardly at my best friend. He stares back and several beats pass.

"You deserve it," he says with a shrug.

"Okay kiddies, we're gonna leave you to your little love fest in just a moment, but first I need—"

"We're not a couple," I say.

At the same time, Harley says, "We're just friends."

"Oh honey, I work in television—you two aren't fooling anybody. Anywho, since your friend here"—he actually puts quotation marks over the word friend—"filled out your forms and forged your signature … illegally, I'm going to need you to fill out these papers, plus read through the contract carefully, initial every page, and sign at the bottom. I've already emailed the itinerary to the store's address. Adorable name, by the way."

"Thank you," I say, but it's clear he isn't done because he actually waves me away. I'm not sure if I should move or not but Harley has me penned in between him and a huge Birchwood aisle arch that's currently hung with white wisteria.

"So, the wedding is one week from tomorrow."

I blink in confusion. "What?"

"You watch the show, right? Harley said you were a huge fan."

"I am, I just thought that maybe that part was made up," I explain, and shrug. "You know? The magic of television."

"No," he says curtly.

"Okay then."

"As I was saying, tomorrow, makeup will be here at 0400 hours. Dale will arrive at 0500 hours sharp. Filming will commence at 0600 hours and we're going to need to make it snappy as he has a flight to New York shortly after. He'll leave, and we'll get all the shots we need of your charming little store for the before. During the week, I'll touch base with you several times to make sure you have everything you need, and we'll need you onsite at 0600 hours come Saturday. You two get some rest now—you don't want to be on television with bags under your eyes. Okay?"

I stare blankly at the man, wondering if perhaps I should have written this down.

"*Comprende?*"

"Er … yes, *sí, comprende.*" I take a deep breath. "I feel as if I'm dreaming. How is this possible?"

"He liked your work. You're lucky; ordinarily, Dale only uses one vendor. You'll still be working closely with them, as I'm not sure your quaint little shop could fill an order for ten thousand roses, but you'll be the headlining floral designer for both the venue and the ceremony flowers." I ignore the fact that he said my shop was *quaint*, as if that were an insult, and I listen with rapt attention as he goes through a few more details about filming and what to expect, and then all three of them clear out of Darling Buds, and I stare out the window as they load the equipment into their van and drive off.

I turn and stare at Harley, and then I launch myself at him again, squealing like a little kid as I smack his broad chest. "I can't believe you did this."

He grabs my wrists to ward off my blows, and presses them tightly to his torso before lacing his fingers with mine. "Nah, it was all you. Now everyone will know how good you are at what you do. You could have your own show, Rose. You could be the next Martha Stewart, but sexy as fuck and without the jail time … or the baking and home making stuff."

I laugh, but inwardly my mind is caught on a loop. Did he just call me sexy as fuck? It's awkward, as I stare at our interlocked fingers my heart beats double time. I gently work my hands free and press them to the sides of my face. "Oh my god, I have so many things to do. I have to wax, I have to wash my hair, I have to—"

"Have a drink with me?"

Damn, there goes my detox ... again. And I've been doing so well. I've made it through an entire day without a glass of wine. The chocolate liqueurs I had for lunch don't count.

"Okay." I walk ahead of him and climb the stairs to my loft. He laughs and shakes his head predictably when he sees what I was watching. I just stare at the TV, unable to believe that my dreams are coming true as Harley heads into my tiny kitchen and opens a bottle of wine, pouring us both a glass.

Two bottles later, I lean my head on his shoulder as we sit on my small loveseat. He's just sat through four episodes of my favorite show—all in the name of research, of course—without complaint. He did pull me close though, wrapping his arm around me and leaving it there. I wasn't going to protest. I feel buoyant, completely alive, and somewhat chilled on account of the wine. I really need to go to bed, but I don't want to move. Besides, I don't think I'll be able to sleep yet anyway.

"You're gonna be there tomorrow, right?" My voice is panicky because for the first time it just occurred to me that he may not be around to hold my hand. "I mean, I know you have work and all, but you're still coming, aren't you?"

He seems to be weighing his words. "I don't know if I can."

"What?" I sit up and glare at him. Then I shriek, "Harley, I need you there with me."

"No, you don't." He tucks a strand of hair behind my ear and yanks it playfully, but his eyes are serious, his expression withdrawn. "You just think you do."

"Are you crazy? You got me into this mess. This is your fault; I can't do this without you."

"I have an appointment in Santa Barbara."

I shake my head in disbelief, because this is the first I'm hearing about it. "What?"

"Yeah, it's kind of an A-list client."

"No way! Get outta here."

"I plan on it, actually. They're shooting right now; I have to interview with him before he flies out for Vegas."

I pick up the cushion between us and throw it at him. It narrowly misses the wine glasses on my coffee table before falling to the floor. "You're just full of surprises today. Why didn't you tell me this?"

"Because I signed a non-disclosure agreement."

"Seriously?"

"Seriously." He pulls me toward him again, and I lean into the warmth of his side. God, he smells amazing. Like citrus, woods, and vetiver. I smile, knowing he still wears the same Tom Ford fragrance I bought him for Christmas six years ago.

"I can't believe you won't tell me," I say, exasperated. "I can't believe you won't be here tomorrow to watch me fall on my face."

"Rose." Harley tilts my chin up toward him, and I lean all of my weight on his side in order to see him better. "You got this. You were born for this."

"I hope you're right, because at the moment I don't know whether to kiss you or slap you," I say emphatically.

"I know which I'd prefer." He leans closer so his lips are just a few inches from mine.

"What are you doing?" I breathe quietly. My heart races uncontrollably.

He moves even closer, and threads his fingers in my hair. "Giving in for once."

"What does that me—"

His mouth crashes down on mine, swallowing my words. For a stunned beat I'm wide-eyed and incredulous, and then I give in too, kissing him back. I shift in the tiny loveseat and climb into his lap. Harley's lips are relentless against mine, his hands rough and so good on my body, so, so good.

He rips open my pajama shirt. The violence of this gesture takes me by surprise, but when his hands squeeze my exposed breasts and he sucks my flesh into his hungry mouth, I forget all about my favorite now-ruined pajamas. With a growl, he feasts on me from nipple to my neck and all the way back down again, repeating the motion on the other side, forcing me to lose my mind.

"Jesus. You look just like you did when we were in college."

I laugh nervously, knowing that's not quite true as his hands and mouth devour more of me. I'm thicker now, thighs, hips, breasts. Gone is the rakish frame of a young woman, and here to stay, it seems, are curves, boobs, and even a small stretchmark or two. "We both know that's not true."

"No, you're right. These tits are lusher, your ass fuller. You're a fucking goddess, love." He tugs at the waist of my pajamas. Those wider hips he was just sinking his calloused fingers into are the reason my shorts won't come off, so I quickly climb off of his lap and remove them, wishing I'd remembered to shave my legs, and also thanking the powers that be that I had the good sense to listen to Izzy when she told me even single snatch needed a wax down.

Harley wets his lips and unfastens his pants, shoving them down his hips while I stand there, mesmerized by his hardness. He's been a fantastic lover in the past. The first time hurt like hell; the second, too; but all of the times after that he'd known just how to move, just where to place his fingers or position his cock so that he'd get me off in a matter of minutes, and the orgasms just kept coming. Whether it was from his hands thrust between us, or my own—it didn't matter. All he cared about, it seemed, was watching me reach those heights, working and waiting and relishing those moments when I'd throw my head back and cry out as I pulsed around him.

But that was a long time ago, and it hurts to think about how many lovers have come and gone since that time. How many women he's fucked, and how little men I've had since then. Crushing jealousy and insecurity hits me in a wave and for the first time I hesitate. I didn't think I'd ever find myself in this position again, and now that I am, my overactive imagination is ruining everything.

"Come here," he says, holding his hand out to me.

I take a step toward him and stop. "What if this is a mistake?"

He grabs my wrist and pulls me down on his lap, sliding his hands up either side of my thighs as I straddle him. He kneads my flesh from hips to ass, his fingertips grazing my labia, forcing the breath from my lungs. "Does this feel like a mistake?"

"No," I pant.

He catches up my hands, causing me to rest a little more of my weight on him, but this makes thought even more impossible to deal with because his thick cock is pressed against me and I can't help but rock gently in his lap. Harley kisses my fingers. His other hand digs into my hip and rocks me faster.

"Tell me this feels wrong," he says, almost as breathless as I am. "And if you can't, then shut the fuck up and kiss me."

My lips crash down on his. He threads a hand in my hair, drawing me closer. His cock slides against my wetness and I close my eyes. He wedges his hand between us and positions himself at my entrance. The tension is ruining me, and when he shoves inside I cry out because it's both delicious and tortuous, pleasure and pain.

I was wrong before—now we're close enough, now we're exactly where we should be. Rocking my hips, I lean back to study his face, so beautiful, so fucking heartbreakingly beautiful. His eyes glaze over as he palms my breasts, and I close my own eyes and arch my back as he pumps into me and these touches, our moans, this closeness, is everything. *He* is my everything. But it isn't close enough for Harley. He isn't like the other men I've been with, emasculated by a woman on top, but he knows I love the weight of his body on mine, that it gets me there that much faster. He eases out of my body, holding me close as he sweeps an arm across the coffee table, shoving the glasses and the bottle of wine onto the opposite side of the floor where they shatter. I stare, wide eyed and taken by surprise, but I'm pushed down on my back. My head hits the dark cherry wood surface of my coffee table, hard, but he doesn't apologize. He devours me instead, consuming every inch of me from navel to neck, driven wild with hunger, and when he thrusts into me again, it's with such force that my hips lift off the table. I squirm beneath him, attempting to put a little space between us because it's too much, the angle, the way he's pounding into me, the table at my back that's as hard and unyielding as his thrusts.

"Harley," I breathe. "Go slow. What's the rush?"

"Fuck," his says, his breathing ragged and desperate. "You feel so good, so fucking good."

He pulls out of me, and with his hands at my waist he flips me onto my stomach, my knees hitting the floor. I cry out in surprise, already missing his heat and the way he'd stretched me tight. Harley jerks my hips back toward him. I suck in a sharp breath when he slowly slips inside me again. His thrusts are gentler now, and though I can't see his face it's somehow more intimate, more intense, just *more*, especially when he covers me with his big body and reaches around, sliding his hands over my breasts and stomach, worshiping every inch with agile hands that know their way around my body so well. His deft fingers find my clit and stroke. Heat builds within me, languorously spreading throughout my insides from the very tips of my toes to the roots of my hair.

"Oh, god," I whisper like a prayer.

"Give me it, love," he says against the shell of my ear, and my skin pulls taut with goosebumps as I smile at his words. "I've waited too damn long to hear those cries come from your mouth again."

I want to tell him that he is the jackass that walked away. He is the one who was marrying another woman; he is the reason he's been waiting as long as he claims, because I've waited for him since he left for college. I am still waiting. But I don't say any of that because his fingers work me mercilessly and my breath steals his name from my lips as I come.

Trembling, every nerve in my body exposed and pulsing, I collapse against the table. I long for respite, for breath, for even more of him. I barely have time to contemplate what has just happened when he eases out and lifts me at the waist, carrying me like a ragdoll the few feet to my bed. A moment later, he lays down on the soft mattress, he doesn't loosen his hold around my waist as he pulls me on top of him, his front to my back, his thick cock inside me, and his arms wrapped tightly around my body, so tight I can't breathe. I say as much but he doesn't let go—he just lies still for a moment inside me, underneath me, around me, until I feel myself unravelling, enveloped in his arms.

Traitorous tears prick my eyes. My throat forms a lump that I can't swallow back as Harley pistons his hips, slowly sliding in and out of me until he comes in hard, hot bursts. With heavy, uneven breaths he kisses the moisture from my face, and I know he's not unaware of my tears. I don't know if he understands what they mean, but he strokes my body tenderly and whispers assurances in my ear about how beautiful I am, how long he's wanted me and how he wishes time would just stand still.

After our bodies are sated and our breathing has returned to normal, our heartbeats steady, he rolls us to the side and spoons me from behind. It feels different. Not filled with promise the way it had in Hawaii, and not raw and tender the way it'd felt while he whispered in my ear, but off somehow, as if he's thrown up a wall around us. No, not around us—between us.

No, no, no. Please don't let that be true.

Warily, as if I'm afraid of what I might find, I turn in his arms and run my fingers through the sweat-soaked hair at the base of his neck. He doesn't look at me, not until I place my hands on either side of his face and force him to.

A million words all clamor around inside my mind, but all that tumbles out is, "Hey."

"Hey," he replies.

"That was intense." I stroke his face,

smoothing the little line that has formed between his brows.

"Yeah." He gives me a half-smile, but his eyes swirl with what looks like fear and regret. He licks his lips. I follow the movement. It appears as if Harley did get his wish, and time is standing still, eking out for an eternity, but it's all wrong—the light in his eyes, the abruptness of his voice, every second that seems to pass as if it's been replaced with an hour.

I frown. "What's wrong?"

He takes hold of my hand and kisses it. "Nothing, but I gotta go. You have an early start tomorrow."

"No, don't leave."

"I should." Harley eases his hand out of my own and leans in to kiss my forehead. He sits up and swings his legs over the bed, climbing to his feet. "You were great. I just have to be up early, and you're going to have a camera crew here in three hours."

"Harley," I say, my disappointment resonating around the tiny apartment. He slides into his pants and throws on his shirt, and then he leans over and gives me a quick peck on the lips before heading for the stairs. "Harley," I say again, with a little more anger coloring my voice.

"Break a leg tomorrow," he says, his own voice thick with emotion I can't place. Then he's gone, down the stairs and out the front door, and I'm left lying on the bed we just made love on, clutching my chest as if all of my insides might fall out if I don't hold them in place.

Chapter Seventeen
Rose

Age eighteen

Being separated by state lines sucks. I've just closed up the cash register, switched off the lights and stepped out onto the pavement when my phone starts ringing, and because I'm juggling keys and rummaging through my bag, which is full of books, notes, and the laptop I've been using to type up my latest assignment for my business management course, I missed the call.

"Damn it," I whisper to the late September fog and rest my head against the shop window—a window I'll be cleaning first thing in the morning because my boss is a colossal bitch. I lock the door and stuff my keys in my bag, finally locating my phone. Harley's number shows up on the screen as my missed call, and I want to cry because school was stressful, the internship I'd wanted so badly was even worse, and he isn't here. Life is sucking with a capital FUCK right now and I really need to hear his voice.

I hit the call-back button. The phone rings

out, but I don't bother leaving him a message. Since he left a month ago it hasn't been unusual for us to play phone tag every day. Sometimes I don't get to talk to him at all between his classes and mine and football, but we make it work. It is hard, but we do it. I hate being away from him, and I've been marking down the days on the calendar until Thanksgiving, so when he told me last week that he wasn't coming home like he'd promised, I'd been gutted.

We all did. Instead of spending the weekend in Carmel, walking through the stone-paved alleyways, past the cottages that are now home to art galleries and boutiques, or sinking our toes in the white sand after Thanksgiving dinner, he is heading to some special football retreat just outside of Louisiana, where the best candidates are chosen and get to rub shoulders for the weekend with previous Tigers who've since been drafted to the NFL. I am so damn proud of him, but I won't lie—I'm heartbroken too. I missed him. So much so that when he told me, and then whispered through the phone that he loved me, I broke down sobbing.

All this time I've tried to keep to myself how much the distance between us affects me, but one thing I know about Harley is that no matter how much he wants this, no matter how many years he's worked his ass off to get to exactly where he is right now, if I told him I wanted him to quit, he would.

There isn't anything he won't do for me, and I know it, and I've worked so hard not to let him see that what he is doing destroys me, because it is his dream, and who am I to take that from him?

I unlock my car and climb in, hitting the keypad on my phone again. It rings three times before he answers, shouting into the phone along with a barrage of sound—a frat party. "Rose?"

"Hey, you're at a party?"

"Just hold on a sec, okay? I can't hear a goddamn thing. Don't hang up."

"I won't," I say, and press the phone closer because I need him. I need him here with me. I don't want to hear the sound of his voice through a tinny, crackling phone line. I want him beside me, in my arms. Fat tears escape my lashes and I close my eyes, resting my head against the seat back. I cover my mouth so he won't hear my sobbing.

"Baby?" he says, "Shit … Rose?"

I sniff and clear my throat in an attempt to keep him from discovering that I'm losing it. "I'm here."

"Thought I'd lost you for a second there," he says quietly.

"Never."

"Never is an awfully long time," he whispers, and I can tell his full lips are curved into a grin the way they always are when we say those words to one another. I sigh, wishing I could see them, wishing I could kiss them and taste him once more. "Long day?"

"The longest."

"God, I miss you so fucking much."

"I miss you too." I clear my throat of the thickness threatening to choke me. "So your frat house is throwing another party?"

"Er … no, it's a cheerleader thing."

"A cheerleader thing?" I might have said this with the smallest amount of incredulity.

"Yeah, they had some championship on today. We couldn't be there because we had practice, so coach made us attend this fundraising party they're having."

"Wow, sounds … like a real punishment."

"Come on. Don't be like that."

"Like what?" I snap, wishing I was a smoker because I sure could use a cigarette to calm my nerves right now. Screw the nicotine—I'm going to raid the shit out of my parents' liquor cabinet the second I get home, and if anyone gives me shit about it, I'll cut someone.

"All pissy and shit."

"Well, I wasn't aware I was being pissy and shit." Okay, so maybe I am, but I don't need attitude from him about it. While he is partying with his frat brothers two thousand miles away, I am here in SF, working my fingers to the bone with school and my internship, and I'm startlingly alone. My best friend is halfway across the country, I live with my parents because I can't afford the rent in this city as well as text books, and I miss him. I don't want to fight, but I don't want to do this anymore either.

"Rose," he says softly, in that way that always tells me without words that I'm being irrational.

I sigh. "I just miss you, is all."

"This isn't forever, love."

"Harley, I've been looking all over for you," a slurred female voice says from the background, and jealousy twists like a knife in my gut.

"Hey Cheyanne, can you give me a minute? I'm talking to my girl."

Cheyanne? What is she, a fucking Garth Brooks song?

"I'll be your girl. You know long-distance relationships never work out anyway. Besides, I'm right here, and I have great tits. See?"

"Don't do that … come on … that's not." He sighs. "Time to go home."

Time to go home? Oh hell no, it is time for that bitch to step the fuck off. And why the hell is she showing him her boobs?

"Rose, I gotta go."

"What the fuck, Harley?"

"I … I gotta help her out, take her home. She's drunk, and I love my brothers, but I don't trust them not to take advantage of her in this situation."

I laugh as if he's joking, because surely this is a bad joke, right? Surely my boyfriend who is currently across not one, but three—four, if you count Nevada—state lines isn't offering to take some drunk cheerleader home after she just showed him her boobs.

"And why are you suddenly responsible for her, Harley?"

"She's a friend."

"Oh she sounds real friendly," I bite out.

"Hey, I'm just trying to do the right thing here. If it were you in her situation, I'd want someone looking out for you."

He's right. I know he's right, and that is why I am so damn angry. Because even though this stupid bitch has just tried to talk my boyfriend into cheating on me by flashing her boobs at him, this is bigger than my petty jealousy. A woman has every right to be as drunk as Cheyanne is and walk through a frat house without any man touching her or taking advantage, but that isn't the world we live in, and I may have the last true gentleman standing, but I know he's doing the right thing. That doesn't mean I have to like it though.

"Rose?" Harley says softly.

I huff. "Just go. I'll talk to you later."

"I love you."

"Yeah, me too," I say and hang up. I start the car and pull out into traffic, heading east on Hayes Street to Masonic. My tears fall all the way to 29th Street where I open the door to my parents' home and trudge up the stairs without a word to either one of them.

I expect Harley to call later that night, but he doesn't. The silence is deafening, and I'm swallowed up by it. We drown in it, in pain, in guilt, and distance, and I'm not sure when or if we'll ever come up for air again.

Chapter Eighteen
Rose

The next morning is torture. The makeup crew show up at 0330 hours to set up, not four like Gray Suit—whose name is Aras, as I'd learn from my email when I finally checked it after Harley left—had said, and I am barely even out of the shower when I hear them knock. I haven't been over the paperwork, but I've signed it anyway, and I hand it over to a flustered Aras before he commandeers my couch to make some necessary phone calls. Then it goes from bad to worse. I'm thrown into hair and makeup and poked and jabbed and forced into clothing that I'd never wear to work in a million years. When Dale Tutela and the rest of the crew show up, I get two words out before he silences me with a look as he pinches his fingers together in a "zip it" motion.

What's that thing they say about meeting your idols? Oh yeah, that you shouldn't, because they never live up to your expectations. Dale Tutela is no exception to this rule. In fact, he is an A-grade asshole. And I am crushed.

I'm also trying to forget about what happened with another asshole just a few hours earlier, but I'm failing miserably. I don't understand it. Harley had been the one to instigate the whole thing. He'd been the one to start it, and he'd been the one to finish it at midnight when he left my house like he couldn't wait to be rid of me. I should never have let him take it that far, but I'd wanted it. I'd wanted him. *God, how I want him*.

Even now as I'm hit with flashes of our sweat-soaked and sweet entanglement, the feel of him inside, hitting the end of me and making me dizzy with that delicious way he gripped my hips and drove into me as if he knew I wasn't going to break beneath him … I want him. He's always been like that, ever since our first time together. He takes me like a wild man, and he's been the man I measure every other by. Every touch, every kiss, every thrust, with any man I've let inside my body since has paled in comparison to the way that Harley makes love to me.

That rat bastard. As if my memories haven't been torture enough, he had to go and give me a refresher course in pleasure that has put all our other times to shame.

A hairy knuckled finger snaps beneath my chin, and I reel back from the shock. "Cut," Dale yells, and I glance between him and the director, unable to believe that I've just been thinking about Harley when I should have been focused on the right here and now.

"Alright, take five," the director says, as he stands and heads toward us.

"I'm so sorry," I say to them both, and then I give the cameramen, who're setting down their equipment, a tight smile. Graham, who I met last night, gives me a chin nod, and they both venture outside for yet another cigarette.

"Honey, you might be a genius with floral arrangements, but there ain't a whole lot going on between those eyes the rest of the time, is there?" Dale says, craning his neck left and right as if working out the kinks. "I need a drink, a tan, and a man. And can someone please do something about this hot mess of a woman." He waves his hand in my direction and turns to the bride, whose flowers I'll be creating. He's right; I am a hot mess. He really doesn't need a tan though, because he already looks like an Oompa Loompa.

God he is an asshole.

"Okay, Rose, here's what we're going to do. We're going to have Dale say his lines again, and then we'll record yours separately. Cutting room will cut it together and *voila*, it will be as if the two of you are actually having a conversation. So I'm going to get the boys back in here, and we'll go from there. Rachel," the director says, squeezing the bride-to-be's arm. "You're doing great."

"Thank you." She smiles coyly, and her gaze shifts to me. The smile dims like a light gone out. "You're not going to screw up my wedding, are you?"

"I … no, of course not," I assure her, a little shocked at her bluntness. "I do this all the time. It's my job. I'm just not cut out for TV."

"No, I don't suppose you would be with that bone structure." She smiles as if she didn't just insult me. My face goes blank and Izzy—who was so excited when I'd messaged at six a.m. to tell her not to bother coming in today that she arrived ten minutes later and made coffee for the whole crew—gives me a plastered on smile and a thumbs up, and then we're rolling again.

I do much better at saying my lines when Dale isn't around, and thank god, because I could be at a real risk of losing this job, and I really need this job. Designing an event featured on *My Wedding Affair* could put my small florist on the map, so I really have no choice but to get it together and pull off the most exquisite arrangements any orange-tanned, egotistical, narcissistic, reality TV-show wedding planner has ever seen.

After the filming has wrapped, Aras sits down with

me to go over what's needed, and when I'll be expected to deliver mock ups for my designs and a floor plan. He tells me the other vendors associated with the show will provide everything I need in terms of flowers and supplies, and Dale will oversee everything from linens to music and the cake, but the ceremony, and the reception are all me. Even the bride doesn't get a say.

I've done the floral arrangements for hundreds of weddings and events around the San Francisco Bay area, so this is nothing new, but designing for an event of this magnitude, worries me just a little, not to mention my terrible filming debut. I'll likely have to close the store, and the lost revenue will suck, but I know it will be good for business in the long run. I love him for laying this opportunity in my lap, but I also hate him at the moment.

I could really use my best friend right now.

I have a mountain of work to do after everyone has left. The shop remains closed, but that doesn't mean I can go upstairs to bed. Izzy is still here, and she pitches in to help clean up without me asking. She's been a godsend, and I honestly don't know what I would have done without her. She is a good friend.

Izzy sweeps the floor as I polish the glass surfaces of my shop until they sparkle. It seems like making television is a messy business.

"So where's Harley today, I thought you guys kissed and made up?" She glances up from the pile of dirt and debris the crew had left behind.

I flinch. Izzy doesn't know how ironic that statement is. "I think he had a job out of town."

She frowns and continues sweeping. "Oh, I'm surprised he didn't reschedule. That boy would move heaven and earth for you."

Someone who would move heaven and earth for you usually doesn't rush out in the middle of the night after you've just had sex, unless it's to bring back ice cream.

I glance up from the counter I'm cleaning and stare at my employee. "Hey Izzy, can I talk to you about something?"

She stills, her sweeping coming to a complete halt, and stares at me. "It's not me getting fired, is it?"

"What?" I make a horrified face. "Oh god no!"

"Oh, okay then." She shrugs. "Shoot."

I take a deep breath, unsure of how much I want to tell her, and then it just tumbles out of my mouth like word vomit. "I had sex."

"Well done." She gives me a thumbs up.

"No, I mean I had sex with Harley."

"Oh yeah," she says scrunching up her nose as if she finds this adorable. "You guys used to date, right?"

"No, I … we had sex last night."

"Get outta town." She squeals in delight. The broom clatters to the floor and Izzy rushes towards me, leaning on the counter I just finished wiping down. "Oh my god. I need details."

"Well, there isn't much to tell, I guess. We were celebrating the show with a few drinks and then we were kissing, and then we were —"

"Getting naked." She waggles her eyebrows. Izzy has great eyebrow game, but this just looks ridiculous.

"Yeah, only he bailed on me afterwards."

Her eyes grow wide as saucers. "Nooo."

"Yes." I nod, making one of those *"I know, right?"* faces. "I don't know what to do. Should I call him? Do I go over there?"

"No," Izzy says, seriously scaring me with the scowl she shoots my way. "Do not do either of those things."

I grimace. "Really?

"Really," she assures. "Maybe he's just freaking out about it, you know? Like exes are super familiar, and it feels so wrong, but it can feel so right, too."

"Maybe," I agree, but Harley and me have been at this game for close to seventeen years now, and I know he felt everything I felt last night because I saw it on his face, I felt it in his touch, and I heard it in the words he whispered to me. I just don't understand why he ran.

"You really care about him, don't you?"

I shrug. "He's my best friend."

She makes a face and gives me her best Mae West accent. "Not any more he's not."

"What do you mean?"

"Best friends don't screw one another," she stoops to pick up the broom and continues sweeping. It's in the handbook."

"Alright, well we're best friends who've screwed one another in the past, and now we're best friends who've accidentally done it again," I say, but I know those words aren't true, because last night was no accident. I puff out a breath of air that sends my bangs flying. "Why don't you put that away? I'll clean up the rest."

"I don't mind."

"Go home, Izzy. I got this." I take the broom handle from her and make a shooing gesture with it, as if I'm going to sweep her up if she doesn't move. "Thank you for being here today."

"No problem. I wouldn't have missed the opportunity to see you fumble all over your lines on national TV."

I laugh and say sarcastically, "You're such a good friend."

"See you tomorrow," she singsongs. I set the broom in the storeroom and come back wielding the dustpan, then I crouch down behind the counter, sweeping the debris into it. "Ooh, Rose, heads up, there's a silver fox sniffing at your door."

I poke my head above the counter and find Dermot standing on the street in the darkening afternoon, his tailored midnight blue suit fitting him like a glove.

"You're like hot dick bait." Izzy grins, and my eyes grow wide because I'm sure he can hear her on the other side of the glass. Izzy pulls back the door, the bell dingles, and Dermot nods and steps aside to allow her to exit the store. "Good afternoon, Mr. Carter."

"Izzy," he says in greeting as he steps across my threshold. I smooth down the skin-tight emerald green bandage dress that I still haven't taken off after shooting. The way his eyes roll over my body makes me wish I'd taken a moment to change. I'll admit, there's another part of me that thinks it might be a good idea just to take it off right here. *Bad brain. Very bad brain.*

"Hi," he says.

"Hi yourself. We haven't seen you in a while." I give him a wistful smile, because I can't help it. My body always seems to be on high alert in his presence, and now is no different. My heart thrums wildly in my chest, and I'm finding it a little hard to breathe, though the dress could be at fault for that.

Dermot closes the shop door behind him and

makes his way over to the counter where I pretend to be very busy straightening things. "I came to see you about that actually."

I glance up, wondering what that means exactly. "Oh?"

"I came earlier in the day, but it seems there was a camera crew clogging your shop. I couldn't even get near the door."

"Oh, I, er … We're being featured on a reality TV show. It's a 'help I'm a hopeless bride who can't plan my own wedding' type of thing." I wave it away as if this sort of thing happens to me all the time. "It'll air next season."

"You're not the hopeless bride, are you?"

"Me?" I squawk, "No, I've had my wedding planned since I was five years old."

Uh-oh.

Dermot raises a brow. He looks a little frightened. "Congratulations on the show. That's extraordinary news."

"Well, let's just say it's been a day." I plaster on a smile, but I feel the weight of the last twenty-four hours slam into me, and I'm suddenly bone-tired. "But you didn't come here for this. What can I help you with?"

"Have dinner with me."

"I'm sorry?" I ask, my brow furrowing.

He holds up his hands as if to ward away any reservations I might have. "I promise to be a perfect gentleman this time. No stumbling and crushing you against my giant erection."

I burst out laughing, I can't help it—the seriousness with which he said that has me giggling like a schoolgirl. And I am not a girl who giggles. "Oh come on now, your giant erection wasn't completely to blame. My vagina is a ninja that likely tripped your penis on purpose."

Did I just say that? Jesus, you have sex one time in three years and suddenly you're Amy fucking Schumer? Get a grip, Rose.

"Thanks for the heads up. I'll tell my cock to be ready for a stealth attack." He grins, but his eyes are all melty chocolate and sinful promises. And there he goes again, being completely inappropriate and sexy-as-all fuck while doing it.

I laugh, nervously. "Well, at any rate, I'm sure your wife wouldn't be too thrilled with the idea of your penis and my vagina getting together to dine out alone … again."

"Ex-wife."

My mouth forms a little *O* as the shock registers with my brain. "I'm so sorry, I … I didn't know you'd separated."

"We filed for divorce the second we returned home."

I swallow hard, hoping this had nothing to do with me. "But I've been delivering lilies to her for the three weeks you've been back. You didn't cancel the delivery, so I didn't know. Oh my god, I feel terrible."

"You've been delivering flowers to the house." He nods.

"But the cards?"

"Yes, I suppose you could stop sending those, unless of course you'd like to write me love notes." He smiles wryly, and my eyes grow wide. "Let's shake it up a little from now on. I find lilies so dreary."

"Dermot, you don't have to keep ordering flowers from me. You've been one of my most valued customers, and I'm grateful to you, but I'd understand if you'd like to cancel that order."

"Now why would I do that?"

I don't have an answer for him. Perhaps he wants to enjoy the scent of fresh flowers in his home—there's nothing wrong with that. In fact, I have several corporate types, all single businessmen as far as I can tell, who ordered arrangements every week for that very reason. You don't have to be a female to appreciate the beauty of nature. Look at Harley—he makes a decent living out of creating some of the most exquisite gardens in the city. "Well, all right then."

"All right you'll have dinner with me?"

"Oh." I pause, unsure of how to proceed. "I meant, all right I'll shake it up a little this week. What's your favorite?"

"Peonies."

I gasp, because most men don't even know how to pronounce that flower let alone have the ability to differentiate between them. My eyes light up, causing me to smile like an insane person, and Dermot smiles too, but it's not a stupid toothy grin. It's just soft enough to have the corners of his eyes crinkling, and just intense enough to have the heat from his gaze set something low in my belly burning. I quickly lose the grin and nod. "Well then, I'm sure I can come up with something perfect for you."

"I have no doubt," he whispers. "Perhaps you could deliver them to the house yourself this time, around eight o'clock?"

"You're relentless."

"I am," he agrees. "Especially when it comes to things I want."

I swear I flush from my neck to my knees. "I can't. I'm sorry."

I couldn't do that to Harley. Even though that jerkoff up and left three seconds after he came inside me last night, even though his silence has made me feel like a dirty whore who just made the biggest mistake of her life, I need to talk to him. And regardless of the outcome, it wouldn't be right for me to accept Dermot's offer because my heart belongs to someone else, and that's hardly fair. While I'm sure the silver fox isn't after anything more than a nice meal and possibly a roll around in the hay—1000-thread count of course—falling into bed isn't only unfair to him, it's unfair to me. I fall fast and hard, I always have, and I think I'm long past the days of empty sex just for the sake of a few short hours of feeling good. As tempting as this man is, I can't have dinner with him.

"I don't date my clients, Mr. Carter."

"I could always stop buying flowers here," he says. "Though I may have a hard time giving up the coffee."

I laugh, because Izzy really is that good. "You're sweet, but no. Thank you, though."

He doesn't look happy, but I think he knows there's no point in trying to persuade me so he accepts this graciously enough. "I think you're making a mistake, Rose. There's chemistry here. It would be a shame not to explore that."

Maybe he's right, but I won't budge on this. I think he sees that stubbornness inside of me, because his lips twitch. He leans in, and to my complete surprise his hand grasps the nape of my neck and he pulls me to him, whispering in my ear, "Such a willful girl. What I wouldn't give to see you restrained and writhing beneath me."

My breath catches in my throat. Dermot kisses my cheek and releases me. There's a brief moment of pause where our eyes meet as he pulls away, and I know he has my number. I know he sees that desire in my eyes because he grins and takes a step back.

"Enjoy your weekend, Miss Perry," he says, as he shows himself out. I'm still standing at the counter gawping at his figure as he stalks around the sidewalk and jumps into a gleaming gunmetal gray Maserati.

It isn't until I see the car speed off that I exhale and slump down onto the floor of my shop, taking deep, heavy breaths as if I were delivering a baby and trying desperately to ignore the lonely cries of my vagina as that giant erection drives away. Instead, I grab my phone from the counter and stride towards the door, locking it up for the night. I pull down the blinds and traipse upstairs where I open a bottle of wine and stare at the blackened screen. Three missed calls from my mother, one from my dad's phone, which is likely just my mother calling from his phone in the event of me avoiding her number, but no calls from Harley.

I guzzle down a whole glass of Pinot Noir and dial his number before I can talk myself out of it. It goes straight to voicemail, and I listen to his gruff recording and sigh as I think about that voice and all the pretty things it said against my ear last night. "Harley, it's me, Rose. Of course you know who I am—I'm sure I didn't need to explain that part. I mean, I'm sure you didn't forget in the time it took you to come inside me and then flee my apartment last night. Or maybe you did." *Oh boy. I really hadn't meant to say any of that.* "Anyway, I'm um … I'm not mad. Just call me back, okay?"

I end the call and take my wine glass over to my couch, plonking myself down on it. I turn on my TV, ready to watch my favorite show, only I find that leaves a sour taste in my mouth after the last twenty-four hours, so I settle instead for the Discovery channel and I drink … far too much.

A bottle of wine later, my phone glares up at me from the coffee table, and I find myself reaching for it. I call again. It goes straight to voicemail.

"You know what? I lied. I am mad. I'm really, really fucking mad. You slept with me last night, and then what? You just vanished off the face of the earth? Who does that to their best friend? You're a shitty friend, Harley, and a shittier boyfriend," I snap, and then think on that for a beat. "Wait, no, you weren't a shitty boyfriend—you were actually pretty good at that, but still. You kinda suck at not being able to stop sleeping with me. And I'm sure most women would take that as a compliment, but you know how I feel about you."

I'm surprised to find my eyes are leaking again, I wasn't even aware of it, which means I'm either really drunk, or … yep, I'm going to go with drunk. I sniff. "Damn it, Harley, you're gonna break my heart all over again, aren't you?"

"Beep! Your message has been recorded," a robotic voice says in my ear, but I'm still angry, and I'm not done, so I dial again, wait for the beep, and say, "Oh yeah, fuck you."

I hang up and throw my cell onto the couch, abandoning my wine for the pint of Ben & Jerry's in my freezer. I dive into the ice cream as if it held my salvation, and I change the channel. *Say Yes to the Dress* is on. I've seen this episode, but I watch it anyway and find myself tearing up again when they pin the veil into a woman's hair and the family gathered in the viewing room bursts into tears. I shovel spoonful after spoonful of ice cream in my mouth as great, fat tears trail over my cheeks, and I sob like a woman who just missed out on a great sale on Valentino shoes at Nordestrom.

I hate men. I hate sex. I hate these squishy feelings I have on the inside. I … *oh shit, I'm gonna hurl.*

I throw the tub of ice cream and run towards the bathroom. I. Don't. Make. It. And I think it's safe to say that this is the last time I eat Ben & Jerry's. Chock chunk monkey fudge does not look the same coming up as it does going down, especially not when it's been drowned with an entire bottle of wine.

Chapter Nineteen

Rose

Age eighteen

I step through the doors and spot him, standing in his football jersey with his hair tied back, flowers in one hand, a Wendy Darling sign in the other, and a big, stupid grin on his face. I smile like a woman possessed and walk toward him, but there's a group of people taking dolly steps in front of me as they figure out where to go, and when my harried steps on their heels don't get them moving fast enough, I push past with a half mumbled apology and shriek as I leap into the air. Harley has no choice but to catch me, dropping the things in his hands in order to grab my ass. I pepper his face and neck with kisses and then when I reach his lips, he groans as I drive my tongue into his mouth. His lips are finally, *finally* on mine.

We garner a lot of really awkward looks from people, and a few even clap at the scene we're making in the Baton Rouge Metropolitan Airport. I slide down his big body, my feet barely touching the floor because I feel as if I'm still soaring above the clouds.

I smile up at him. "Hey Tiger. Nice jersey."

"Hey." He leans down and presses a kiss to the tip of my nose. "You're here."

"I'm here," I agree. He gathers me up in another embrace so tightly I can barely breathe, but I don't care because I've missed his arms around me like this. I've missed that spicy scent of his aftershave and green grass that always accompanies him off the field no matter how many showers he takes after practice. His hair is damp, and I'm betting he's just come from the field. I press my nose to his jersey, breathing him in. "Purple's really your color."

"Don't be hating on the jersey," he says, hooking his arm around my shoulder. "Come on, let's go get your bags."

I smile over at him. And heft the small duffle bag at his chest. "Actually, this is all I brought with me." He frowns, clearly not comprehending. "I wasn't sure I'd be wearing clothes for much of the time that I'm here."

He hefts the bag onto his shoulder and pulls me in close to whisper in my ear as we walk, "If it wouldn't get us arrested, I'd push you up against that wall over there and fuck you right here in front of everyone."

My cheeks flush, and my vagina does cartwheels in the very expensive panties I put on this morning just for our reunion. I keep up with his great, loping stride as best I can and then we exit the airport, jump into his truck and speed down Route 110.

It takes just fourteen minutes to get from the airport to the LSU campus, but I swear to god, Harley runs every red light between here and there and gets us home in eight.

We park in front of a huge red-brick frat house with a well-lit, immaculate lawn. On that pristine lawn sits two guys in loungers; they're drinking from beer hats and wearing ridiculous oversized clown glasses. The house itself is gorgeous, at least from the outside, and you'd never know it was home to twenty guys.

Harley climbs out of the truck and runs around to the passenger side before I can open it, and then he pulls me from the cab and pushes me up against the vehicle, kissing me hard. A cheer goes up from the guys on the lawn. I glance at them over Harley's shoulder, and then I gasp as he picks me up and I feel how hard he is beneath his jeans. I wrap my legs around him, and he strides up the walk with his hands on my ass and his lips crushed to mine.

"Dude," someone says. "Get a room."

"I plan on it." Harley grins at me, and all I can think is *yes, yes, yes, god yes.* It's been far too long, and I'm not sure I even remember what sex feels like.

"I wouldn't leave your car there, man," Clown Glasses says. "The parking police are gonna have your ass for it."

"Don't care."

"You're gonna get towed," the guy shouts as Harley climbs the porch and stops just outside the front door.

"You wanna give me a hand here?" Harley whispers, chuckling as I cover his face and neck with kisses. "Mine are kind of full."

I reach the door handle behind me, and then we're inside, banging into furniture, and walls, doors, and I'm pretty sure that was even a person that we ran into on our way up the stairs. I don't care. I don't care how it makes me look to Harley's frat brothers; I don't care how much they hear or that they were yelling shit from the front yard—all I care about is him. All I want is him.

We enter a room on the second floor. I don't know if it's small or large or if it's a damn supply closet because his lips smash into mine and I close my eyes as his fingers knead my ass. I groan and writhe against him, breaking our fervent kisses to remove my shirt and whisper, "I need you inside me, now."

"Fuck, baby," he says, trailing his lips over my neck and breasts, devouring me as if he's been starving this whole time we've been apart. "I plan on burying myself so deep you'll walk funny this entire weekend."

"Um … hi," a voice says, and my eyes shoot open to find a tall, sort of nerdy-looking kid standing not three feet away. His cheeks are as flushed as what I'm betting mine are right now. "You must be Rose."

"Oh my god," I say, covering my chest. I deliberately didn't wear a bra because though my boobs are big, they're still perky, and I know it drives Harley nuts when I go out with just a T-shirt on.

"Out!" Harley commands, and the guy slips past with a nervous look on his face, as if he's afraid that at any moment Harley might rip his head off with his bare hands. I can't say I blame the poor kid. My man is kind of terrifying when he gets going.

"Nice to meet you," I call after the door snicks closed quietly behind him, and then I'm launched across the room and onto what looks like a hastily made bed. I shriek as Harley's big body cages me in, and he presses his hips to mine.

He slips a hand between us and unfastens the button on my jeans, unzipping me and slipping his thick fingers into my panties. His brows knit together, and he tilts his head questioningly as he pulls away. His hands come out of my pants, and he leans back on his ankles as he removes my Keds and tosses them across the room, then he yanks the denim down my legs, exposing my very scant black panties. He takes me in, appraising my body from head to toe. "Goddamn it, Rose. Are you trying to give me a fucking heart attack?"

"Nope, just showing you how much I missed you." I give him a coquettish smile, and slide my foot over the bulge in his pants. He catches my ankle and presses a kiss to my inner arch, and then he widens my legs in order to get a better look. In the past this always made me nervous, him studying my body so closely, but I'd lie here forever just to have him look at me this way.

"I missed you, so fucking much," he says, climbing up the bed and dipping his head low to my crotch. "Okay if I tear these with my teeth?"

I laugh. "Whatever you want, QB1."

"Fuck I love it when you talk football," he growls.

Harley lowers his head and covers me with his mouth, panties and all. I moan, because it feels so damn good to have his lips on me again, and I grasp a fistful of hair, tugging until he looks up the length of my body to meet my gaze. He sinks his teeth into my panties and pulls them like a dog with a chew toy caught in his mouth. They don't break the way he was so obviously hoping, and I erupt into peals of laughter.

"What's the matter, QB1? Couldn't hit a

homerun?"

"Stop," he says seriously. "You're mixing your sports metaphors. It's embarrassing."

"Eat me."

"Oh, I plan on it. Don't you worry." He takes the thin wisp of fabric hooked around his fingers and pulls, hard. The stitching breaks, the fabric tears, and the elastic snaps against the sensitive skin of my hip and inner thigh. I gasp, and a bright red welt forms on my flesh.

Harley presses his lips to the injury. His tongue darts out, soothing the raised welt like a balm. He trails his mouth over me, separating my labia with his tongue. He licks my wetness and groans, closing his eyes, and I can't help but smile, because I've missed this too.

My quiet laughter quickly turns into a cry of pleasure as he buries his head in my pussy, eating me out as if I were his favorite meal. I writhe against his face, gripping his hair hard enough to pull it out by the roots. Heat rushes through me, and my orgasm begins building, but just as I'm about to fall over the edge of that precipice he draws away, pressing a kiss to my inner thigh. I groan in frustration, my heart pumping furiously against my ribcage as Harley removes his jeans and climbs up my body. His erection digs into my belly as he leans his lower half on me and I wriggle against him, tasting myself on his mouth. I always loved kissing him right afterward, when his lips and chin were slick with me. I wrap my legs around his hips. Harley slides a hand between us to guide his cock to my entrance and then he slowly pushes inside. Our eyes lock as, inch by delicious inch, he moves deeper, and I can read exactly what he's thinking because I'm thinking it too.

"Welcome home," he says with a grin.

"Oh," I cry out, as he seats himself balls' deep. "Shouldn't I be the one saying that, given that you're inside me and all?"

"Fuck, fuck, fuck, Rose." He sounds close to losing it, but his thrusts are slow and measured, and I know he's setting a pace that's comfortable for me because if it were up to him, he would have jackhammered me through the wall by now. *Not that a bit of that isn't nice.* "Stay with me."

He's not talking about right here and now, because I'm exactly where I should be, present and feeling every second of his thick cock moving inside me. "I can't."

He shoots me a warning look and pulls out almost all the way, and slams back in, as if he's punishing me for that little reply. "Stay. We'll get a place, just you and me."

"I have school," I pant, and squirm beneath him as he pistons his hips.

"So? You … can do … that anywhere. Jesus, fuck." He supports his weight on one hand

and slides the other between us, softly stroking my clit, so different from his sharp, punishing thrusts. Still, it's a heady combination, and I arch my back as I come, clenching tightly around him. I don't know if it's the time apart, or that we just need furious and primal fucking to reconnect, but whatever it is, it's hot, and it's enough to tip him over the edge, too. I squeeze my muscles the way he likes as he comes in thick, hot bursts.

"Fuck, fuck, fuck, love," he groans, sucking in a sharp breath as the last of his come spills inside me. He collapses against me, caging me in with both arms and legs and that large torso that seems to have only gotten bigger since he left. Everything about him looks bigger, though perhaps it's just the distance between us playing tricks on my mind. I'd forgotten how it felt to be dwarfed by him, enveloped and made whole again as I lay beneath him.

Panting hot breath in my ear, he says, "If you stayed, it could be like this every day."

I laugh, but the way his body stills tells me he's not joking. "Harley—"

"I miss you too much, Rose." He leans up on his elbows, our bodies pressed together at the waist, his cock still firm inside me. "I can't concentrate. I fucking hate this distance between us."

"I do too, but—"

"Then stay. You can get a new internship; it's not like they don't have florists in Baton Rouge."

Is he serious? This internship might be a pain in the ass, but it's my pain in the ass. I've wanted to study under Sara Lau since I first saw her designs in *Vogue Weddings* six years ago. She might be a bitch, but she is a genius, and I still have a lot to learn from her. I'm not the one who changed the plans—*he* is. LSU was never a part of our plan.

I don't say this, and I let his blasé comments slide because I know he's just feeling everything at once the way I am. I should be glad that he wants me to stay so badly, but it bothers me that suddenly my career path isn't as important to him as his is to me. We'll talk about this later, no doubt. For now, I don't want to argue, so I concentrate on being here with him after so long apart, and I marvel that our bodies haven't forgotten one another in our long absence.

I lie naked in Harley's bed, save for his arms around me and his leg thrown possessively over my thigh, and we drift in and out of sleep for several hours. It feels right; I do feel as if I'm home, and I never want to leave, but something in the back of my mind tells me that this is just the endorphins and my vagina talking.

"You know I'm never washing these sheets again." Harley burrows his face in my neck.

"Eww."

"I'm serious," he says, sliding the palm of his hand over my exposed nipple. He lowers his head and bites down over the sensitive flesh. I cry out, but he kisses it better and all is forgiven. "Not until the next time you come to see me."

"That's seriously disgusting."

He shrugs. "Say whatever you want, but this way I'll get to smell you every time I climb into bed. I don't want you to leave."

"Enough talk of leaving, already. I just got here, and you promised me all the flavors of Baton Rouge, so get dressed. You're taking me to dinner." I climb out of bed and start searching the dimly lit room for my clothes.

"I'd rather just stay in and eat you."

I laugh. "Well, I'm not sure vagina is one of the four main food groups, so get up."

"I love it when you talk dirty," he says, grabbing his junk, which is already thickening and ready to go again.

I pick up a pillow and swat him with it. "Get up."

"I'm already up," he says, fisting his beautiful cock. Long fingers glide over his length, and I watch with rapt attention. I also let out a huff, because I know I'm not going to be eating anything that isn't penis any time soon.

Harley pulls me back to bed, where we stay until well after midnight when we run through the house half-dressed, me in his football jersey and no panties and him in a pair of workout shorts, no shoes, no shirt. We hit the drive-through Five Guys on campus and garner some very strange looks from the cashier. She shouts something about Sunday's game as she hands us our food, but it's drowned out by the blood pumping in my ears and the whoosh of butterflies that take over my stomach when Harley presses his lips to the back of my hand, allowing just the smallest hint of tongue to graze my flesh.

I scarf down three French fries before Harley pulls over in the lot of a darkened building. The night around us is pitch black save for the streetlight several yards away, but I don't need light to see by because I've known every plain and angle of his face and body from the time I was five years old. I learned them all again when he changed at puberty, and then again after that when he became the hulking, gorgeous man he is today.

He unfastens his seat belt and slides across the cab, taking the bag of food from my hands and tossing it over his shoulder.

"Hey," I protest. "I'm hungry."

"Me too." He kisses the sensitive flesh of my neck, and trails his lips over me as if he could devour me with each kiss.

In the morning, I wake to warm hands on my body and Harley's mouth on my neck. I groan and turn onto my side. I ache all over, and it's barely even light outside, so why is he trying to kill me?

"Let me see those pretty eyes," he whispers, kissing my shoulder, my collar bone, and finally trailing his lips over my bare breast. He sucks my nipple into his mouth hard, and my eyes fly open as I take a slow, hissing breath. I run my fingers through his hair and stare down at him. "I gotta go. Coach is making me run drills before practice for cutting out early yesterday."

"No," I complain. "It's snuggle time; how does he not know this?"

"I got a game tomorrow night; I'm pretty sure snuggle time is the last thing on Coach's mind." He chuckles darkly. "You gonna be okay here? I hate to leave you in a house full of frat brothers, but they know better than to fuck with you."

"I'll be fine. I've been dealing with unruly assholes my whole life."

He raises a brow. "Oh really?"

"Yup, lived right next door to the very worst of them."

"Cute," he says, biting my flesh as he moves down my torso.

"What are you doing?" I whisper, because I'm afraid if I talk too loud he'll stop. "Aren't you late for practice?"

"Yeah, but Coach can wait just a little longer. It's not every day I wake with this gorgeous a specimen in my bed. I may need to examine it more thoroughly."

"I better be the only specimen waking in your bed."

"Always," he says, pulling the sheet away before covering me with his mouth. It's exquisite, and as he leaves me with a long, hard kiss and the taste of me on his tongue, I think that I could get used to waking like this every day, just the two of us, no parentals around, no climbing in through windows and sneaking back out before we get caught. Just us, getting lost in one another for hours, the way we did last night. Just us.

I can't put off going to pee any longer, so I stand and stretch next to the bed. My eyes roam the floor for my clothes when the door opens and the tall, nerdy guy I met briefly last night stands in the doorway with his jaw hanging open, his eyes roaming my body unchecked.

"Oh my god," I squeal and reach for the sheet, wrapping it hastily around my body from chest to ankle. I curse the fact that it's white, and with the early morning sun streaming in through the window, he can probably see everything anyway.

"Shit! I'm sorry," he says, turning and giving me his back.

"What are you doing in here?" My tone is sharp and accusing, and I think I may have frightened him a little because he flinches.

"Er, just trying to get some clothes." Covering his eyes with his hand, he turns around, and peeks through the gap between his ring and pinkie fingers. I'm still shielded by the sheet. *Too bad if I wasn't.* He drops his hand. His eyes dip from my scantly covered body to the ruined panties on the floor, and he presses his lips tightly together. Then he drags his gaze back up to my face. "So I'm not late."

"What?"

He points to the built-in wardrobes across the other side of the room. "My clothes. I need to get dressed."

I inhale sharply in surprise. "Wait, is this your room, too?"

"Yeah," he says nervously. "I … er, Harley asked me to take the couch while you're here."

"Oh my god, I am so sorry. I didn't know."

He shrugs, and the gesture just looks so odd while he's standing there with his hands fidgeting at his sides and his cheeks are beet red. "It's okay. Though could you maybe not tell Harley that I walked in on you naked. He's … kind of likely to beat my head in."

I laugh nervously. "Don't worry. Secret's safe with me."

"Thanks, so … I'm just going to get some things."

"Okay. I'm really sorry we kicked you out of your room."

"It's fine. Happens all the time."

My smile falters, and my heart skips a beat. "Wait, what?"

"In the house, I mean, not in this room, but in the others. There's always someone getting kicked out and sleeping on the couch."

"Right, of course."

"Harley isn't like that."

"I know," I say, though not very convincingly.

"I mean, plenty of other guys would. QB1 gets offered more pussy than he can handle, but he doesn't ... he's not ... well, he doesn't pay them any attention. He's not interested in other girls. He jacks off to your picture a lot, but ..."

I laugh, and he runs a hand over his face.

"Okay, I'm just gonna ..." He trails off and heads to the closet, grabbing a handful of clothes without even really looking at what he's doing. Then he moves to the desk and stuffs pens and books and a laptop inside. "See ya."

"Bye," I say. The door closes softly behind him. I let out a huge puff of air and fall back on the bed.

This distance between me and Harley has me losing my mind. I know this man; I know he'd never break my heart that way, so why am I always waiting for the other shoe to drop?

Chapter Twenty
Rose

I've always cried at weddings; it's what I do. It's more than just the idea of two people coming together to say their vows. It's more than the dress, the cake, the flowers, or the way a groom watches with bated breath and a tear in his eye as his beautiful bride walks toward him. It's so much more than that. Over the course of several months, and in some cases, years, I develop a relationship with the bride, and it becomes more for me than just helping her big day be as beautiful as she imagined it would be as a little girl. It's more than just a job—it's about creating a memory and a snippet in time that they'll remember long after the petals have fallen from their bouquet and turned to dust, when their groom is driving them mad by not putting the garbage out every week.

TV weddings are largely different from a regular ceremony. There's the grueling hours, numerous takes, and what seems like cameramen and crew everywhere, but there is still something magic in this wedding that extends beyond the enchantment of TV, and it's here in the wisteria wonderland we've created. *We did this.* Dale Tutela might be a 'roid-raging Oompa Loompa in desperate need of a Xanax, but he'd given me a gift with a big budget and TV airtime. Though I guess Harley had been the one to make it all possible.

The wedding was taking place at the Legion of Honor, SF's finest art gallery. I'd dressed several weddings here in the past, and each one was classic and beautiful. I didn't know how they'd booked the venue so late, because ordinarily they were reserved months in advance, but that's the magic of Hollywood for you.

I kept the ceremony in the Court of Honor elegant, reserved and all white to match the huge stone pillars around us. Rose pomanders hung from each aisle seat, and the altar was set with stone column pedestals overflowing with snowy white orchids, roses and anemone, but it was inside the Rodin Gallery where the arrangements were really spectacular, and this was the current cause of the tears that threatened to spill from my eyes. The entire room was strung with wisteria in pale lilac, frosty pink and whites. Guests dined under great arches of it, huge vases of it lined the table as centerpieces, and the bronzed statues of Rodin juxtaposed the soft feminine feel of the room. The bride had been wanting roses everywhere, and I'd given her that in her ceremony, but they weren't the flower for her.

I didn't much like this woman, and I knew

she didn't like me from the first time we'd met right up until last night's cast and crew rehearsal dinner, but that didn't matter. Because I'd seen her face when she'd seen her ceremony decorations and met her groom at the altar, and I'd seen the way her eyes misted over and her mouth fell open when she entered this room. She'd been transported back to her childhood when she'd dreamed of a day just like this. I know, because that's what all of my brides do. They light up when their dreams are realized. It's what I hope to do one day, light up like a damn Christmas tree when I walk down the aisle surrounded by lush peonies and orchids, paper lanterns and an April sunset—my best friend waiting at the altar in a tux, a soft smile on his face and a glimmer of tears in his eyes as he watches me take those final steps toward him.

But it's a little hard to marry your best friend when he clearly doesn't love you, or even return your calls, for that matter. One week. That's how long I've given him. One week. I must have dialed that number a thousand times. I walked by his apartment; I banged on the door. I shouted up at his window, and nothing.

I know it is pathetic. I know I am pathetic, but this whole time I hadn't given up on him, and that's wrong. I need to let him go, because he's already released me and I've been too stupid to see it. I have to put childish things aside and give up on the idea of having him love me back. And so, with a heavy heart and a guilty conscience, early this morning I'd sent a card with Dermot's arrangement with only one word on it: *Dinner.*

He hasn't called yet, and maybe that's for the best, but I'd had to do something.

Dale sidles up beside me. I plaster on a smile, but all at once the weight of the last week rests heavy on my shoulders, and it falters. He clears his throat. "It's a celebration. You're supposed to be having fun."

"I am," I say, sipping my drink. All I really want to do is gulp it down but I don't, because you never know who's watching, especially with a camera crew involved.

He gestures toward the room with his drink, sloshing a little of it on the floor. Apparently Oompa Loompas can't handle their liquor. "I knew you'd pull it off."

I arch my brow but figure it's best not to say anything because even though he's been a complete douche-canoe while filming, he's still offered me a boon that I'd never be able to repay.

"Oh! And I saw the footage Aras shot of you and the hot lumberjack." His eyes widen as if the thought just struck him. "We're including it in the show."

My blood turns ice cold.

"You call me when you want your own

wedding planned." Dale goes back to gesturing wildly, punctuating his words with his martini glass as if they were a news headline. "We'll do a follow-up exclusive: San Francisco's hottest floral designer weds childhood sweetheart."

"Sounds great," I say, looking for an excuse to get as far away from that idea as possible. "Excuse me. I need a refill."

With filming wrapped, or my part of it anyway, I bid the bride and groom farewell. She actually hugs me, which comes as a huge surprise, but I hug her back and congratulate them again, telling her new husband to call the store on Monday and arrange their first anniversary floral arrangement in advance. I'm only half joking. Still, he promises that he will.

I exit the museum in order to call an Uber, but it's a nice evening so I stand on the steps in front of the building for a beat and stare up at the sky. A few stars peek through the curtain of fog. It's nothing like the sky in Carmel, where if you walk down the beach a way, far enough from the houses, a blanket of stars shines back at you.

Normally I'd stay at an event until takedown, but after talking with Aras I was assured that the crew had that part handled. Besides, I've decided I've earned the right to head home, slip out of my heels, and pour myself a very stiff drink.

My phone rings, and for a beat I dare to

dream that it's Harley, but I don't recognize the number when I glance down at the screen. I answer it, assuming it might be Dale or Aras or some other member of the crew insisting I come back. "Hello?"

"Rose." It's Dermot. My heart stutters a beat, and I suck in a deep breath.

"Hi." *Oh crap. Oh crap. Oh crap.* I don't know if I'm ready for this conversation.

"You were expecting someone else." It isn't a question.

"No, you just caught me off guard, is all," I say, tugging at the high-necked collar of my dress. Did the temperature gauge suddenly ratchet up to seventy degrees? "I didn't think you'd call so soon."

"I don't like wasting time," he says. I already know that about him. I suppose it's why I sent him that card in the first place. Only now that he's actually calling me, I'm having second thoughts about the state of my mental health and decision-making ability. "Where are you?"

"Leaving the Legion of Honor."

"Alone?"

"Yeah, we filmed the wedding today for the—"

"Hopeless bride who has no idea how to plan her own wedding, I remember," he says, and something in his voice tells me he's smiling.

I laugh and shake my head, though I know

he can't see the gesture. "Wow, you really pay attention, huh?"

"Only when my interests are piqued."

"So, you're a reality-TV fan then?"

He chuckles. It's a dark sound that sends a shiver down my spine. "My interests are in you, Rose. I'm not sure how I can make that any clearer."

"Oh … I—"

"Now, about dinner," he says. "Have you eaten yet?"

I haven't. Not really. I'd snagged a couple of hors d'oeuvres from the waiters as they made their rounds, but I wasn't involved in the sit-down dinner, as you'd expect. "No," I say, drawing out the word as if it were a loaded question. "It's almost eleven."

"I'll be there in five minutes."

"Dermot—"

"Hang up the phone and wait for me, Rose."

I sigh and find myself staring at my nude peep-toe Louboutins. I wore a Ted Baker Bowkay print dress. In a powder blue. With a dreamy floral print, it's just the right amount of color for a wedding like this without detracting from the bride or the color scheme, even if it is a tad short for a cocktail dress.

"Okay, I guess I'll see you soon."

"Do try to curb your enthusiasm," he says,

and I know he's grinning now because I hear it in the teasing tone of his voice.

That does make me laugh, and I hang up the phone with a smile on my face. I don't know what to expect with this man—from one second to the next, every exchange I've ever had with him has left my head spinning, my heart tap-dancing in my chest, and my stomach in knots. And it might not be smart, but maybe that's exactly what I need.

True to his word, Dermot's gleaming grey Maserati pulls to a stop in front of me just five minutes later. I knew he lived up on Seacliff, but I didn't realize he was that close. I reach for the door handle but find it locked. He puts the car in park and climbs out, and I stare at him over the roof, confused. "Are we not leaving?"

Dermot walks around to my side of the car. He wears a deep brown leather jacket, a white T-shirt, and a pair of black jeans with russet-colored boots. He looks good, younger without the suits and briefcase. He slips a hand around my waist and leans in to kiss my cheek. I try hard to ignore the flutter in my stomach as he whispers in my ear,

"You look positively—"

"If you say radiant, I may have to hurt you," I blurt out, putting my hands on his arms to allow myself a little breathing room.

He steps back, cants his head, and grins, those warm brown eyes spearing me where I stand. "I was going with fuckable, but radiant works too."

A shiver runs down my spine, and guilt slams into me at the thought of the two of us … fucking. Even after Harley left me the way he did, it still feels as if I'm betraying him by seeing Dermot tonight, which is stupid. Perhaps the real betrayal lies in me denying myself the opportunity to feel anything other than heartbreak again. But I am too raw to think about my best friend and the way he continually crushes me, casting me aside like an old toy he no longer wants to play with. I shouldn't feel any guilt. I didn't break us—he did. And attempting to move on isn't wrong.

"Rose, what's wrong?" Dermot asks, pulling me back to the here and now.

I blurt out, "I need to take this slow."

He raises his brows and says, "The *friend* friend?"

"I … it's not…" I exhale loudly and glance at the huge glimmering water fountain nearby. "I'm sorry. I know I sent you that card, and I don't mean to give you mixed signals. I'm just …"

He takes my hand and kisses it, the way

Harley always did. Something in it forces my breath to catch in my throat, and I snatch my hand away. My gaze meets Dermot's confused one and I glance at my shoes. *He can't have that gesture.* He can touch me, he can kiss my cheek, he can slide his hand up my waist or place it at the small of my back. He can open doors for me, and say wildly inappropriate things that make me want to lean over the hood of his car and give in to him right here in front of a wedding I just designed, but he can't have that.

Maybe this was a bad idea.

"Rose." He cups my chin between his thumb and forefinger and tilts my head up toward him. "I'm not a patient man. When I want something, I take it, but I just ended a twenty-two-year marriage with a woman who never gave me her heart. If there's a chance I'll win even just a slither of yours, I'll learn to wait."

I don't understand, so I say as much. "Why?"

"Because extraordinary women don't come along every day."

I laugh, because it's completely cheesy, but somewhere inside, a frisson of excitement moves through me. "Oh, you are layering it on thick, aren't you?"

He chuckles and opens the passenger door. "Get in the car, Rose."

I do, and Dermot circles around to his side, climbing into the driver's seat. He starts the engine and takes off before my belt is buckled, and I quickly learn that he's a speed freak when behind the wheel. *Boys and their toys.*

Our first date goes nothing like I'd expected when I sent that card with his arrangement. He doesn't take me to a fancy restaurant in the Bay area, but a warehouse on 20th street in The Mission that houses a trendy bar full of hipsters. Over burgers that are served on a sesame-seed hotdog bun—that Dermot claims are the best in the city— and cocktails cleverly based on the Pantone color chart, we try to hold a conversation, but mostly just wind up screaming at one another to be heard over the noise. We stay until closing, and at two a.m. when he drives me home, he doesn't attempt to take things further, nor does he ask to come up.

Dermot presses a soft kiss to my cheek and waits until I open the shop door before getting back in his car and driving away. And I pretend as if I hadn't seen the light from Harley's apartment still on, because if I think about it too hard and too long I'll likely fall apart again, and I've had too good a night to have it soured by men who think I am anything less than extraordinary.

Chapter Twenty-One

Rose

I take Dermot's arm as we walk up the steps of the Bentley Reserve. It's a cool San Franciscan night with fog so thick you could get lost in it. *But I'm not lost.* I am currently on the arm of my … boyfriend? God, that just sounds so juvenile, and can you really call us that when we haven't even slept together? It's been three weeks since our first dinner date—not including the mess of a meal in Hawaii—and he's been so understanding. He doesn't push. We've kissed a bunch of times, and though I've always enjoyed those moments, it still feels … well, wrong. Like I'm cheating on Harley. I don't understand that at all, but I'm clearly a crazy person.

I love spending time with Dermot. He's charming and sweet, and surprisingly witty, not to mention gorgeous. He's a fantastic guy, and we have chemistry that can't be ignored. The only thing that's missing? He isn't my best friend.

"Ready?" he asks, and I nod. He knows how apprehensive I am about this. I've been a SF native all my life, but tonight, I am crossing to the dark side. Rose Perry is attending a stuffy charity auction like the ones the parentals frequent. *And I'm going willingly.* After I'd agreed to Dermot's invitation, I'd hung up the phone and considered going to my parents' house to have my dad check my temperature and vitals to make sure I was alright. Thankfully, I didn't need to see Dr. Dad because, as it turns out, Dermot has a doctorate too.

He isn't a surgeon like my father; he's the CEO for some multi-billion-dollar stem cell clinical trial company founded right here in SF. He knows my father, they've worked together several times, and though my dad has never paid much attention to my sex life before, I get the feeling this is one partnership he isn't going to be happy about. After all, Dermot is just five years younger than him. Which is kind of creepy, I know, but they may as well have been born in different centuries. Dermot's young at heart, adventurous, and so incredibly sexy. And my father is … old.

"Rose?" he whispers, leaning in and pressing a kiss to the curve where my shoulder meets my neck. As always, the ache begins low in my belly when he touches me like this.

I close my eyes and breathe in the sweet and

spicy licorice scent of him. "I'm ready."

Dermot chuckles and places his hand at the small of my back. "We haven't even entered the building, and already your attention is waning?"

"Well, can you blame me with how dreamy my date looks?" I straighten his bow-tie, which of course doesn't need to be straightened at all because he looks just as downright delicious as always with it slightly off-center. And if I thought Dermot was edible in jeans a T-shirt and a designer leather jacket, he is devastating in a tux.

"Dreamy?" His brows furrow, and he leans in and murmurs, "Where is the bastard? I'll kill him."

I laugh and let him lead me into the Banking Hall. It's filled with the sounds of a string quartet and tables that are dressed elegantly in black and white linens with blood red roses, women dressed to the nines, and men in tuxes looking ridiculously dapper. It's beautiful and terrifying all at once.

"Drink?"

"Oh god yes," I agree, and Dermot takes two elegant champagne flutes from a nearby waiter. He hands one to me and holds his out in a toast, but I've already drained the thing dry. "Sorry."

"Relax, Rose. We'll only stay as long as absolutely necessary."

And now I feel bad, because I know from my parents that these tickets aren't cheap, and neither is the sizable donation they give every year. I've lucked out this year though because both the Perrys and the Hamiltons have decided to make their sizable donations from the comfort of the cottage in Carmel, and thank god, because all I need right now is my mother showing up.

Dermot sets his champagne down at a nearby table and checks the seating chart for our names. He leads me over to a half-empty table and takes my clutch from me. "Dance with me." It isn't a question. Dermot does that a lot—demands rather than asks—but in a strange way I like it.

"When do we get to the part with more drinking?"

"When you show me you can be a good girl," he says and taps me on the ass. I swivel my head as if possessed, wondering what the hell that was about, and why he decided to do that in a room full of people, much less at all. His responding grin has me reeling as he takes my hand and leads me out onto the dancefloor. It's filled with men and women his age and aside from the waitstaff and the musicians in the corner, it appears there's only one other female my age, but she looks like she belongs on *Housewives of Beverly Hills*, so she doesn't count.

I put one arm on Dermot's shoulder and link my hand with his. The smile he gives me catches me off guard, and I find myself blushing to the roots of my hair because there's a world of promise in his eyes. It forces my heart to trip all over itself, but a knot of fear tightens my insides. I glance around the room, feeling awkward and out of place and so strange in his arms, as if I don't quite belong here either. There has always been one place, one person to whom I belonged, but he doesn't want me, and even now, four weeks on, that cuts like a knife. Because it could have been perfect and real, and he threw it all away. *He threw me away.*

Dermot's hand brushes the hair back from my eyes. He leans in and gently presses his lips to mine in a whisper of a kiss. I swallow around the lump in my throat. My eyes prick, but I blink back that moisture.

"What I wouldn't give to be the man consuming your thoughts," he whispers.

I stop dancing, staring up at him, my eyes pleading with him to forgive me, or change the subject or just go back to ignoring it like he usually does.

He doesn't. His gaze bores into mine, and my skin feels hot and prickly all over, and just when I'm about to lie, I hear it. A shrill laugh that strikes fear in the center of my heart.

Wild-eyed, I grab hold of Dermot's arm and spin us so that my back is to her. I wince and hold very still, praying she hasn't seen me. Dermot wears a vaguely amused expression. Seconds later, I'm tapped on the shoulder. I exhale loudly.

"Rose, darling, I thought that was you," my mother says. I pull away from Dermot and feign my surprise, pretending I didn't just deliberately ignore her. "What are you doing here?"

She pulls me into a hug and air-kisses me, likely eyeing Dermot over my shoulder. "Is this your date? Mr. Carter, I thought you were a happily married man."

"Separated, actually. It's a pleasure to see you again, Mrs. Perry." Dermot doesn't bother shaking hands—he pulls her close and plants a kiss on her cheek. I glance around the room, and find my dad at a nearby table. He watches us like a hawk, and he is not happy. Harley's parents stand with him, and when I meet Rochelle's eyes I have to swallow back bile. God. I'm not the one to blame here, her stupid, stubborn asshole son is, and yet I'm riddled with guilt and shame and remorse, because just like me, she knows this situation is … well, kind of fucked, actually. There is no other word for it.

"Oh please, call me Evelyn," Mom says.

"Evelyn," Dermot says with a nod.

Mom turns her attention back to me. "This dress—oh, Rose, it's stunning. Wherever did you get it? And those shoes—who are you and what have you done with my daughter?"

I smooth my hand down the front of my

black strapless Elie Saab gown. It's the most gorgeous thing I've ever seen, even though the thigh slit almost comes to my hip and has me breaking out in hives about showing so much skin. "They were a gift from Dermot."

Mom grins. It looks dangerous. "Really?"

"You look lovely too, Evelyn," Dermot says. "It's not hard to see where my Rose gets her beauty."

My Rose. My thoughts are echoed by my dad repeating the term of endearment as he sidles up to Mom and glares at my date.

"Hello Herb," Dermot says, offering his hand to shake. My dad glares harder.

"Herb," my mother chastises, at the same time as I say, "Dad."

He shakes his hand, though it's clear he'd rather be doing other things with it, like punching Dermot in the face.

"Nice to see you both," Dermot says, completely unfazed by my father's rudeness.

"Yes, what are you doing here?" I stare at my mother with a Lucy-you-got-some-'splainin'-to-do look. The only reason I decided to come was because I knew she'd be out of town. Okay, so maybe that wasn't the only reason—I did want to see if Dermot in a tux lived up to my fantasies. Which was just plain stupid because … Dermot. In. A. Tux. "I thought you were headed to Carmel?"

"We were, but Rochelle decided she wanted to stay close to the city this weekend, and it seemed a shame to go without them. I mean, we've never done that, so here we are." She waves Rochelle and Dean over, then she grabs my arm and whispers, "She needed some cheering up. She's been awfully down lately."

That makes two of us.

The Hamiltons join us, and it's just one big frosty reception as they shake hands with Dermot and Rochelle pulls me in for a hug. She holds on a beat too long, and it makes me wonder if she knows about what transpired between Harley and me. She couldn't know though because then my mother would know, and that's one thing she would not have waited around to talk to me about. She would have been up in my face demanding details before Rochelle had even finished that sentence.

"Well, don't let us keep you kids from dancing," my mother says. *Kids? Urgh!* I cringe because, again, Dermot isn't that much younger than she is. Which a fact I'm finding more and more disturbing now that I'm confronted with it face to face.

"I believe Rose was after a drink, anyway," Dermot says, placing his hand at the small of my back. Every pair of eyes before us follows the movement.

"A drink. What an excellent idea," Mom

says, and I could just die. My only solace comes when the event host announces that we should take our seats because the first course is about to be served. I exhale in relief, because surely my parents won't be seated beside us, only when Mom heads for our table and asks one of the couples to switch seats with them so we might all sit together, I think the only way this night could possibly get worse is if Harley were to come strutting in and wedge his way between Dermot and me.

As if he doesn't already come between us enough.

That isn't what happens though. In a way, that might have even been preferable, but no, fate must really have it in for me, because when the final party joins our table it seems there's a standoff between them and Dermot.

The woman is tall and slender, and has glossy raven hair that falls down her back. Her eyes are just as dark, and her face looks as though it's been Botoxed to within an inch of its life, but there's no denying she's beautiful. Beyond the lip filler and the smooth-as-alabaster skin—pulled unnaturally taut for what I assume is her age—she's stunning.

Dermot, ever the gentleman, nods his head and says, "Mireille,"

This is Mireille? You have got to be kidding me. Not only does his ex-wife look like that, but her name sounds like poetry as it rolls off of his tongue?

"Dermot," she greets him with a French accent, stepping forward until they're toe to toe and kisses him on this lips. He turns his head and takes a step back.

"What are you doing here?" he says, curtly. "You know how I hate to miss a charity event," she says, and then she glances at me over his shoulder. "And who is this? A student from your lab?"

"This is Rose," he says, and I think for the first time ever he sounds a little flustered. "My … girlfriend."

It's no less awkward when he says it. It certainly isn't the poetry of *Mireille* that rolled so beautifully off of his tongue.

She laughs. "You Americans and your labels. Why can't you just say this is Rose, my lover? Or this is Rose, the woman half my age who I'm fucking?"

I glance at my father's unimpressed face and desperately wish I could melt into the floor.

"That's enough," Dermot snaps. Mireille smiles. It's catty and yet still stunningly beautiful. *I hate her*. It's illogical, seeing as he's the one who filed for divorce, but it's there all the same. Mireille turns, as if only just remembering her date and introduces him as her lover James, or as the French apparently say, "James, who also happens to be half *your* age, and who *I'm* fucking."

Dermot doesn't wait until she's even finished that sentence before he pulls my chair out for me. I promptly sit down, half afraid I might earn a spanking for not complying fast enough. Frenchie and her little lapdog take the chairs opposite us and all sets of eyes settle on me and Dermot.

This is why I shouldn't tempt fate, because no matter how bad you think things are, they can always, *always* get worse.

Chapter Twenty-Two

Rose

Dermot pulls to a stop in front of my apartment, and I stare out the windshield at the ever-present drizzle that dogs San Francisco at this time of year. He doesn't speak; I know it's my turn. I know I need to invite him in—but I don't think I can. Every time I kiss this man, every time I feel his hands upon me, and every time I wonder about sleeping with him, I see Harley.

Four weeks and not a single call, no texts, nothing. And that hurts like hell because I begged him not to break my heart again, and he did.

"I had a great time tonight," I say, because it's expected. I anticipate a chuckle, or a wry grin from him—we both know it's a blatant lie—but neither of us are laughing. Dinner with my parents and his ex-wife does not equate to a *great time*. Not even close.

Dermot slides his hand onto my thigh,

pushing the fabric of my dress aside until my whole leg is exposed by the generous slit. I both want to pull away and shift closer. Clean, well-manicured fingers trace soft patterns on my flesh. I squirm, because despite the reservations my head has, my body likes Dermot a lot.

Slowly, he edges his hand farther up my thigh. My eyelids fall closed and my lips part. His touch is sensual, and it's not the first time I've thought that he'd make an excellent lover. "Rose, invite me inside."

"I can't," I breathe, and lie my head back against the deep tan, buttery-soft leather headrest. Dermot shifts, leaning in to kiss my cheek, but his exploration doesn't end there. He trails his lips across my jaw, down my neck, and along my collarbone, stopping just above my cleavage. I let out a moan as he nibbles the tender flesh spilling out of my dress. His free hand grips the side of my neck as the one on my thigh climbs higher and traces the outside of my panties. I gasp, thrusting my hips forward, until that delicious warmth spreads out from the very core of me. He latches on to my earlobe and my whole body goes electric, and then I remember the last time I felt like this, and Harley's face appears unbidden in my mind.

I shove Dermot's hand away abruptly. "I can't. I'm sorry."

"Rose—"

"I … oh god, I'm such a head case." I bury my face in my hands, unable to believe my own stupidity. This man, this gorgeous, fucking incredible man wants me, and I want him, but I want my best friend more. *What the fuck is wrong with me?*

"You're not ready," Dermot says softly, as if in answer to my silent question.

"I'm so sorry."

"It's fine. This is my fault." He pulls my hands away from my face, his thumb grazing my cheek. "You told me you wanted to take it slow. And feeling you up in the front seat of my car like a horny teenager isn't taking it slow."

"Dermot, I …"

He grasps my face with his hand and pulls me closer, pressing a kiss to my forehead. "Shh … I can wait. Now go on inside before it starts to pour."

I nod. "Thanks for tonight. Parents and ex-wives aside, I like spending time with you, Mr. Carter."

"I like spending time with you too, Rose," he says, and there's no edge to his voice, there's no anger or disappointment, which makes me wonder why? *Why is he still here?* It's been weeks, and this little encounter is the closest he's ever been to getting me naked beneath him.

This isn't fair. I can't keep stringing Dermont along and torturing myself over a man who clearly doesn't want me and doesn't respect me enough to have a conversation about what happened to us.

"I'll wait until you're inside," Dermot says, pulling me from my thoughts.

I need to tell him why I won't ask him up. I need to explain that I'm afraid if I sleep with him, I won't feel anything. I won't be able to pretend that I can leave Harley and me in the past. I don't tell him, because I'm weak. I'm a horrible person. I don't tell him because I'm selfish and all the things I let go unsaid pile up around me, layered, stacked high, one horrible truth on top of the other, until they surround me like a fort.

"Well, goodnight." I lean across the car to kiss his cheek, and inhale the sweet masculine scent of his cologne: amber, sandalwood and a hint of licorice. For a beat I contemplate climbing into his lap to finish what he started, but I don't. Instead, I whisper, "Dermot, would you come inside for a drink, and nothing more?"

He lets free a humorless laugh. "I wish I trusted myself to say yes, but as it turns out, my kryptonite is beautiful women who are in love with other men, so no; I think in order to save my own heart, I won't come up tonight."

Tears prick my eyes, and I can't look at him as I say, "Oh."

He collects a drop of saltwater that runs

down my cheek. "And here I was hoping you'd correct me."

"I'm trying not to be … in love with him, I mean," I say quietly, and for the first time in weeks I feel the smallest sense of relief. "I really am."

"And I'm trying to make you forget all about him, but it seems I'm a poor distraction."

"Don't say that." I clutch his hand at my face and kiss it. My tears soak his skin.

"Don't feel bad, Rose." He smiles solemnly. "It's my lot in life to fall for women who can't love me back."

I want to tell him that it's not true, that I'm the one who's ruined. I'm the one at fault, but all that comes out is, "I just … I need time."

"Then I'll wait."

I give him a sad smile, take a deep breath, and open my door. I don't glance down the street towards Harley's apartment, and I don't look back at the car as I dash from the passenger's side to my shopfront and fiddle with the keys in the lock. I open it, walk inside, and lean against the door as Dermot's car roars down the empty street. And then the rain starts, fat heavy drops hitting the windows of my shop. My tears swell with it, and so does my anger and my sadness.

I slept with my best friend. I gave in, though I knew it would hurt me. I screwed up royally, but I thought we meant more to him. I thought I meant more than this silent treatment he's giving me. I want to know why, and I think I deserve a fucking explanation.

In that second, I decide I'm done with avoidance. I'm done with waiting. Wiping my eyes dry, I yank open my door, and stalk out into the night without even bothering to close it behind me.

Rain beats down on my head, quickly drenching my clothing, forcing my mascara to run into my eyes and soaking me to the bone, but I just keep stalking towards his apartment. When I'm out on the pavement below his window, I screech into the night, "Harley! I know you're home, you jackass. Your lights are on; you never leave the lights on when you go out. You know how I know this? Because I know you. I know you'd rather conserve energy because that's just who you are. And you know me. Why didn't you answer my calls? Why did you ruin it?"

There's nothing from the window. Who knows? Maybe I'm being drowned out by the rain, and he can't hear a damn thing. "You ruined me. You're still ruining me, even though you promised you wouldn't." I lean against the brick façade of the building. "I wish it had never happened. I wish I'd never met you." I'm sobbing openly now. All my bravado is gone, washed away by the rain that beats down relentlessly on my trembling body. "I'm dating someone. I almost slept with him ... no, that's not true. I didn't even get close, because do you want to know what happened when he touched me tonight? I thought of you. That's all I ever do, think about you, and I can't … I like him a lot. He's a good man, a better man than you, because he would never hurt me the way you have. You broke my damn heart."

I lean against the wall, feeling as if my chest will cave in, feeling as if I have no heart because he stole it from me. He smashed it into a thousand tiny pieces, and I'm the fool who let him.

"I'm going to sleep with him. I'm going to move on because there is nothing for me here. You broke me, Harley. Maybe he'll be the one to put me back together again."

I walk away, back up the street to the open shopfront. I'm trembling when I climb the stairs, and I'm sure it's more to do with the shock than the rain. After all this time, I'd still expected him to say he was sorry, to rush out and throw his arms around me and tell me that he'd screwed up, to beg my forgiveness, but of course fantasy and reality are two very different things.

I don't bother to run the shower and get warm. I don't bother to take off my makeup or dry my hair or even remove my drenched gown. I just shuck off my ruined heels and climb into my bed, wrapping myself up in the duvet where I cry for so long that all the hemorrhoid cream in the world won't be able to reduce my puffy eyes in the morning.

Tomorrow will be a new day. I'll climb out of bed, I'll put on a brave face, and I'll forget Harley Hamilton was anything more than a boy I knew from my childhood. I'll forget him the way Peter Pan so often forgot Wendy. After all, we all have to grow up sometime.

Chapter Twenty-Three

Rose

Age eighteen

The roar as the Tigers run onto the field is deafening. I thought I'd seen football fanatics—what with my Dad and Harley's, the game is religion in our households—but this is another thing entirely. They take their football pretty seriously down here in the south, and the thrill of watching my man run onto that field had been intoxicating, but it quickly turns brutal in the first quarter. The team have their asses handed to them after their middle linebacker takes a hit to the head and has to be carried off the field. And things get worse from there. The rivalry between the Tigers and Ole Miss is an old one and tonight it is as if both sides are playing dirty.

In the end, they scrape in a win in the last quarter with the Tigers digging deep and a score of

23–20. Once the game is done and the players shake hands, the Tigers are swarmed with cheerleaders, and Harley is no exception. In fact, one of them even goes so far as to pull him down to her and press a hard kiss to his lips. I see red. On the inside, of course, because I am trying really hard not to dampen his win, but it hurts like a bitch. Harley's eyes seek mine in the crowd. He finds me, and the responding grimace tells me he knows I am pissed.

An hour later, I sit on the bleachers, enjoying the quiet of the empty stadium and the tepid night. It's hard to believe it's fall here; there's barely even a chill in the air. If this were SF I'd be covered in a cloud of fog.

Footsteps sound on the stadium bleachers behind me and I turn, half expecting some random guy to come kick me out, but it's Harley. He sits down on the seat and bumps his shoulder against mine. "Hey."

"Congratulations."

He smiles wide, looking out on his home field. "Thanks."

"I'd kiss you, but apparently someone beat me to it," I say.

Harley's smile fades. "Cheyanne was just excited."

"Well, at least she wasn't getting her tits out this time."

"Here we go," he says, letting out a puff of

air. "I knew we weren't done with this conversation."

"No, you're damn right we're not." I glare at him. "What happened that night?"

Harley shakes his head. His lips form a tight line and he won't look at me. "Why don't you just come out and say what we both know you're thinking, Rose?"

"Why don't you try being honest for a change?"

"Are you fucking kidding me?" he says, exasperated. "All I've ever done is be honest with you, but you're still determined to throw shade on this, so I got to ask—when did you stop trusting me?"

I reel back as if his words were a slap in the face. "Right around the time you told me I wasn't good enough."

"Did you smoke something back at the house? When have I ever told you that you weren't good enough?"

"You left me," I accuse, and my words ring out across the empty stadium, echoing back to us.

"Yeah, to give us a better life."

"No, you left for you. And this distance is killing us, Harley," I snap. "I don't want to do this anymore. I can't. It's too hard. I can't breathe without you and I'm turning into something I don't want to be. Someone I didn't think it was possible for me to be. I can't do it anymore."

"I know it's hard right now, but it won't always be that way. You could finish up the year and move out here."

"I don't want to live anywhere else. SF is my home. Don't you get it? You changed the playbook, not me," I shout, getting to my feet. "We had plans, and you changed them, and I'm happy for you, I really am. Watching you tonight? I was so damn proud, but we're running defense for different teams."

"What are you saying?"

"I wanna go home. Please, just take me to the airport."

"No! I'm not taking you anywhere." He stands up, towering over me. "You're leaving over some bullshit kiss with a cheerleader that I didn't even instigate? I'm not taking you to the airport. I'm taking you home."

I move to push past him, but I should have known he'd never let that fly. He grabs my shoulders tightly and studies my face. "You're gonna sit and talk to me until this shit in your pretty little head is sorted out."

"You're hurting me," I cry. Harley winces, as if the thought causes him physical pain, and he loosens his hold. "This whole thing is hurting me. It killed me to watch you walk away, but I let you go because I knew that was what you wanted. Now it's time you do the same for me."

"This is bullshit," he sneers. "You don't want your freedom any more than I want to give it to you. I'm not taking you to the airport."

"I'll call a cab."

"Rose, no. I have you for another three days." He tucks my hair behind my ears, holds my face between his big hands, and kisses my forehead. His voice is choked with emotion when he says, "Don't take that from me. Stay. Please?"

"Why? So we can continue to hurt one another even more when it comes time to leave?" I say around the lump in my throat. "A few days changes nothing, Harley. By Wednesday it will just be worse because we'll have to go through this all over again."

He runs a hand through his hair and leans back as though he's exasperated. "I don't understand why we're going through this fucking shit in the first place." He shakes his head and takes a step back. "Tell me, what the fuck is going on here, because I haven't got a goddamn clue."

"We just need to be on our own—you here in Louisiana and me? I need to be at home. San Francisco is my home."

"You leave now and we're done," he warns, and those bright blue eyes hold so much anger. Anger I never thought he could direct towards me.

God, it kills me to do this, especially after

winning tonight's game. *But you can't win them all.*

I give him a slow, crushing smile and walk away.

"Shit, I didn't mean that. Rose, come back."

"Congratulations on the win, Tiger," I say through my tears, and hurry down the stairs.

"Fuck, Rose!" he shouts, but he doesn't come after me.

I know I created this, but somehow it makes it so much worse that he lets me walk away. I want to run back up the stairs, fall against his big chest, and tell him I take it all back, but I don't. Instead, I flee through the stadium doors and hop into an awaiting taxi, telling the driver to take me to the airport.

In the car I call my parents, and ask them to rearrange my flights, and I don't bother going back to the frat house to get my things. I have my purse, my phone, and my ID, and that's all I really need. An hour later, I'm boarding a flight to LA, and I cry the whole way home.

Never in a million years did I imagine we'd end like this. As tempting as it might have been just to stay in Baton Rouge, I won't change my plans for him, and I wouldn't expect him to give up that scholarship for me. He earned it, he deserves it, and even if we could work things out, we'd just be facing the same thing all over again when he went pro. And there is no way we can go back to being friends now, not after we've been so much more. Not after I've seen my future with him.

I haven't just lost my lover this night, I've lost my best friend, my soul mate, and a piece of myself. A piece of me will always remain in Louisiana because that's where I broke my own heart.

Chapter Twenty-Four

Harley

I flush the toilet and wipe my mouth with the back of my hand, staggering over to the chair by the window because I'm sick of the sight of my bed. I wish Rose were here. Whenever I was sick as a kid, it wasn't my mother I sought out, but a tiny blonde who lived right next door. It was her cool hands that stroked my forehead when the fever hit, and her smiling face looking down at me as I lay in my bed, wallowing in my own misery. She'd pretend to be my mother, just the way Wendy had pretended to be Peter's. Always playing pretend, an entire lifetime of it, and now was no different.

I wish she'd come now, but I made that impossible. I pushed her away, and for what? We're both miserable because of it. Of course, I'm just going off what my mother tells me. I haven't had the guts to face her since I left her lying naked in her bed with that freshly fucked glow on her cheeks. She always was the most beautiful thing I've ever seen, made-up, not made-up, dressed, undressed, but I particularly love her messy bed hair and sleepy face. When she rolls over and looks at me like I just kicked her puppy for waking her? God, she's the most beautiful fucking thing walking the planet.

"Rose," I whisper to my empty apartment. *Jesus Christ, I need a drink.* But at the thought of more poison entering my body, my stomach heaves again. No. I don't need alcohol; I just need her. With the exception of my time in Louisiana, this is the longest I've been away from her, and it hurts like fuck.

I close my eyes, and when I wake I'm on the hard floor, slumped against the wall. I must be still dreaming or fucking hallucinating, because moments later I think I hear her voice outside my window,

"I wish it had never happened. I wish I'd never met you," she says, and my heart thuds in my chest as I start to think maybe I'm not hallucinating after all. Because if I was, why the fuck would I imagine her screaming at me from outside my window? If I was hallucinating I wouldn't have lost my guts to the porcelain god countless times tonight, and Rose would be in here, naked, straddling my hips and bouncing up and down on my cock. Which means she really is outside my window and I'm in hell, because the pain in her voice hurts worse than the pain in my body.

"I'm dating someone," she says, and fuck if that doesn't feel like a knife to the gut. Blood whooshes in my ears. I crane my neck to hear her over the pouring rain. "I'm going to sleep with him. I'm going to move on because there is nothing for me here. You broke me, Harley. Maybe he'll be the one to put me back together again."

No, no, no. I squeeze my eyes tightly closed. *No.*

I get up, determined to go to her though every muscle in my body screams. I make it three steps, but I fall on my ass, and the sound of her footsteps running away from my apartment echoes through the empty street.

Maybe he'll be the one to put me back together again.

Is she fucking kidding? I don't know who this guy is, and a part of me wants to just let her go, to let her be happy, but another part wants to choke the life out of the bastard. Too bad I can't move to save myself.

I study my rug up close, counting the threads as if I have all the time in the world. The thought of her with another man makes me physically sick to my stomach, and I puke all over the plush carpet. I created this; I'm the cause of this. I wanted this.

So why does it hurt so fucking much?

Chapter Twenty-Five

Rose

Age eighteen

I set my belongings down on the single bed in the room we shared at the cottage, and I stare at the bed opposite. The one that should hold Harley's things. The one that should have my best friend on it. This is the first Thanksgiving we've had without him. And it sucks.

As far back as I can remember we've shared this room on the holidays. We'd sit up talking well into the night, and when we got a bit older I'd stay up even longer just to watch him fall asleep. I used to dream about climbing out of my bed, crossing the room, and waking him with a kiss, but I was never bold enough to do that. I was always too worried about ruining our friendship, and for what? It is all shot to hell now anyway. Our parents used to say there was no Rose without Harley, and no Harley without Rose. That's still true, for me at least. There is no Rose without Harley because she died that night in Baton Rouge.

I haven't heard from him since I left. When I got off the plane, I'd had thirty-two missed calls. Thirty-two. I didn't listen to a single one of them. I couldn't. He didn't call me after that, and I didn't call him. It hurts too much. Just like this room and the gardens where he threw a makeshift prom, and the rug in front of the fireplace where he took my virginity. These walls are filled with sadness and regret now, and we've done that.

I grab my paperback and head outside, passing the parentals with their mournful faces and the silence that fills the room every time I enter, as if they're afraid I'll go off like a time bomb at any second. I ignore the front gardens where we danced under the stars, and head instead for the old hammock in the tiny backyard, that Harley's dad hung between two huge leafy trees two Christmases ago. I test its strength with my arms first, and when I decide it seems okay, I jump in, awkwardly landing with my legs up in the air over my head. After a few wobbly attempts to right myself and get comfortable, thanking god the whole time that I'm alone and Harley isn't here to see my graceless attempt at climbing into a hammock, I settle in with my book.

I read the same damn page eight times. I

don't mean to, but as soon as I am comfortable in the quiet, everyone in the cottage decides to come outside, and when the parentals get together, it's loud, and generally followed up with a whole lot of drinking and several rounds of poker.

I eventually get sick of reading the same line of *Wuthering Heights*—Heathcliff is a douche— over and over again, so I let the book fall to my chest and I close my eyes. It feels good being here, even though it hurts. The fresh briny air, the quiet, the peace, and even though there are a thousand memories of Harley everywhere, it's still as beautiful as it is soul-destroying.

I wake with a start and pull the book from my chest and glance at the table that the 'rentals were occupying. The smell of Dean's barbeque ribs is in the air, but everyone is gone.

"Thanks for waking me, Mom," I say, shooting daggers at the cottage as if my gamma ray glare could slice through walls. I attempt to sit up, but forget that I was sleeping in a hammock and I wind up falling out on my ass.

"Ow!" I throw Heathcliff off into the nearby

bushes. "Fucking Heathcliff." Tears sting my eyes and then I'm caterwauling like a baby because it's all just too much. The memories of this place, being here without him—everything.

"Hey, now, it wasn't entirely his fault," a voice, *his* voice, says from behind me. I still as if I'm in some terribly cruel dream conjured up by all the memories that the cottage stores like a vault. "Rose?"

Nope, not a dream. I scrub my hands over my face, wiping away my tears. I'm sure I'm smearing dirt and everything else over my cheeks too, but as long as he doesn't see me cry, we're good. Slowly, I turn and face him. "What are you doing here?"

"It's Thanksgiving," he says, as if that's explanation enough. It's been two months since I left him in Baton Rouge, but every second that's passed since feels like a lifetime.

"But you had that camp."

He nods solemnly. "I quit."

"What?" My chest goes through the motions, my lungs too, but I can't get any air.

"I walked out."

"Why?" I say angrily, because if he's not taking the thing that tore us apart seriously, then what was the fucking point of all of it? The long nights, me tearing my heart out when I said goodbye, him being in Louisiana—all of it. What was the fucking point?

"I love the game. There's nothing better than setting foot on that field, but it didn't feel like a game anymore." He lowers his voice and smiles softly. I don't smile back. "It didn't have the same joy in it. I didn't feel it."

"So you just threw it all away? You're just giving up?"

He shrugs. "I can't do something I don't love, Rose. I switched to horticulture."

"What?"

"I like getting my hands dirty," he says, as if this is a fact that I should have known by now. "A few days ago I walked out of the frat house, saw the sprawling lawns and magnolias, and decided that I wanted a different career path."

"But you've been working toward the NFL for forever."

"Football fell in my lap. I've always done it because I loved it, because everyone else told me I should, because I was good at it, but even if I got lucky enough to go pro where does that leave me when I'm thirty and had two knee replacements? I love it, but I don't love it enough."

"What did your parents say?"

"Dad yelled, a lot. And really loud. I'm surprised you didn't hear it, actually. Your 'rentals made themselves pretty scarce. Guess I ruined everyone's weekend."

"Not everyone's." I give him a sad smile.

"You wanna go get drunk with me in my truck?"

"I don't think that's a good idea."

"Please? I don't wanna walk back in there and have it start all over again."

I let out a sigh and run a hand through my sleep mussed hair. "Fine, but you're taking me to the beach. I'm not drinking in the parking lot of Lopez's Liquor store again and getting naked in your truck."

He smiles uneasily. Guess I should hold off on talk of getting naked from now on.

He walks away, and I follow. *Nothing new there.* When we make it through the front gate, Harley opens the passenger door first. I'm about to climb up when he snags me around the waist and pulls me toward him. For a beat I think he's going to kiss me. He rubs his thumb over my cheek. I stare at him, uncertain, wanting more of his touch and wanting to pull away, but he holds up the pad of his thumb, showing me the dirt he wiped from my face. "Now you're perfect."

God help me. My stomach does flippy things, and my heart beats double-time. I don't want it to, but it does. He turns away, walking around to his side of the truck, and I stand there staring at the imprints of his shoes on the ground, wondering how we go back to anything from here when it hurts every time he touches me.

With a prompt from him, I climb into the truck and stare out the windshield on the setting sun as it ignites the horizon. I avoid looking at Harley as we pull into a parking space on Scenic, but we don't get out of the truck because there are too many people around and we have underage drinking to do. Harley hands me a beer from the cooler on the floor beneath our feet, and he clinks his can against mine.

"To new beginnings," he says, though it sounds rather sad.

We talk about a lot of things, including school, my course load, where I'm living now—he's surprised to find I'm still in my old room, and yeah, it makes me feel like a grade-A loser, but rent in the city ain't cheap. He doesn't talk about football or Louisiana. A part of me hates that, that I've been gone from his life for close to two months but that it feels a lot longer. I know nothing about what he's doing now, who his friends are, and what he does with his free time since quitting the team, but I don't push him for answers because I know my best friend. He tells you what he thinks you need to know when you need to know it, and nothing more. Luckily for me, that has been pretty much everything from the time we were five years old. I guess I always liked that about him—that he let me in, that I was privileged enough to know

Harley's secrets when no one else did. But it sucks being on the other end. In fact, it hurts so bad that I want to shake him and demand he talk. I don't, because we're not there yet.

Silence falls over the car for the first time, and I stare out at the empty beach and the black waves beyond. It's dark now, and I gaze at the halo of light from the streetlamp, remembering the last time we were in this truck. Heat claws at my face and neck as I recall the way his hands and mouth devoured me.

Harley hands me another beer, and I accept it gratefully. The drinks are warm. This is my third, his fourth, and I'm vaguely aware that we should stop or we'll wind up having to spend the night here, or worse, call our parents to come get us.

Harley's eyes are on me. Waiting—I think—for me to meet his gaze. I pretend not to notice. "Why were you crying?"

"What?"

"At the cottage. You were on your hands and knees in the dirt, crying."

"I wasn't," I protest, but I feel his eyes burning into me.

"Rose," he says in that tone that he uses when I need to be reasoned with.

I glance at him and decide to give him the truth. If nothing else, he deserves at least that much from me. "Because everywhere I turned I saw you, only I didn't see you because you weren't there, just the ghost of your memory taunting me. I was crying because I miss my best friend." I take a deep breath and meet his gaze, though I can barely get the words out. "I miss you."

"I miss you too," he says, as if he's in a hurry to tell me I'm not the only one suffering.

"You do?"

"Course I do," he says, and apparently that's enough for me because I throw myself at him, climbing into his lap in the small space and bringing my lips crashing down on his. My ass leans on the horn, and his tongue slides into my mouth, meeting my own with equal vigor. Harley's hands roam my body, digging into my hips, squeezing my breasts, tugging my long honey blond hair back to expose the line of my neck to his mouth.

Desperate and hungry for more of him, I cup his face in my hands and bring his lips back to mine. He lets out a groan, and I match it, taking more of him into my mouth. I reach between us in the cramped space and stroke his erection through his jeans. His lips graze mine hard enough to bruise. I don't care that it hurts—all I care about is that I've missed him, that I want him here in the cab of his truck, in the parking lot. I unfasten his zip and pull him free, and then I stroke my hand up along his gorgeous shaft and bring my lips back to his.

"Rose, mmm." My mouth against his

drowns out his words, and I laugh a little and quicken my pace. "Rose … wait."

"What? Is it too hard? Sorry, I'm getting carried away. It's just that I missed you so much." I pepper his jaw with kisses, stroking him slower.

"Rose, I can't." His Adam's apple bobs. His hand grasps my forearm and gently pulls me free from him.

"Why?" I say, breathlessly.

"I have a girlfriend."

I have a girlfriend. Four little words that tear my entire world apart. They seem to bounce around in the cab, slicing the air between us, slicing into us, into me. All the air leaves my lungs in a rush, and my head spins from the confession, and maybe a little of the beer too.

"Oh," I say pathetically as I slide off his lap and land heavy on my seat.

I have a girlfriend.

I don't even know how to deal with that information, so I don't. I think a part of me just turns catatonic. I don't cry. I don't say a word. I just stare out the window through the fogged up glass.

"Shit, I'm sorry. I didn't mean to tell you like that. I shouldn't have let it get this far." He rests his head on the steering wheel. "Ah fuck, I didn't want to tell you like this. And I certainly didn't bring you here for—"

"It's fine," I say absently, because I'm afraid

that if I don't just be okay with it I'm going to break down, or worse, I'll start screaming at him because I'm so angry. I've never been angrier. I've never felt more betrayed. We had one fight. I mean, it was a big fight, and he tried to call, but I just assumed that he'd try harder and for longer than just one day. I thought even though I'd let him go, one day he'd find his way back to me. But I was wrong. And this is on me as much as it is on him, because I didn't fight for us either.

I have a girlfriend.

One little sentence that makes me want to die.

"Rose," he begins.

I turn my face to the window and whisper, "Take me back to the cottage, Harley."

"I'm sorry," he says quietly.

He's sorry. He's sorry. Not half as sorry as I am, and now there's nothing to be done about it. He didn't come home for me. He didn't miss me at all, because he has a girlfriend.

By the time we pull into the drive at the cottage, I'm seething. I climb out of the car before Harley even brings it to a stop. Within seconds he's on me, grabbing my arm.

"Don't touch me," I say, as I whirl around.

"Rose—"

"Fuck you! I loved you. I still love you," I spit the words as if they were venom. "I left for you so you wouldn't have to choose between me and football, and you gave us both up."

"I know, I'm an asshole. Please just talk to me."

"You let me think there was a chance for us again. Coming back here, kissing me?" I throw my hands up in exasperation. My heart squeezes until I feel like I can't breathe. "God, you just can't help but break my heart, can you?"

"Hey, I loved you too," he says sharply. "It shattered me when you walked away."

"Well, how convenient that you found someone to help put you back together," I say caustically. "And just two short months after breaking up with me. I can tell I meant a lot to you."

"You walked away from me, remember?"

"I left you because I didn't want to hold you back, not because I stopped loving you, or because I was looking to replace you with someone else," I say, feeling as if my chest caves in a little more as each word leaves my mouth.

"No one could ever replace you, Rose."

"They already have." I walk away and yank the screen door open. It slams against the brick wall, and I know I should be quiet. I don't need Mom or Rochelle coming out to try and smooth things over with us. Hot cocoa and a couple of Kumbayas aren't going to fix this. We're broken, shattered, crumbled to sand and dust beneath his feet.

I stalk into the cottage as I hear a round of expletives leave Harley's mouth. The truck door opens and slams, but he doesn't turn on the ignition. He doesn't come into the room either. I don't know where he's sleeping. I know it's not beside me though. Gone is the comfortable and reassuring sound of his breathing as he slept in the bed across the room, a bed so close to mine that when we were younger, far too young to know what it meant, or what those memories would mean to us later in life, we'd stretch our arms across the divide and hold hands as we fell asleep.

None of that will ever be the same. Thanksgiving will never be the same. This cottage will never be the same, because we're not the same, and we never will be again.

Chapter Twenty-Six
Rose

I feel like hell, and it isn't just because I stood on the street in the rain pouring my heart out to him and hoping—no, begging—him to open the door and let me in. It's more than likely because I went to bed soaking wet, and that's pretty much how I stayed all night. This morning, I can barely lift my head from the pillow.

Everything aches. My head is filled with fogginess and my nose runs like a tap. I lean over and turn off the alarm. It's a Sunday; I should be at the flower market collecting blooms for this week's specials, but I can't do it. I reach for my phone; I don't know why. Every day for a month it's been devoid of calls and messages from him, but this morning I'm surprised to see two missed calls. I squint at the screen and dial the number to retrieve my voice messages. A computerized voice tells me I have two new messages, and I skip past my mother's straight to the second.

Dermot's smooth, warm voice fills the earpiece. "Rose, it's Dermot. Obviously." He sighs. "I can't stop thinking about you. I was an asshole. I should have walked you to your door. I should have taken you up on that offer for a drink, and only a drink. I'm ... I'm sorry. Goddamn, I hate these things. There's no need to call me back, unless you want to, and I want you to." I smile a little to myself, because it's possible that Dermot is even worse at talking to voicemail than I am. "Shit, I'm not even making sense. How do I put this more succinctly? I know your heart belongs to someone else, but I'm—"

Beep.

The message cuts him off. *I'm what? What was he going to say?* Without pausing for even a beat, I hit the 'return call' button and field a couple of sneezes as I wait for it to ring. He's probably out jogging or doing breakfast with a client or winning a freaking Noble Prize. Hell, maybe he's out hiking in Muir Woods. Whatever he's doing, I'm betting it's something active, because I can't understand how the man could be almost old enough to be my father and still have a body like that. I make a mental note to join a gym because somehow I doubt he's sitting around eating a pint of Ben & Jerry's every night.

"Rose," he answers, sounding a little

breathless. In the background, some kind of machine whirs.

"Are you in the middle of something?"

"No, just jogging. Are you okay? You sound terrible."

"I feel terrible," I admit, hating that even though he's a little out of breath, he still sounds so put together, and me? I sound like I stuffed that pint of Ben & Jerry's up my nose. "I got caught in the rain last night after you drove me home."

"You left your apartment?" I hear the barest hint of accusation in his tone.

"Yeah. I had some words to say to a friend."

"I see," he says, so calm and collected. I wish I could see that handsome face, catch a glimpse of those warm brown eyes that seem to give everything away and nothing at all. "So what can I do for you, Rose?"

"I don't know. I just—I wanted to hear your voice."

He chuckles, but I'm not sure if he finds that funny or ironic after last night.

"I know you've been hurt before, and I wouldn't blame you if you wanted to just cut your losses now and a … a … choo."

"You're sick," he whispers.

"It's nothing."

"It's not nothing. I tell you what—save that thought. I'm going to clear my schedule, and I'll be there in twenty minutes."

"You keep to a schedule on Sundays?"

"Of course. Doesn't everyone?"

"No," I say automatically, and then I realize that my Sundays are ordinarily filled with flower markets, inventory, online ordering, and anything else that might make my week a little easier. "Actually, yeah, I guess I do too."

"I'll see you soon."

"Dermot, don't come over. I'm snotty and gross."

"I'll be there soon," he repeats, a little more firmly this time. "Don't argue, sweet Rose, you won't win."

"Dermot," I say before he can hang up. "Can you bring ice cream?"

"Sure," he says and disconnects. I fall back against my pillows and sigh, and then it occurs to me that I probably look like hell, so I get up and shower, brush my teeth, and change into a sweater and leggings. Ordinarily I wouldn't consider wearing anything like this around him, but I guess there's only one way to find out if he's serious about me: have him see me at my worst. Though we might need wine for that.

Close to half an hour later, a knock comes from downstairs and I crawl out of bed, my muscles protesting each movement and practically screaming at me when I use the stairs. Dermot stands on the other side of the glass in a sweater, jeans—likely designer ones that cost more than a month's rent for me—and a charcoal gray blazer. The man certainly knows how to dress. In his hands he juggles two big black and white striped bags. My eyes zero in on the label and I realize he went all the way to Soma for this. And not only that, but he bought ice cream from the best creamery in town. Warmth fills my chest.

"Hi," he mouths.

"Hi," I say, feeling marginally better now that he's here.

"Let me in," he says. I give a little scoffing laugh because he's right, I need to let him in, and not just because he's standing on my doorstep with ice cream that's likely melting. *I need to let him in.* I have to take a chance on this gorgeous man because he hasn't broken my heart, and if gut feelings are anything to go by, I dare say he never will.

I pull back the locks and he steps inside, out of the morning mist. Dew clings to his dark salt-and-pepper hair, and I want to run my fingers through it, I want to smell the moisture that's settled with his skin and cologne, but I guess that's kind of creepy and I don't want him to get sick, so I don't. Instead, I let him enter the shop, and I close and lock the door behind us.

"I'm glad you came," I say, leading the way

up the stairs.

"Me too. I didn't know what kind of ice cream you liked, so I bought one of everything."

"What?" I turn and face him with a dubious expression. "My freezer is not that big."

"I didn't want you to be disappointed."

I keep walking up the stairs, turning once I reach the top in order to see his face. "Okay, what's wrong with you?"

His brow furrows as if he doesn't understand the question. "I'm sorry?"

"There has to be something wrong with you. You're gorgeous, you're sweet, you're thoughtful and considerate, and you're successful—what woman in her right mind wouldn't want that?"

He laughs. "You tell me."

I pause, suck in a deep breath, and look into his eyes, really look. I have so much to say, and no idea where to start, but I suppose an apology is as good a place as any. "Dermot, I'm sorry about last night."

He takes a step forward, and I move away from the stairs in order to let him come up. I realize this is the first time he's actually setting foot in my apartment, even though we've been dating for weeks. "There's no need to apologize."

"Yes there is."

"You want to show me where to set this stuff down?"

"Right, sorry. In here," I say, and lead him into the tiny kitchen. The bags barely fit on the counter, and I don't know where the hell I'm going to store that ice cream because my freezer is only so big, unless of course I use the cooler downstairs.

Dermot opens the freezer, putting away pints of expensive homemade ice cream.

I snatch the Matcha green tea flavor from the bag and hold it to my chest. He raises a brow and looks as if he's storing that information away for later, but once he's done filling my freezer—all but three pints, including the one I'm holding, fit inside—he takes it from my hands and pulls out another bag. This one contains fresh fruit, cinnamon rolls, bagels, and a small container of soup. "It's early. I wasn't sure if you'd had breakfast or not, but everyone should have chicken noodle soup when they're ill."

"You're like my sexy fairy godmother right now."

"I'm not sure the words 'sexy' and 'fairy godmother' should be used in the same sentence, but I do like to be thorough." He grins, and something tells me he's not talking about being a boy scout. "Now, go lie down. Patients should be in bed."

My belly backflips, and heat scolds my cheeks. At least I can blame the blushing on my fever. I sit on the couch, because I'm not sure I'm ready to jump into bed with Dermot just yet, but I do feel a little odd about having him wait on me in my own house. It's clear he doesn't feel the same way because he sets the food down on the coffee table in front of me, along with a nip of brandy from my cupboard.

"Brandy?" I question.

"My mother always swore on brandy for a sore throat."

I smile at that. I like the fact that he has a mother and a whole life I know nothing about. He's a mystery to me, and one I don't mind uncovering. "Where is she now?"

He removes his blazer and lays it over the wingback chair. I expect him to sit, but instead he crosses the room and settles on the loveseat beside me. Though my nose is stuffy, I can smell his licorice spice aftershave. It's intoxicating. So grown-up and mature, but not stuffy, and nothing like vetiver and green and citrus. "She passed ten years ago."

My smile falters. *How did I not know this?* How have I not asked him about his parents? I'm a sucky … girlfriend. I'm selfish and thoughtless, and I've spent this whole time focusing on what was behind me, that I forgot to look ahead. I couldn't see a future outside of the one I'd imagine with Harley. But there is a future, just not one with my best friend in it. "Oh, Dermot. I'm so sorry."

"She had emphysema. In the end, it was easier to watch her go than to watch her struggle," he says, and damn if that doesn't just break my heart. The idea that someone you love could be in so much pain that it is easier to watch them die than it is to fight.

"That must have been horrible." I reach for a tissue and blow my nose. I might have discreetly wiped away the tears springing up in the corners of my eyes too.

"It was." He pauses for a beat and smiles, as if he's remembering her with fondness. "She'd smoked these imported dainty menthol cigarettes her whole life, convinced they couldn't kill her because she was smoking half of what a regular person would."

"That's terrible." I sniff.

"That's life."

I nod, though I'm not sure I'm free to comment. I've never lost anyone close to me, apart from my grandmother when I was thirteen years old. My mom may drive me bat-shit crazy, but losing her would kill me.

"And your dad?" I'm almost afraid of the response, but I want to learn more about him, and I can't believe it's taken me this long to figure that out.

"He passed too, when I was just a boy," he gives me a gloomy smile. "I do have a sister and a niece that live just outside the city that I rarely get time to see because of work."

"You should make time for them."

"I should," he agrees, and clears his throat. "I'm supposed to be taking care of you and here I am making you feel worse."

"I like learning more about you." I chew my bottom lip in an attempt to hide my smile. Dermot reaches out and runs his thumb over my cheek.

"I like you asking." His gaze turns molten and my face gets hot, my skin prickles all over, and I swallow hard. My head hurts, but I'm sure it's not just the fever that's making it swim. I glance away, searching for an escape.

"Should we watch a movie?" I say, too quickly.

"As long as you eat something first." He gestures towards the coffee table laden with food.

A slow smile spreads across my face. "You're pushy, huh?"

"Oh, Rose, you have no idea." He grins, and there's something wildly sexy and sinister in it, but then it's gone. "I don't like to see pretty girls wasting away to nothing."

"I'm hardly wasting away."

"You're incredible. Your body is incredible. I'd like to see it stay that way."

"Okay Mr. Bossy Boots." I pick up a cinnamon roll that's almost as big as my head and attempt to hide behind it because I'm blushing again. I nibble away at it for a bit just to appease him. It's not that I don't want to eat in front of him; we've been on several dinner dates already, and I'm not one of those girls who is shy about food. SF has some of the best restaurants, food trucks, and farmer's markets in the country, and I'm not afraid to try all of the gastronomical delights the city has to offer. The problem lies more in my throat feeling like I swallowed razorblades. The only food I want to eat when I'm sick is ice cream.

I set the pastry down and field the look Dermot gives me. "It hurts my throat," I explain without looking at him. I flick past my recommended viewing options on Netflix, afraid he'll see how wedding crazy I am, and I settle on a movie that seems ruggedly manly and intellectual, if such a movie exists. He takes the remote from me, flicks it to the main menu and settles on *Crazy, Stupid Love*. I stare in shock.

"You don't mind, do you?"

"Of course not," I say, because Ryan Gosling.

Dermot picks up the spoon and my ice cream from the coffee table and hands them to me. I snatch them greedily and stroke the carton as if it's my own, my precious. He looks amused but doesn't say anything, he just grabs my ankles and settles my feet into his lap.

"What are you doing?" I'm not sure we're at this juncture in our relationship. I mean, I love the feel of his hand at the small of my back, I love his mouth on mine, but my feet in his lap?

"Quiet," he commands, and I promptly shut up because he rubs them with smooth, sure strokes, and it feels divine. *Maybe we are at this juncture after all.*

"You don't have to do that," I say, because I feel like I should. Not because I actually want him to stop.

He turns to glare impatiently at me and grips my ankle, pulling me down farther on the couch so my legs are in his lap now, and my butt is flush with his side. "Rose, we don't know each other well, but if there's one thing I hate, it's talking during a film. So shut up, eat your ice cream, and enjoy my hands on your body."

That makes my eyes grow wide as dinner plates. *His hands on my body?* "Your hands on my body?"

As if he felt words weren't enough to convey his meaning, his strong hands smooth my calf muscle and I groan, a little louder than perhaps I should because Dermot's deep chocolate eyes have turned predatory again, and I'm pinned by his gaze. I gulp, and the man smiles. *Bastard.*

With one hand, he takes the ice cream from me and sets it down on the coffee table. His other hand slides up my calf and pulls me farther down the couch and when he releases me, he climbs up my body, wedging himself into the space between my legs. His arms pin me into place on either side of my head, and he leans in to kiss me.

"What are you doing?"

"What does it look like?"

"You'll get sick," I warn.

"I don't care," he whispers and presses his mouth to mine. At first I try to pull away, because I can't fathom what he sees in me right now with my rheumy eyes, my hair in a messy knot on top of my head, and my nose red. I try to resist but I can't because this stunning, sweet man came running the second I called, and it's nice to be someone's priority for once. So even though I know he will likely get sick too, I kiss him back.

Dermot's hand slides up under my sweater. His touch is soft and cool against my burning flesh. His palm grazes my breast, the sheer lace of my bra providing no protection against his hands, and my nipples stiffen and form two hard peaks. He rocks his hips against me and I squirm, Delicious heat engulfs me from the core up. His mouth devours mine; he pinches my sensitive flesh, and I pull away because I can't breathe. "Dermot ..."

"You're right, I should stop."

"No. I want you closer," I pant, reaching for the hem of his sweater and lifting it up over his head. He pulls it the rest of the way off but his eyes search mine as if he's uncertain. "I want you."

He grins, and as quickly as flipping a switch, the man snakes his hand behind my back and flips me onto my stomach. I gasp in shock as he pulls me up by the hips and slides my leggings and panties down over my ass. Cool air rushes across my body, and I'm completely exposed to him. Shock and fever both have me stunned, and I don't dare move a muscle.

I'm rewarded with a warm, wet tongue plunging into me. I let out a sharp breath, and Dermot shifts me so that my torso is bent over the armrest of the small loveseat and my ass is offered up to him for the taking. His whole mouth devours me, and if it didn't feel so amazing, I might have had the good graces to be embarrassed. I tremble as I try to keep my balance and not fall over the edge of the couch, as if that were even possible considering the grip Dermot has on my hips.

His tongue laves at my flesh over and over. He's relentless, merciless, and I think he gets off on control because the more he keeps up his ministrations, the closer I am to coming, and the more he orders me not to. I moan as the orgasm builds within me, wracking my frame and making me feel as if I've lost complete control over my body. And just when I'm close, he slides two thick fingers inside me and hooks them toward my belly in a 'come hither' motion, hitting my G-spot. His tongue slides over me again, but not on my clit. This time his whole mouth greedily eats my pussy and ass, and I come so hard it's as if for a moment I cease to exist. *Bliss*. That's the only word for it.

I pant. My whole body goes limp as I collapse against the couch, but it seems Dermot's not interested and letting me rest because he moves up my back, rubbing his stubble against my buttocks, awakening my skin to the bittersweet agony of it. I feel the wetness left behind long after his mouth leaves my flesh. His leanly muscled body hovers over mine.

"I've waited a long time to do that," he says, coolly. My core muscles tighten again, sending a thousand little mini aftershocks through me. "You taste like a fucking angel, Rose. So goddamn sweet and so fucking tasty."

Jesus. He's so vocal. Somehow, knowing he has a dirty mouth makes me that much more attracted to him. He grinds himself against me, and even clothed I can feel how hard he is. I moan, and he lifts my sweater up my back and over my head, then grabs a rough handful of my breasts through the bra I'm wearing. He doesn't bother to take it off.

"I wanna fuck these tits. I wanna see my come spread all over them later, but first I'm going to bury my cock inside your sweet little cunt and fuck you until you beg me to stop." He pinches me hard, and his mouth kisses my neck with the barest hint of teeth.

"Oh," I moan, wrapping my arm around his neck and drawing my back up against his front.

Behind me, I hear the tearing of a foil packet as Dermot angles his body away, unzips his pants and rolls the condom on. His palm rests between my shoulder blades, and he pushes me down as he guides himself inside.

"Oh fuck," he grunts, as he eases in inch by inch. I'm ready and soaking wet, but I still grip him tightly, contracting my walls around him so he gasps. "Jesus, Rose, stop or I'm going to come much sooner than you want me to."

To punctuate his words, his hand comes down on my butt cheek and I gasp, jumping a little beneath him and squirming with my smarting flesh. "Keep still, baby, or I'll do it again."

I can't keep still though. My brain tells me to, but my body moves because I can't have him inside me and not writhe. I want more, more heat, more delicious stroking, and more blows from his hand. So I rock my hips back and forth. He growls, and that hand comes down upon my ass again, striking even harder than the last time.

"Oh god," I cry. "Again."

He does it again. In fact, I lose count how many times he strikes me, because the smooth, cool strokes of his hand on my stinging flesh soothe like a balm, and his thrusts make me lose my mind. I come over and over again until I lose count of this too, lose focus on everything around me.

Dermot pulls me up flush against him. His hand is at my throat as he comes inside me, and I tremble on shaking knees as he sags into a kneeling position on my couch, taking me with him. I lean back against his rigid body, the hand at my throat now softly stroking my face, my hair, and my breasts as he nibbles my ear. I don't know why, but I feel both empty and satiated, raw and numb. Too many emotions clamor for my attention—I don't know whether to laugh hysterically or cry. All I know is I want sleep, and I want Dermot to hold me as if that meant something to him because the last man I let inside my body hadn't.

As if he can sense this, he shifts on the couch, removing the condom and disposing of it, and then he lifts me up and carries me to the bed. He pulls me on top of him, my back against his front.

"I have no control around you," he whispers sleepily against the shell of my ear. "I couldn't help myself. Fuck, Rose, the way you came alive under my hand ... beautiful."

Reverently, he caresses my body from my hips to my chest. He snakes his fingers between my thighs and strokes the wet flesh, paying particular attention to my clit. I squirm against him. My muscles clench. "Let me take care of you."

I don't protest. I come hard as he whispers in my ear the sweet and brutal things he wants to do to me. I feel as if I'm coming down from the greatest heights. My feet barely touch the ground, and yet I'm still afraid, afraid he'll leave, afraid to let him in—afraid that at some point I'll fall, and no one will be there to catch me.

When I wake, I'm alone.

There's a note on the pillow. I squint at the darkening sky and wonder what time it is. Afternoon, for sure. Did I sleep all day? I pick up the note and read it with bleary eyes.

Rose,

You are fucking incredible. I want dinner tomorrow night, my place, you naked and sprawled across my dining table at eight p.m. sharp.

Don't be late, or there will be another spanking in your future.

D.

Holy shit. *Wow. Just wow.*

I'd been aware of him pulling me closer, holding me and kissing my neck and cheek and telling me how perfect I was, how wanted, as I drifted in and out of sleep. Though I don't know how long he stayed, I do know that I woke several times with his warmth at my back, and every time he seemed to wrap me up in his arms tighter than the last.

Now, I press my hands against my head to stave off the headache. I ache with need as I read the note once more. The idea of being with Dermot again is both exciting and terrifying, and I don't know if I'm dreading or eagerly awaiting eight p.m. sharp.

I drop the piece of paper. It flutters to the pillow beside my head, and I smile as I fall asleep again.

Dermot doesn't come in for coffee the next morning, and I'm a little disappointed. I know we have plans for dinner tonight, but I'm jumpy and full of nervous expectation and nothing will calm me down. Of course, that could have something to do with the two cups of coffee I've had Izzy make me already this morning.

I slide my empty mug toward her again with

a sheepish smile. She gives me a puzzled expression, then a smug smile lights her face and she shouts over the high-pitched squeal of the machine frothing the cream, "You got laid on the weekend."

My eyes bug out as I glance at the longline of customers waiting for their coffee. They all look at me, and then their eyes dart back to Izzy like zombies hunting a fresh brain. One of the hipsters is actually slack-jawed. "Did not."

"You did," she shouts. "Someone rocked your world; it's written all over your face, and you're walking like you got a good dicking. Did Harley come around after all?"

I feel a pang of regret when she mentions his name. "No."

"Then who?" she says, her grin widening. "Oh my god, Silver Fox?"

"His name is Dermot."

"His name should be *Yes Please*. You have to tell me everything. When did this happen? I didn't think you were that into him." She sets the stainless steel creamer jug on the counter and begins creating her masterpiece. I still haven't worked out how she makes little flower patterns in the foam, but every single one is different. She hands them off to the awaiting customers, three at a time and I keep manning the register.

There's still a line halfway to the door, so I

know I'm not going to get away with telling her I'll give her details later. She'd likely halt all coffee production until it was done, and we can't afford to lose their business, so I angle my body away from the customers.

"Um … we've sort of been dating for weeks."

"And you didn't tell me?" She slams the paper cup down, spilling coffee over the sides. I glance at the next customer; it's zombie hipster guy. He doesn't even seem to notice. He just picks up the cup and draws it to his face, getting foam in his trimmed yet strangely unkempt beard, then he closes his eyes and groans in ecstasy, shambling out of the store.

"I didn't know how much there was to tell."

"Well clearly there's something to tell, because you've been walking bowlegged all morning."

"I am not." *I'm not. Am I?* "I told him I was hung up on someone else."

She raises a brow at me. "Okay, I'm bored now. When did the sex happen?"

"I went to Harley's," I blurt out.

"And now I'm confused."

"I walked over there after my date with Dermot on Saturday night. I stood at his window screaming up at him … in the rain."

"You what?"

"I don't know; I just couldn't stand the silence between us anymore. I was angry, and I thought if I confronted him something would happen."

"And did it?"

"I wound up with a head cold." I shrug and take the money from the next three people in line while Izzy hands them their coffee.

"Are you getting to the sex anytime soon?" Izzy makes an impatient face.

"Have you ..." I pause and look at the line. Just two people left—one a middle-aged woman in sweats and a tank, and the other a tall blond man in a navy suit. They're both engrossed in their phones, so I lower my voice and say, "Have you ever had anyone spank you?"

"Oh god, he's a control freak too?" She pouts, as if I'd dangled a piece of candy in front of her face and eaten it myself. "You know if you ever let him go, feel free to send him my way. I love those domineering alpha types."

"I second that," the woman in the workout gear says.

"Third," Navy Suit says, without looking up from his phone.

I blush and smile awkwardly at the customers before turning my attention back to my employee. Then I decide I should at least look like I'm doing something now that the line has dwindled, so I take out my appointment book from beneath the counter. I stare at the pages, seeing but not taking anything in. "I really like him, Izzy, but I'm—"

"Still hung up on Harley, I know," she says. "You know sometimes what we want isn't the best thing for us."

I pause in my perusal of our appointments and glance up at her. "Is that what you think Harley is? No good for me?"

"I just think he's had you so long, in so many ways—friends, not friends, lovers, friends again, and fuck buddies—that I think he's taken that for granted. You have to do what's best for you. If that means moving on with the fantastic Mr. Fox and forgetting Harley exists, then so be it. You can't be at his beck and call forever, Rose. Eventually, something has to give. You have to let him go."

She's right. I hate that. I've already come to this conclusion, of course, but I hate that it has taken her a few short months to see what I hadn't noticed in a lifetime. Maybe we never saw what was best for us until the damage was already done, until hearts were already broken with no way to put them back together. As far as I'm concerned, hindsight could suck it.

Chapter Twenty-Seven

Rose

Age eighteen

In the morning I wake late. It's the first time that I haven't woken with the sunrise on Thanksgiving, but even without me waking the entire house, the moms have got up and are in the kitchen, preparing the turkey for dinner.

I lie in bed and listen to the clatter of pots and pans, the moms endless chattering and the dads complaining that their noise is interfering with the game. I can't hide out in this room forever, and after ten minutes of quietly chanting 'there's no place like home' as I click my heels together—and likely bruise my ankles—I get up. I shower and dress in jeans and an old T-shirt, and head downstairs. I don't bother doing anything with my face or hair, because who gives a shit, right? Certainly not Harley. He has a girlfriend. *Rat bastard.* Besides, no makeup in the world could hide the fact that my eyes are puffy and practically rubbed raw.

"Oh, darling, you look terrible," my mother says as I plonk myself at the kitchen table.

"Thanks Mom," I mutter, burying my head in my elbows.

"Are you coming down with something?" She places her cool hand against my forehead to check my temperature.

"I'm fine."

"I don't think Rose has a fever," Rochelle says, nodding her chin towards the window.

I know what she's referring to without having to look, but still, I do it anyway. Through the living room window I see him closing the front gate. His movements are stiff, and he looks like hell. He wears the same gray T-shirt and jeans he had on yesterday, and his hair is mussed from sleep. I suck in a sharp breath because looking at him hurts, and I turn my back to the window before he can notice me.

The worried look our mothers share doesn't go unseen, but I ignore them both, resting my head in the crook of my elbow again. I just have to get through this weekend, that's all. It's not like he intends to stay for good, because he has a girlfriend that I'm sure he'll want to get back to. I'm struck with uncertainty. What if by some cruel fate he brought her to my city? What if they move to SF and I'm forced to spend all of the holidays with the two of them, pretending I don't want to shank her with my fork? *No, Harley wouldn't do that*, I tell myself, but fear strikes my heart because the Harley I used to know isn't the same guy as the one opening the front door to the cottage.

I guess I can't avoid this forever. Our families are ... well, family. I make a promise to myself then and there that next year, I'm going to Maui for Thanksgiving. Alone.

I can't help it. I lift my head and watch Harley step inside. He removes his Chucks and sets them down on the shoe rack that we used to try to break as kids. His eyes meet mine, and he walks across the room and sits on the barstool beside me. Agitated, I get up and storm around the small kitchen, collecting a bowl, a spoon, and a box of cereal that I return to the counter. Harley rises too and starts banging things around: a mug, a canister of freshly ground coffee, the sugar bowl. Our moms look on dumbfounded while our dads, who are sitting on the couch in the open plan living room, tell us to pipe down because they can't hear the game. Ordinarily, Harley and I would be watching it with them, cozied up on the loveseat like we have every year since we were seven years old, but there is no more cozying in our future. Harley stands in front of the refrigerator, looking for juice or cream or his cold dead heart, I'm not sure which, but the fact that he's blocking my way annoys the shit out of me.

"Excuse me," I snap.

He turns to look at me as if I'm interrupting a very important clandestine meeting he's having with the contents of the fridge. He steps back a little as if to let me in, and when I reach for the milk his fingers get there first and wrap around the bottle. I attempt to yank it out of his hands, but he holds it tightly to him and brings it to his chest. And then the rat bastard twists off the lid and guzzles down the rest.

"You ass."

"Sorry. I didn't know you wanted it," he says, wiping away the milk moustache that I so badly want to lick. Even now.

"Harley," Rochelle chides.

"There's another out in the icebox," Mom says, like the jackass didn't just drain it dry on purpose.

"It's fine. I'm not hungry anyway." I brush past him in a hurry because it's the stupidest thing, but tears are forming in my eyes. Not from the milk, though that was a douche-canoe move, but from the aching in my chest, from the blackness that I fear will swallow me whole if I can't just put my arms around him, or have him hold me and tell me that though we're broken now, we're going to be okay. *But we're not okay.* We both made decisions that led us to this point, and we were both selfish assholes. What I'd done might have seemed selfless, leaving him so he wouldn't be held back, but it wasn't. I could have given up my studies; I could have moved to Louisiana and opened a shop there, but I didn't want to leave my city. *So I left him.* And in turn, he left me for someone else.

I walk down the hall to my room and close the door firmly behind me. It doesn't have a lock on account of the 'rentals insisting that we didn't need one, as our relationship had only turned romantic a year ago. I wish there was a way to bar the door but then I wonder what's the point? Harley won't come after me—why would he? When Harley wants something he makes sure he gets it; that's how I knew he wasn't coming after me when I left Louisiana. Because despite everything he said, he didn't want me enough.

It's another hour before my door opens and snicks softly closed. My back is to the door, so I don't see who it is, but I don't need to—I feel him. I'd always thought that when I read that in novels or when I saw the protagonist in a film turn because she felt her lover's eyes on her that it was complete bullshit. But I know it's Harley standing behind me because I know that flippy feeling in my stomach, and I know that scent of citrus and spice mixed with a little sweat. And I know that presence because I know his energy better than my own. It's comforting, even though he is the cause of my hurt, and isn't that the definition of irony?

"Go away," I beg pathetically. "Please? I can't fight with you anymore."

He doesn't answer, but I hear the bedsprings groan in protest as he lies on the mattress. Even this makes me cry, because he won't leave, and it seems he's never happy unless he's tormenting me. I sob, and I can't stop it. He doesn't touch me; for a long time he doesn't say anything, and it makes me both grateful and angry at the same time.

"I don't know how to fix us," he says, exhaling softly. "I don't know how to not have you in my life."

"I don't know how to have you in mine," I admit.

Harley sighs, and a beat later the bed squeaks as he gets up and crosses to the door. "I know it hurts now—believe me I feel it too—but I hope you can find a way to be okay with me, with us, again, because you're my family, Rose. You're it. Everything is fucked up now, but I can't live my life without you in it."

"Get out," I whisper, and I'm proud that my voice doesn't sound as broken as I feel. "Just get out."

He leaves, closing the door behind him, and for a second I think I hear him slump against it, but then his footsteps sound on the worn floorboards and I'm alone again.

Mom comes to collect me for dinner a few hours later. I tell her I'm not hungry, but she insists I eat, and she doesn't leave the room until I'm trailing along after her. I can't even look at Harley. I take the empty seat next to my dad, and I silently thank my mom for ensuring we aren't at least sat together this year. Even being in the same state is too close to him now.

After dinner, the 'rentals pull out the cards and set up for poker like they do every year. I can't entertain the thought of having to spend one second longer with Harley, so I excuse myself and head to my room. Moments later, his truck pulls out of the drive. I don't know where he's going, and I don't care. The sooner we leave and put this weekend behind us, put our love affair and our childhood behind us, the better we'll be.

Chapter Twenty-Eight

Rose

I stand outside Dermot's house. It's huge, a four-level white façade residence reminiscent of the French renaissance. It sat on a cliff-side lot overlooking the ocean in Sea Cliff. I've known Dermot had money, that much is obvious in the way he carries himself, the clothes he wears, the car he drives, but this is … this is intimidating as hell. My parents are smart, hardworking people. They live in a nice house and drive nice cars, and my mom wears designer everything, so it isn't as if I'd grown up in a poor house, but staring at Dermot's Mc Mansion I decide I am definitely in the wrong business and I need to go back to school in order to learn how to become a CEO and founder of some billion-dollar stem cell clinical-trial company.

I also don't understand why, if he lives here, does he come all the way across town to slum it and buy his coffee from my store in Noe Valley? It can't have been because we have the best coffee in the entire city. Izzy is good, but with this kind of money Dermot could afford a thousand live-in Izzys to fetch him coffee beans dipped in gold and ground by virgin hands from the Peruvian Andes.

I don't know how long I stand there gawping at the brilliant white house, but the front door opens and Dermot leans against the doorjamb in a white button-down shirt rolled at the sleeves and charcoal suit pants, black belt, black shoes, and no tie. He runs a hand through his salt-and-pepper hair, and it strikes me that I have no idea how to approach him now. Do I kiss him? Throw myself at him, or just be casual? I have no idea what the proper response is when greeting a man the day after he's spanked you on your couch and fucked you senseless. All I know is that I want more. I don't even know what more I want—the amazing sex definitely, but the spanking? I don't know. I do know that I want to know more about him, where he is from, how he became so successful, what his favorite food is. Does he watch football? Did he play it in school? Was he a nerd, or was he part of the in-crowd? Does he really like the fundraisers with stuffy socialites that he attends? Did he spank Mireille, his stunning ex-wife? That thought has me reeling, and it takes a beat before I realize Dermot just said something.

I shake my head, as if I could clear these

thoughts that fog my brain. "What?"

He's so cool and casual, leaning against the doorframe, as if he knows I'll be eating out of the palm of his hand the minute I cross that threshold. "I said, are you planning to stand out here all night?"

I smile sheepishly. "I'm thinking about it."

"I won't bite, Rose."

"What if I want you to?" From the looks of it, I've surprised the both of us with that comment, because Dermot's gaze goes from warm to glacial in zero-point-two-five seconds.

I take a deep breath and brush past him, but he reaches out and grips my arm tightly, leaning in to whisper, "Do you have any idea how much I've been dreaming about seeing you sprawled on my dining table all day? It's very distracting, Rose. I've had to leave no less than two meetings to sort out my giant erection."

I laugh, but clearly this is the wrong thing to do because Dermot's gaze sears me where I stand. He guides my hand to his crotch, showing me just how sincere he was being with that last statement. "God, I can't help myself with you."

"Then don't."

The door closes behind him with a resounding thud, and I gulp. Dermot grasps the nape of my neck. I gasp and break out in goose bumps. His touch is firm, yet tender, as he leads me down the hall toward the dining room. The view is incredible: a panorama of the Golden Gate Bridge, Pacific Ocean, and Marin Headlands, and I feel a sweeping sense of peace watching the fog waft over the bridge. A huge antique mirror dining table with sage gray upholstered chairs stands before us. One end is dressed for two with fine crystal and Chinese takeout, and the rest is left bare. I glide my hands along the shiny surface as Dermot bends me over the table with his hand splayed flat against my spine. I go willingly, with knots forming in my stomach and the smallest pinch of fear in my heart. I let him slide up my dress and fuck me senseless right there on his exquisite dining table with the fog and the Pacific as our witnesses.

And I barely even think of Harley at all.

Chapter Twenty-Nine

Rose

Age eighteen

When I agreed to tag along with my parents to the cottage for Thanksgiving, it was under the condition that they'd drive me back to SF before Saturday. I have to work this weekend and my car is in the shop and unable to make the two-and-a-half-hour drive to Carmel and back. My mother insisted that this would not be a problem and that she would drive me myself, but come Friday, it is a huge fucking problem. Unfortunately for me, Harley happens to be driving back to SF this very afternoon and it "just makes sense" that I catch a ride with him. I know this is our mothers' plan to get us talking again, but it's not going to work. I have nothing left to say to the man, so when they pile me into his truck with my belongings I sit stubbornly silent the whole ride up the coast to the city.

Harley pulls into his parents' drive, and I open the door before the car has even come to a complete stop and jump out. I grab my things from the bed of the truck and stalk across the pavement and onto the drive of my own house. It's only when I get to my front door that I realize I didn't bring my keys. I was with the 'rentals; I hadn't planned on leaving early and now I'm locked out of my house. I bang my head against the door and sigh, as the car door slams. I glance over at Harley, who's watching me closely as he leans against the truck.

"I forgot my keys," I explain.

He grins. "Looks like you're stuck with me a little longer then."

I shake my head. "My window. It's closed, but unlocked. I just need to get into your room."

He smiles sadly. "Been a while since I heard that."

"Just don't. Please, don't pretend like everything is the way it was, because it's not. It's not ever going to be."

His mouth forms a hard line, and he turns and heads towards his front door. "Come on."

When we make it inside, he gets to the stairs before me and takes them three at a time. I curse his long strides and attempt to race him the way I used to, as if there was ever a possibility of winning with him. Now is no different, and when I enter the room I find him climbing up onto the sill as he's done a million times before. He slides his big body through the tiny window frame, stepping across the empty space between our houses, and pushes on the glass.

It doesn't budge.

"It's not opening," Harley yells.

"It has to. It's unlocked."

"You still leave your window unlocked?"

I shrug like it doesn't mean anything, as if it wasn't an invitation for him to come to me whenever he found himself back home. When I'd returned from Louisiana and ventured up to my room, my window had been closed. It looked wrong, as if it was just another door closing on the two of us, and though I'd felt miserable doing it, I'd let it remain shut, but I'd never turned that latch a day in my life and I didn't plan on it ever.

"It's always been unlocked," I tell him sadly.

"Maybe your mom locked it this time. Either way, we're not getting in that house unless your folks come with a key, or you want to break the window and set off the alarms."

My mom would never come, citing instead that it was the perfect opportunity for me and Harley to sort out our shit, and my dad would have kittens if I broke a window and called out the security guy on a holiday weekend. So, resigned, I flop down hard on Harley's bed.

I've always loved this room. It isn't the

decor or the fact that it's the polar opposite of mine; it is just so intrinsically him. The smell, the color of the walls—even the bedding is Harley, no fuss and a little bit lumberjack for a high school kid.

I smooth my hands over the checked quilt and smile to myself, remembering how soft that flannel felt against my naked body the few times I'd grown impatient waiting for him to come to me and I'd climbed in his window instead. Even though he'd been away all this time, Rochelle kept it exactly the same, only stripping the sheets and duvet to wash them every few weeks in case he came home.

"You remember the last time we were in here? The night before I left and we made one hell of a mess of the sheets?"

"I remember." I smile fondly at the memories.

"That was a good night."

"We had a lot of good nights," I say, and the smile leaves my face.

Harley's does too, turning instead to a serious expression. "Come on. Come have a drink with me."

"Because that worked out so well last time?"

"I promise I won't let you kiss me again … or touch my dick."

"You're such an ass," I say, throwing the pillow at him. I can't help but laugh a little too, because I've never been that forward with him. While I might have snuck across the gap between our houses a time or two, Harley had always been the one to initiate sex.

Eventually, after I get over the heartbreak of those words he told me when I straddled him in the truck and grabbed his junk, I'll likely chalk that experience up to a humorous one, but I can't move past the pain of it just yet.

"What else are you gonna do?" His mouth tips up in the corners, the very start of a Pan grin forming. "Wait out on the doorstep in the cold just to avoid me?"

"Maybe," I deadpan. "As far as ideas go, it wouldn't be my worst."

"No, it wouldn't," he agrees, and I know he's talking about my decision to break it off because it landed us exactly here. Then again, Harley is seeing someone else now, so who knows? Maybe in two, three, four years' time he'll be thanking me for walking away first as he gets down on one knee to propose to his girlfriend.

"What's she like?"

"Who?"

"Your girlfriend."

"Nothing like you," he says, too quickly. The knife twists in my gut because I don't know if that's better or worse.

"What's her name?"

"Emma."

"And what does Emma look like?"

Harley runs a hand through his hair, it's longer now. It suits him, resting just above his shoulders in one of those shaggy Jared Padalecki cuts. "Rose, what are you doing?"

"I just want to know. We told each other everything once."

"That was before." He shakes his head and glances at the window. "She's insignificant."

I laugh humorlessly. "Insignificant? But not enough to throw away what you have with her? Not like with me."

He scrubs a hand down over his face. "She's not insignificant—that was the wrong word. She's important to me."

"But not as important as me?"

"No one will ever be as important as you."

"Right, but then, I'm not important enough to wait for. Not important enough to come back for." I swallow hard around the lump in my throat. "Do you love her?"

Harley's temper flares as he meets my gaze. "Rose—"

"Do you?"

"I don't know." He rakes a hand through his hair. A beat later it falls right back in his face. I long to reach out and touch it, but that isn't my place anymore. "Yeah. I think so. When I'm with her I'm

a different man, but when I'm here with you, I'm …
I'm me."

"God," I breathe. "That's so much worse."
Fresh tears prick my eyes. I cover my face, as if I
could hide my torment or the despair that I feel in
this moment.

As if I could hide anything from this man.

"I know." Sadness chokes his voice, making
the words almost impossible to hear. Harley pulls
me close, folding me in his arms, holding me the
way he has a thousand times before, but this time
it's infinitely different.

This time, it's the end of us.

I cry into his big chest. This hurts, having
him close, having him hold me after these lonely,
never-ending months, but it's also cathartic. Yes,
I'm still mad. I'm furious at him and a part of me
will always be angry, just like he'll always be angry
at me for doing this to us in the first place.

First love is always hard to get over. It's
been that way since the beginning of time, and it
won't end with Harley and me. I don't know where
we go from here. I wish we didn't have to go
anywhere. I wish he'd stay, I wish he'd choose me,
but I know that he won't because somewhere along
the way we became different people. We changed.
Not for the better, not the worse—we just changed.
We grew up. The boy who never wanted to grow up
did. And it came at the cost of everything we were.

"I could use that drink," I say, stepping back from him, but he pulls me in again and presses a soft kiss to my lips. For a beat I'm stunned, and then I begin to understand. It isn't a romantic kiss—it's a goodbye.

It rings in a new dawn, one where Harley isn't the center of my Earth and I'm not the center of his, and just like that, I'm lost. I'm no longer tethered to this man. I'm no longer his future—I'm his past, and he's mine. But that's all we are. Ex-lovers. Friends? Maybe one day, but for now are just two people who've clung to one another for so long we forgot we weren't the only two to exist. We forgot we weren't a whole, but two separate pieces.

It will kill me, but I have to let go of Harley Hamilton, because he's already let go of me. And there is nothing sadder than a woman clinging to a ghost.

Chapter Thirty
Rose

Dermot and I fall into a strange sort of rhythm over the next two weeks. We very rarely go out anymore. A part of me wonders about this, and the other part doesn't think too much of it once he puts his mouth and hands on me. Staying in means we can get naked, so that's what we do.

In the mornings he's gone before I wake, citing exercise or work at the lab, and I find a romantic note on the pillow and a coffee on the nightstand. Those nights that we stay at his place, I wake to a damn buffet breakfast … alone. I try not to be disappointed in that; we're both very busy people, and I understood that to own a house like this, you have to work a lot. So even though we hardly ever got out, there is no doubt we're becoming more and more serious.

I've spoken to Dermot's sister on the phone a handful of times and though we haven't met in person yet, I like her a lot. The two of us nag him constantly about setting aside time for his baby niece. Mom dogs me with questions about Dermot and me almost every day. I think she's just glad I'm not spending my weekends alone, but dad was not happy about me dating a work colleague, much less one only five years his junior. I guess when you think about it like that, I'm not so happy either.

But Dermot is a very different man from my father. He's young at heart, adventurous, and so incredibly sexy. He is also late, but I am too. Dermot has booked a table at a French restaurant in the Bay area thirty minutes after his flight lands from LA, and I am running so late that I've only just sent Izzy and Ginger home. He was due to arrive ten minutes ago and I still haven't showered or freshened up my hair and makeup, not to mention found something to wear.

I duck into the cool room and return a bucket of roses to the ledge, and then I lean against the metal shelving unit and breathe. Like all businesses, the lead up to Thanksgiving and Christmas is chaotic. Izzy, Ginger and I haven't stopped running all day.

I check my phone, which happens to be conveniently resting on the cool room shelf where I left it and is almost out of batteries. Ten after seven. *Shit*. Dermot is going to kill me … or spank me. *I rather like the idea of that second option.*

The bell above the door rings and I crane my neck, listening for signs of my man. He knows where to find me, and since I can't hear a pair of very expensive leather shoes walking across my floorboards I roll my eyes, just knowing I'm going to have to deal with some irritating hipster who ums and ahhs over spending twenty dollars on a bouquet. I really need to start locking my door.

"We're closed," I say from the cool room.

Nothing.

So I walk out and let the door slam behind me, wiping my hands on my apron and wishing like hell I didn't have to deal with this right now. That's the thing about floristry—people think it's all roses and beautiful-smelling blooms, but it's not. It's messy, and it's work, and sometimes it downright stinks, and no matter how you try you can't get the stench of rotting flowers off of you.

"We're closed," I say again, exasperated as I round the corner and see Harley standing in the middle of my shop. He looks like shit—thin, gray around the eyes, and gaunt. I want to go to him, but my feet stay glued firmly to the floor. "What are you doing here?"

"I was in the neighborhood." My brow furrows at that. He's always in the neighborhood; he lives just a few doors down from me.

I swallow back the panic rising in my throat, because something is wrong, something is very wrong. This isn't my Harley. "What's wrong?"

"What's right?" He gives me a small pained smile and takes a step toward me, but I hold my hand up for him to stop. "I had to come see you."

"You had to come see me? Six weeks,

Harley. I haven't seen you in six whole weeks, and all of a sudden you had to see me? You look like shit, by the way."

He smiles at that. Actually smiles. *Bastard*. "Feel it, too."

"Good." He flinches, and I soften my tone and say, "What have you done to yourself?"

He ignores the question and moves closer. "Can we talk?"

"I have a date."

His brow creases, and he raps his knuckles on the counter. "With who?"

"With Dermot."

Harley shakes his head, biting down on his lip before levelling his eyes on me. "The cheater, Rose? Really? Why him?"

"He never cheated on her, and nothing happened. He filed for divorce the second they came home," I say, caustically. "You know what? I don't even know why I'm justifying anything to you. Dermot isn't the one who fucked me and didn't return my calls. My best friend did that."

His Adam's apple bobs. "Rose—"

"You know I never could keep up with you and your fucking bipolar disorder when it came to me," I say, and mimic his voice, "I want you; I don't want you. Which is it, Harley? I'm getting a little bit sick and tired of being at the end of your puppet strings."

"I want you, Rose. I've always wanted you. Since the day you pushed me over in that sandpit I've wanted nothing else, but—"

"Then why the hell would you do that to me?" My voice cracks until it's shrill and doesn't sound like my voice at all, but some kind of childlike cry. "How could you do that to me? To us? You knew how I felt about you."

He nods somberly, but he doesn't meet my gaze.

"Why?" I demand on a sob. "What reason could you possibly have for breaking my heart after I asked you not to?"

"Because I'm sick."

Everything stops. As soon as the words are out of his mouth, everything. Just. Stops. And I know, I know in my heart and down to the very last cell that makes up all of me, that it's the truth.

"Stage IIB seminomas."

"What does that mean?" I cover my mouth. I'm certain he's not speaking English anymore, and I silently plead for him to explain or to tell me he's kidding. Maybe I'm dreaming. Maybe this is all some terrible dream and all I need to do is just wake up.

"I have testicular cancer, Rose. I had surgery to have it removed, but it's spread to my lymph nodes. So now I get a cocktail of chemo pumped into my veins every three weeks."

"Surgery?" I whisper, and he nods gravely. "When?"

"The morning after I made love to you."

A horrified gasp escapes my throat, and I shove him hard. He stumbles. "You asshole! You let me think you were avoiding me, and you were in surgery? All this time you've been sick?" An odd, animal sound rips from my chest, and my legs go out from under me.

Harley catches me up in his embrace. He sinks to the floor and cradles me in his lap, and then the tears come. Thick, fat droplets fall into my lap, soaking my apron front, and even though he's just told me that he's sick, I feel as though I'm the one dying. I'm no longer the sum of my parts, but I'm shattered, wrecked, ruined. I'm a million pieces broken off and scattered to the wind.

When I find my voice again, it's quiet and wracked with guilt for all the terrible things I've said about him, all the horrible thoughts, all the hate and the anger. "Why would you keep this from me?"

"Come on, Rose. I couldn't do that to you. I didn't know how to tell you."

"Then why now?"

He lets out a breath, and his shoulders sag as he slumps against me, and I know the reason without him having to tell me.

Because he doesn't think he's going to make

it.

smoothing the hair back from my face. "I was terrified, Rose. Alecia had been at the doctor's office with me when I found out, and it was the scariest moment of my life. All I could think about on the way home was your face, and how it would destroy you when I told you. I panicked. Alecia said yes. It was shitty. I hurt her, I hurt me in the process, and I hurt you. And I never ever wanted to hurt you."

"Then why did you ask another woman to take my place?"

"Because I didn't care about breaking her heart." He cradles my head in his hands and presses his lips to my cheek. "But I sure as hell care about breaking yours."

"Then don't break it now." I kiss his forehead, his nose, chin, and lips. "You do right by me, Harley Hamilton. You fight like hell, and you win, and then you put a ring on my finger because I've been waiting twenty-five goddamn years to marry my best friend."

Chapter Thirty-One

Rose

In the morning, I hear the key sliding into the door downstairs and I roll over. I don't want to deal with the world today, but apparently the world has other plans, because my mother sings out and I find myself wide awake and blinking up at the roof of our blanket fort.

"Darling, are you awake? I found a handsome gentleman waiting on your doorstep. It's very rude to not answer your phone, Rose."

Oh god, Dermot. I forgot all about our date. Oh shit. Where is my phone?

"Shit." I sit up. The weight of everything that happened settle on my shoulders. I carefully climb over Harley so he doesn't wake, and wrap the sheet around me. I'm wearing a silk chemise that I'd put on last night in order to be comfortable, and Harley, being Harley, never sleeps in anything at all, so though we didn't do anything, I'm still wearing too little clothes to face my mother and Dermot.

I stumble out of the fort and come face to face with Dermot and my mother. Dermot's features are full of concern, but Mom is staring wide-eyed at the blanket fort, because I'm pretty sure she knows what that means.

"Er … hi. What are you doing here?"

"My flight from LA was delayed. No one was flying in or out of SF on account of the fog. I couldn't reach you on your cell."

"Oh, I think it might still be locked in the cool room. Why didn't you try the shop phone?"

"I did," Dermot says, and I know I look guilty. Mom takes a seat in the wingback chair, with a rapt expression, watching our conversation unfold. Harley yawns and rolls over on the bed, causing the blanket fort to sway. "He's here, isn't he?"

"He …" I trail off. My heart squeezes painfully, because even if I tell him that nothing happened between Harley and me last night, I'd be lying. We may not have had sex, but I boxed up what was left of my heart and gave it to Harley for safe keeping. I love him, I've never stopped loving him, and judging by the look on Dermot's face, I've broken his heart in the process.

He shakes his head. "Jesus Christ, I should have seen this coming."

"Dermot, I didn't mean for any of this to

happen," I say, begging him not to turn away from me before I can explain. "We didn't sleep together."

"But you let him back in."

It really isn't a question, but I nod all the same. I feel as if I drive a blade right through his chest. Dermot has a knack for loving women who can't love him back, and I'm just another one who's screwed him over. Though I can feel the controlled anger vibrating off of him, he cups my face in his hands and kisses my temple. "Goodbye, Rose."

"Dermot …" I begin, but what is there to say? I'm sorry? It's not you it's me? They're all just words, and I think he knows that as well as I do.

He walks down the stairs, disappearing from my line of sight. A moment later, the shop door snicks quietly closed behind him.

I exhale a puff of air and glance at my mom. She's looking behind me at the rustling fort. Though I know none of what just happened is her fault, it might have been nice to have a heads up so Dermot wasn't faced with seeing that. I suppose, though, she wasn't to know that I wasn't answering my boyfriend's calls while another man was occupying my bed.

Harley comes up behind me and pulls my back against his front. I'm not entirely sure where his clothes ended up last night, and judging by the way my mother ogles him, raises a brow, and swallows back her smile, he's still completely naked. I glare at my mother, and she finally quits staring long enough to study my expression and clue in.

"Right, well I better get going." She has her phone out, and if she hasn't already, I know she'll be texting Rochelle like a mad woman the second she leaves. "Bye, darlings."

She blows us both a kiss and hurries down the stairs as fast as her Jimmy Choos will take her. I was wrong; she doesn't text, but calls instead, squealing, "It happened, it finally happened," before she's even left the store.

Harley tightens his grip on my waist, leaning down to press a soft kiss on my shoulder. "You okay?

"Yeah, I just … God, it just sucks, you know? Feeling like you're breaking someone's heart."

"I know, love." And I suppose he would. He drags me back to the bed and we tumble into it, almost knocking down the walls of our makeshift house.

"Maybe we're too old for forts and fairytales," I say wistfully, snuggling into his chest.

"No one is too old for fairytales," Pan answers back.

Chapter Thirty-Two

Rose

I wake with Harley's body wedged against mine, his arm around my waist and his head resting on my pillow, and I know he's not sleeping because his breathing is shallow and he's not snoring the roof off of my apartment. I roll over and meet sad blue eyes.

"Morning," I say. He traces patterns over my collarbone and down over my breast, circling my areola. I squirm and bat his hand away.

"What are you doing today?"

"Um, you're looking at it." I stretch in my bed and yawn. Harley's hand slides in between my legs, and I squeeze my thighs tight. He doesn't move against me, just rests there in "his spot". A place to warm his hands, he'd once said. *And drive me crazy.*

He runs his fingers through his hair and makes a fist, waiting until it's just a few inches from my face before he opens his palm and several strands of hair fall onto my floral duvet.

"Oh, Harley."

"I knew it was going to happen. I'm coming up on my third chemo session, so it's kind of a given, and I don't wanna hang onto it just for the sake of it, you know? Why prolong the inevitable?"

"You want me to cut your hair?" I ask, panic rising in my voice.

"Shave it, actually?"

"All of it?"

"Yeah, Rose." He grins and kisses my forehead. "That's usually what 'shave it' means. You think you'll still find me attractive with no hair?"

"Are you kidding? It'll even the playing field for once, and you and I might finally be on equal terms."

"I don't know. I'm pretty fucking handsome with a bald head," he mocks, and I slap at his chest. He winces a little, and I bite my lip, worried I've hurt him.

"When do you want to do this?"

"Now. Only let's get dressed and go over to my place. The two of us won't fit in your tiny bathroom."

I pout, and he pulls me closer. "While we're on the subject of cancer shit, you think you can clear some time in your schedule for me tomorrow?

There are some people I want you to meet."

"Of course."

"Cool. Bring a strong stomach though."

I frown, not sure what he means by that, but I nod anyway. "And don't wear fancy shoes."

"Do you know me at all? I own like one pair of heels and I only bought those for your stupid pseudo wedding."

"Right. For a minute there I thought I was talking to a real girl."

"Fuck you, Hamilton."

"Okay," he says, and rolls on top of me. He swivels his hips. His rigid cock presses against me and I allow him to take me where he wants to, but too quickly he pulls away. "Hair first."

I pout and climb out of bed after him. I don't want to do this. Not his beautiful hair. But cancer doesn't care what we want.

Cancer can go suck a bag of dicks for bringing its shit into our world.

Standing behind Harley, I meet his gaze in the mirror. "Are you sure?"

"Yeah. Just do it."

I tense my fingers around the weight of the clippers in my hand, and switch the gadget on. It vibrates loudly, and my bones ache with my white-knuckled grip.

"Do it, Rose."

I run my hands through the length of his gorgeous hair. Hair that I've tugged in my fingers while his face was buried between my thighs; hair that for so long had been his crowning glory, beautiful—just looking at it made you want to slide your hands through it. For the longest time, Harley's hair has been one of the things I've loved so much about him, and I think I am having a harder time with this than he is.

"Come on, love. Before I lose my nerve."

"Right, sorry." I smile, but inside I'm dying. It's just a haircut, but it represents so much more. On the outside, he doesn't look all that sick; he has deep shadows beneath his eyes from the lack of sleep, and he can't keep up his fitness regime, not the way he used to, so in the six weeks that he's been gone from my life he's lost a lot of muscle mass, making his face look gaunt, but all this aside, you couldn't tell that he had cancer by looking at him. So even though this is just a haircut, it's infinitely more.

I raise the clippers to his head. He doesn't flinch when the blades snip away the first few strands. He doesn't even flinch when the entire back is done. Instead, he turns his head to the side and laughs because he looks like he did that one time in high school when the football team shaved one side of his hair off. He'd worn it like that for a whole week, just to show them how much it didn't matter and how they hadn't rattled him.

I lift the clippers again and begin on the front, and when it's done he pulls me down on top of him and kisses me hard on the mouth. I set the clippers aside on the bathroom counter and run my hands over his freshly shaved scalp, marveling at the unfamiliar spikiness of it, and how it makes his face seem a little rounder, his stubborn jaw a little more prominent, and those beautiful eyes of his gleam.

He pulls away and whispers, "Still sexy?"

"Was there ever any doubt?" I kiss him on the lips again. The few spots where his head is missing hair give him a little bit of an edge. "I like it. All you need now are a handful of tattoos and you'd look like you were straight out of *Prison Break*."

He laughs and shifts beneath me. I leap up off of his lap, frightened that I've hurt him. He stands, sending a torrent of long locks to the floor of his bathroom, and he lifts me onto the vanity, knocking off several bottles of aftershave and beard oil. I swipe at a strand of his hair that tickles my neck. His lips meet mine again, and I cup his face in my hands as he unbuttons my shirt and palms my breast through the lace of my bra.

Harley has said that the chemo only makes him weak in the days after his treatment, and though I want to reconnect with him so badly, I'm unsure if this is the right thing to do. I don't want to stop, not if he's fit enough to keep going, and not if it's one of the last times … *No. I will not think that way.* Harley is going to beat this thing. He promised. Five, ten, twenty years from now we'll be doing this very thing, when our skin is sagging and our faces are crinkled and weathered from a life well lived. He'll take me like this, perhaps in the kitchen of our home, or on the floor, the bed—it doesn't matter where.

"Hey, where'd you go just now?"

"I …" I swallow back the lump in my throat and close my eyes. It doesn't stop the tears from sneaking out of the corners. Harley pulls away, and for a second I think he might leave, so I wrap my legs around his hips and grab his biceps, feeling the strong muscles that have already wasted away so much in just a few short weeks. "You had better fight this."

He rakes a hand over his head, his brow creases with confusion for a beat as his fingers meet no resistance and glide across his now short hair. He swallows hard and glances at the remnants of his hair on the white tiles. "Rose ..."

"No, I mean it. I can't …"

"No more," he says cupping my face and leaning in to place a gentle kiss to my lips. "I need you here with me, not here with my cancer."

"I'm sorry."

He dips his head, so he's looking directly into my eyes when he says, "It's okay. Just, can we just pretend I'm a regular guy and this isn't a pity fuck?"

"This isn't a pity fuck," I say, confused.

"Well, maybe not for you …" He trails off with a grin, and I make a shocked face and slap him on the arm. He flinches and then he leans across the small bathroom, pulls the shower curtain back, and runs the water. "I need us to be here, with one another. I need you to pretend I'm not sick, and that I'm still the guy who had a starring role in all your wet dreams."

"You ass. I never fantasized about you."

"You didn't?" He makes a face. "Jesus, that stings like a bitch, Rose, because I spent every day since my teens jacking off into my sports socks as I thought about your glorious ass bouncing around on my dick."

I slap him again, but this time he catches me mid spanking and runs my hand down his body, shoving it into his pants where his erection presses into my palm. He waits until I meet his gaze before saying, "I need this to be about us."

I nod and slide down off the counter, forcing him to back up a step or two. I pull off my top and let it fall to the floor, and then I step out of my jeans, kicking them into the cabinet behind me. I lift his shirt, and together we pull it over his head and toss it onto the floor with the remainder of his hair. I slide my hands up around his neck as he pulls me into him, and Harley shoves down his jeans, shuffling us toward the shower recess where I help him step out of them. He backs me into the shower and warm water covers us both. Grabbing the shower head, I hose him down, rinsing the hair from his body, running my hands over the smooth expanse of his chest.

He'd told me his body hair started falling out within the first few days of chemo. I've always preferred a little chest hair on men, not a full-out rug or anything, but Harley had always had chest hair and I'd loved running my hands over it when so many other guys waxed it all away. Harley losing his hair is in no way unattractive to me. I've always wanted him, no matter if he gained a hundred pounds or lost all his hair to chemo. I guess that is the definition of true love, isn't it? To love someone exactly as they are, faults and all.

But Harley never had any faults in my eyes, though he does have awful taste in stand-in brides, and he is stubborn as an ox. Once he gets something in his head, there is no swaying him. Kind of like right now, as he pulls me closer and dips his head to kiss my neck. He cups my breasts and takes my nipple in his mouth.

I can already see the fatigue in his eyes, but I don't try to stop him or sway his actions. Instead, I place the nozzle back in the holder and turn the shower off. Taking his hand, I lead him from the bathroom without bothering to dry off. He palms my ass as I walk across the expanse of his apartment. I'm sure there's hair stuck to the bottom of my feet, but I don't care. I climb onto the bed and wait there on all fours, my ass in the air, ready and waiting. Harley groans and slips a finger along the crease. He hovers over me, his erection jutting up against my lower back as he whispers in my ear, "Not that I don't love this view, but I wanna see your face."

I crane my neck back and kiss him. Slow, deep kisses, as if we have all the time in the world. Harley flips me over, slides his hand beneath my back, and moves us up the bed, his hips coming to rest between my thighs. He trails his lips over my neck, kissing my breasts, tugging one of my nipples between his teeth. I slip a hand between us and guide him into me, agonizingly slowly, inch by inch, until his thick cock fills me and he's buried to the hilt. He rocks inside, hitting the very end of me, and I pepper his face and neck with kisses as he keeps this slow and tender pace. I don't know if that's for me or for him, or because he's tired, but I don't care because each time with him is different and new and nothing has ever felt as good as having Harley inside me, as giving myself over to the man I love.

When we're both spent and he's soundly sleeping, I climb out of the bed. I don't want to leave the warmth of his embrace, but I don't want him to have to face another reminder of the way his body is changing when he wakes, so I pad softly into the bathroom and pull together a few strands of his glorious hair. I take an elastic from his bathroom cabinet and tie it off, setting it aside to slip it into my purse when I'm done here. It might seem creepy as fuck, but that hair is as much mine as it is his, and though I love his new shaved look too, this is a part of Harley that I'm not willing to let go of just yet—maybe not ever.

Chapter Thirty-Three

Rose

I walk into the oncology ward holding Harley's hand and see the sick faces smiling back at us. *He doesn't belong here. He's not sick like them*, my mind tells me. *This must be some kind of cruel joke.*

But it's not a joke; there's nothing funny about cancer. Though it seems Harley doesn't agree, because as he walks into the room, he kisses an unenthusiastic nurse, and trades insults with the tall male nurse about Ole Miss's latest ass-whooping from the Tigers. He introduces me to them both and they share a mildly surprised exchange, but I'm guessing they've talked about me and they'd thought that maybe Harley was making me up.

There are several stations set up around the room with recliners and TVs and privacy screens, but no one is in them. The patients all seem to be sitting in a circle on big wingback chairs with IVs in their arms and mobile drips and monitors by their sides. When the nurse tells Harley to go take a seat, to my surprise he doesn't move into one of the makeshift booths, but to the middle of the room with the other patients. It's like we're back in high school again—he's the star quarterback loved by everyone and I'm just, well … me. He knows everyone. Everyone knows him, and apparently everyone knows me too, judging by the way they greet me … and use my name while doing it.

Harley fist bumps a kid who's probably no older than sixteen. He has a gaunt face. He's ashen, and far too skinny with not a single strand of hair on his shiny, smooth head. "Nice hair."

Harley smiles sheepishly and runs a hand over his shaved head. "Thanks. I heard the Chemo Cut was in for the winter."

The boy's eyes settle on me, and then his gaze rolls appreciatively over my body, coming to rest on my boobs. *Seriously?* "Dude, you weren't kidding,"

"Told you she was hot," Harley says with a grin. "Now pay up."

I watch on in horror as the kid lifts a gangly arm and grabs his wallet off the table next to a pile of old *Rolling Stone* magazines with yellowed, doggy-eared pages and ripped covers. He fishes out a twenty and hands it to Harley. My eyes widen. *He did not just take this sick kid's money?*

"Aww, you gonna cry, pretty boy?" Harley taunts, and I smack him hard on the chest. He glares at me. "Ow. What the hell, Rose?"

I just glare back, and give him an *are you freaking kidding me* face. "I bought you something," Harley says, and pulls a long black case from his back pocket. It must have been hidden beneath his sweater, because this is the first time I'm seeing it. There's a logo on the front—*TAINT*, written in a white, bold brush font surrounded by splatters. The kid's face drops, his jaw going slack and his eyes growing wide as saucers.

"No fucking way! No fucking way!" the kid shouts, and the nurse that Harley kissed with a sweet face and—ironically—a very unsweet expression moves away from the nurse's station.

"Language," she says in a booming voice.

The kid covers his face; he still hasn't taken the box from Harley yet. "Carissa, fuck me, do you know what this is?"

The woman in question walks toward us, and the kid snatches the box from Harley, running a reverent hand over the outside of the case before snapping it open. "Looks like drum sticks to me, honey. Ones I'm going to shove where the sun don't shine unless you keep it down. People are trying to stave off death here."

"Holy shit, they're signed." He glances at Harley, who's grinning his Pan grin. "Fuck dude, they're signed by Zed Atwood himself," he crows. "The Grim Reaper can take me now and I wouldn't give a shit because I got to hold Zed fucking Atwood's sticks in my hands."

"Mmmhmm," she says, and turns her back on him. She points to Harley as he sits in an empty seat across from the kid. "This is your fault."

He winks. "Just trying to brighten your day, Carissa."

"Oh, honey, the only thing brightening my day would be getting rid of the lot of you," she says, and I gape at her in horror. "I'll be back in a minute with your pre-med cocktail."

I sit down hard on the seat beside Harley, and he places his large hand on my thigh and gives a reassuring squeeze. The male nurse comes and takes Harley's blood and tells me he's checking to make sure all his white blood cell counts are stable, then Carissa returns with a mobile monitor and a drip attached to it. I stare at the bag; there's a label with Harley's name on it and the prescribed drug, and for a moment I feel as if all the air has been sucked out of the room. I can't breathe, and I can't leave, so I look away as the nurse inserts the line into Harley's arm and presses a series of buttons on the machine.

With a tight smile, I turn my attention back to the kid. He strokes the beaten wood of the drumsticks Harley gave him, and his eyes become rheumy.

"Styx, dude," Harley says. "You know the rules."

He nods, and he looks Harley dead in the eyes when he says, "You're pretty fucking cool, man."

Harley nods, as if this was something he already knew, but there's a tightness to his smile, and his Adam's apple bobs as he clears his throat. "Rose, this is Styx. He's been bugging the shit outta me since my first cycle of chemo."

"We're chemo buddies," Styx says. "It's like fuck buddies, only not gay."

"Just as messy though, right?"

"Only when Jan's here," Styx says, tilting his head toward the elderly woman beside him, who I'd previously thought was sleeping, but quickly realize isn't because she sticks her middle finger up and closes her eyes again.

The boys laugh, and Styx's gaze lands on me again. "I hope you jacked off into a cup before you started chemo, dude, cause your babies would have been like little fucking cherubs or something." I stare at Styx, unable to believe I heard that right. "What is she, mute? What's the matter, darlin'? Cancer got your tongue?"

I glare at Harley. "Is this kid for real?"

"Styx? Yeah, he's kind of a douche." He laces his fingers with mine. "I should have given you a heads up."

"Nah, you're just jealous you ain't all up in this, pullin' bitches and livin' the high life." He laughs, making a lazy hand gesture that encompasses all of him, and then that laughter quickly erupts into a fit of coughing.

"You okay, dude?"

"Yeah," he says, and then grabs the bucket at his feet and vomits into it. His body's reaction is so violent I almost don't know what to do, so I sit here with my hands over my mouth in shock as the male nurse comes over and pats him on the back. Styx flinches away from his touch, and the nurse holds his hands up and checks the drip. "Okay, rock god, you're done anyway. Let's get you back to your room."

Styx nods but doesn't say anything. He just leans back in the chair as the machine beside him is turned off and the line is gently pulled from his arm.

"Rock on, fuckers! See you next time 'round." He waves the box of drumsticks in the air at us, and the nurse wheels him from the room.

I glance at Harley's solemn face and burst into tears. He cups my chin with the hand that doesn't have the line in it and tilts my face up towards him, gently shaking his head. "No, love. There's no crying in this room. This is the only place we get to come and be with other people who know what it feels like to fight this war. There's no crying in here, only assholes, laughter … and sometimes vomit."

"I'm sorry. I can't do this," I say and run through the same doors that Styx just exited. I know Harley can't follow me because he's hooked up to an IV, and I know I'm being selfish, but I can't help it. I can't watch him go through this. I can't watch a sixteen-year-old kid have the life drained out of him and stand there joking as if it isn't happening.

Sick to my stomach, I collapse against the wall, and a beat later Carissa finds me. "You okay, honey?"

"No!" I sob, covering my face with my hands because I feel like a complete pussy. "How do you do that every day?"

She smiles, but it doesn't reach her eyes. "Girl's gotta earn a paycheck."

"It doesn't get to you?"

"Every single one, but that room is the only place they get to walk into and not be crushed by pity. That room is their safe haven. It's the one place they can go to know that they aren't alone, and that everyone in there knows what's going on inside their head. It's why Styx does his chemo without his parents. It's why Harley's been coming here by himself since his cycles started. Because there's no one to comfort. The fact that he's sharing that with you now is huge, so you got two choices, girly—either you dry your eyes and get your ass in there and give him hell for trying to die on you, or you wait out here until he's done."

I nod and swipe my hands under my eyes to dry my tears, and I follow her back inside.

When I enter the room, it's quiet. Harley looks lost in thought, and Jan still has her eyes closed. I take the seat beside him and he grabs my hand and squeezes. I squeeze back, hard.

"You okay?"

"Yeah, I'm just …" I glance at Carissa, who leans against the nurse's station again, watching me with one eyebrow raised. "I'm just hoping you'll hurry up so I can go get a Big Mac."

Carissa laughs. Harley does, too, and then he reaches for the bucket and throws up. *Good thing I'm not a sympathetic puker.*

"With extra cheese," I say, and I don't know whether the tremor that runs through his body is him losing the rest of his guts, or if he's chuckling into his plastic-lined puke bucket. Carissa's howl of laughter practically brings down the roof on our heads, and when she's done, she nods at me and sets about her paperwork.

After we return to his apartment, I put him to bed and climb in beside him, but while Harley falls into a fitful sleep, I can't even close my eyes without seeing him clammy and throwing up, without seeing that kid Styx's face as he held those drumsticks in his hands.

I can't be here right now. So, as quietly as I can, I get up and get dressed and I leave. I head to my parents' place, just a few blocks away, and ordinarily I wouldn't walk through SF at night by myself, but tonight my head's not really in the game.

I bang on the parentals' door. They're asleep, it is close to midnight after all, but I scratch, and I howl and plead for them to let me in.

The front door opens, and I fall into my dad's arms and sob. My mom is there too, stroking my hair, asking me what's wrong, but I have no words for them other than, "What's right?"

So I don't say anything but garbled nonsense. My parents hold me as if I were five years old again. As if this cancer were inside me and not the man I love. Since Harley has finally come clean with me about his illness, Rochelle and Dean have since told my parents. I haven't really talked to either one of them about how I feel. I haven't talked to anyone, because it isn't about me. Now, as I lie on their couch and my dad strokes the hair back from my face as Mom makes me hot cocoa in the kitchen, I allow myself to let out a little of what I've been feeling these past few days. And it's a good long while before I have the strength to tuck it all away inside and ask my parents to take me home.

Dad is the one to drive me back to Harley's. "I know this isn't the life you two wanted. It's not what you should have had, and it's not right that it happened to either one of you. It's not fair," my dad says, startling me as I grab the handle to open the car door. He's a man of few words; he uttered maybe four in the entire time I lay on their couch crying. I twist in my seat to see him better. "If I could take it from you both, I would."

I give him a sad smile.

"You're going to need to be strong for him, pumpkin."

"I know."

"I don't think you do. You need to give that boy a reason not to give up when he's tired and wants to just stay down."

"What?" I ask, uncertain why he's telling me this. It had never even entered my head not to be there for him—I just wish I'd known earlier. I wish I hadn't wasted time being angry at him when all I wanted was to love him, to make him let me in.

"I didn't give her a reason to stay," he whispers, and it takes me a beat to realize he's talking about his sister, who died of MS at the age of twenty-three.

"Dad, you couldn't have saved her."

"I didn't try. I just accepted it, you know? Doctors tell you one thing, and it's almost as if whatever they say is finite. She'll live to twenty and no more, they told us. She lived another three years, but she had more in her. I know she did, just like he does. You make sure he fights for every goddamn second."

"I will," I whisper and squeeze his hand. He pulls me into a hug, and then I step out into the drizzling rain and climb the stairs to Harley's building.

My father waits as I fumble with the keys in the lock and push inside. Bone weary, I climb the stairs slowly and then unlock Harley's apartment and move as quietly inside as I can. The acrid stench of vomit hits my nose, and I swallow back bile. Tomorrow, I'll make sure to bring plenty of flowers from the shop, but for now I take off my clothes and climb into bed beside him. Careful not to wake him, I roll onto my side, giving him my back.

His hand reaches out and pulls me closer. "Where did you go?"

I sigh. "To my parents'."

"Did it help?"

"Yeah, it did."

"Good," he mutters sleepily, and his body

goes lax against mine as his soft snore fills the room.

Sleep still doesn't come for me, and I thank God that Izzy and Ginger are covering the store because I can't fathom having to go in to work and greet customers like this. I laugh silently at myself, as if work matters. As if anything matters when my reason for living is dying of cancer.

Chapter Thirty-Four

Rose

Thanksgiving comes and goes, and we spend the holidays in Carmel, just like every year, although this time it's weighed down with fear and indecision. Everyone tries to act normally, to put away our worries of what the future holds, but it's there in the stolen glances at Harley's face, in our dads conceding their annual argument over whose turn it is to carve the turkey by allowing Harley to do it, and in the way Rochelle breaks down when she thinks we're not looking.

Because the shop is covered and few people in SF are getting married around Thanksgiving anyway, we stay an extra week in the cottage after the parentals have gone home. Harley feels good. We spend time on the beach. We talk about moving to Carmel permanently, about getting a dog and being those people who've left the city and the rat race behind. It's bliss. No hospital, no blood tests, no PET scans, and no chemo. No cancer. At least, that's what we pretend.

But all vacations come to an end, and as we walk through the oncology ward for Harley's next treatment, I have this sick sense of foreboding. These past three weeks my father's words have bounced around in my head, and I've bolstered false courage and pinned it to my chest as if it were armor. I've even thought up several new lines to feed Styx, but when we enter the room the tone is completely off, and even Carissa—who seemed as immovable as a mountain three weeks ago in her demeanor—looks a mess. No one says anything, and I have a terrible feeling I know what is coming.

"Where's Styx?" Harley glances around the room. The quaver in his voice tells me he already knows, just as I do.

"Have a seat, Harley," Carissa says. "I'll get your pre-meds."

"Where is Styx?"

"He's gone."

"Gone as in left the hospital on a day trip or gone as in dead?" His voice is at fever-pitch now.

Carissa just looks at him. She doesn't need to say any more.

"No!" Harley sinks into the chair, burying his head in his hands. "No!"

"Hey," I say, reaching out to him. He knocks my hand away. It stings. He grabs it and presses it to his lips, peppering my fingers with kisses.

"I'm sorry, I'm so sorry." His voice cracks, and then his whole chest shakes. "Fuck! He was just a kid."

"I know," I whisper. I wish I knew what to say. *God, it's just so fucking unfair.*

"Fuck cancer!" he says. This is echoed by Jan, who's sitting in the same spot she was last time we were here.

"Fuck cancer," Carissa agrees solemnly, handing Harley the pair of sticks that he'd given the boy three weeks ago. "His mom thought you should have them back."

"No, they're his. What the hell am I going to do with them?"

"Learn to play the drums and annoy the shit out of him in the afterlife," Carissa says with a shrug, but even her voice is choked with emotion.

"It's a little late to be learning anything," he mutters and lets go of my hand.

Chemo is quiet for the next six hours. It seems everyone feels the loss of this kid, including me, and I met him only once. When we're leaving, Carissa pulls us aside and tells us that Styx's funeral is on Monday, and she expects us to be there. I promise her we will.

In silence, we walk through the hospital. The acrid stench of bleach and sickness makes it hard to breathe, and when I leave Harley at the entrance in order to bring the car around, in a far corner of the parking lot where he can't see or hear, I lose it. I bend double against his truck and gasp in great big lungsful of air, and they're not enough. I choke, devoid of oxygen, suffocating on my grief for what's past and what's to come.

He promised. It'll be okay because Harley promised me he won't give in. He'll fight. He'll win.

The truly terrible thing is that Styx likely promised someone, too. Sometimes, no matter how we try, we can't help but break our promises.

Chapter Thirty-Five

Rose

One week out from Christmas, Harley sits by the window in his apartment, staring out on the cold winter night. It's strange to see him so beaten down by illness. He's sallow, his cheeks sunken, so different from the strong, healthy athlete I've known my whole life.

He's been moody and withdrawn since Styx's funeral, and I haven't been able to shake the feeling that he is just done, with talking, with sickness, and maybe even with me, and that eats away at me as surely as the cancer is eating him.

"Can I get you something?" I dry the dishes and put them away, waiting for a response, but I get none. He just continues looking out the window. "Harley?"

"What?" He turns his attention toward me, his eyes vacant.

"Are you okay?"

"I'm fine," he says impatiently.

I sigh and give him my back, leaning my hands against the counter. I fight back tears because neither one of us has the strength for this tonight.

"Okay," I say on a shaking breath. I'm afraid if I say any more than that, I'll break down.

"I'm just tired, Rose," he says softly, but the words are hollow. "Nuking every cell in your body will do that to you."

"I know." Anger swells within me until it can't be contained, and I go back to putting away the dishes because it actually feels therapeutic to slam things. To make noise and say, *I'm here, and I won't be ignored because it's easier for you.* I'm not sick, so maybe I have no right to judge, but he isn't trying. He isn't opening up to me; he's just switching off. "I've been here, remember? I haven't left your side for a single day, not for a second, and I don't intend to, but I just wish you'd talk to me."

"And say what?" he snaps, causing me to drop the bowl in my hand. It shatters on the floor, and the broken pieces sting my feet as they bounce off the tiles and land around me. "That every day I feel more and more like shit? Do you want to know what's in my head right now? I'm worried I won't make it to Christmas. Fuck, I'm worried I *will* make it to Christmas."

I cover my mouth with my hand to stop the sob escaping but it comes out anyway. "How can you say that?"

"Because, Rose, I'm tired." He closes his eyes, and a tear escapes them. "I'm so fucking tired."

"So you're just giving up? What about fighting? What about beating this thing like you promised?"

"You can't fight a monster that's determined to kill you."

"What are you talking about?" I ask in disbelief. "You have been fighting. You've cut it out. You've done the chemo—"

"And it's spread anyway."

"What?"

"Dr. Hanson called today. I went to see him while you were at work, yesterday. I had another PET scan, lit up like the fucking Rockefeller Centre in December." He runs a shaking hand over his bald head. "It's spread, Rose. It's everywhere."

I can't keep it in any longer. With a cry that rips from my chest and doesn't sound even remotely human, I sit heavily on the ground amongst the broken shards of our crockery and my broken heart. I don't even feel it digging into my flesh until Harley pulls me from the wreckage and grabs the tea towel to stem the blood. "Shh, love. I'm sorry. I didn't mean to tell you like that. I … fuck!"

"You can't leave me, Harley. You promised."

"I know." He presses his lips to my hair and I lean into him, crying so hard that no sound comes out.

"Promise me. Promise me you'll fight." I know it isn't fair of me to demand this. I know he doesn't want to die any more than I want him to, but I can't be the only one fighting for us. I grab his shirt and draw him to me, sobbing into his chest the way a toddler might with a banged up knee. "Promise."

He holds me, but he doesn't promise a thing, because we both know it's one he can't keep.

Chapter Thirty-Six

Rose

"Nine one one, where's your emergency?"

"3920, 24th street. My boyfriend's not breathing," I scream into the phone in a blind panic.

"3920? Okay, what's your name, ma'am?"

"Rose."

"Rose," she repeats, so calm. *Why is she so fucking calm?* "And you say your boyfriend's not breathing—where is he now?"

"He's on the bed."

"He's on the bed. Can you move him to the floor?"

"I don't … yeah, just, oh my god, Harley. Please wake up. Please." I suck in deep breaths and set the phone down as I drag him from the bed. He hits the floor with a thump. I wince.

"Ma'am, ma'am, are you there?" the woman's voice says from the receiver, and I snatch up the phone and put it on speaker.

"I'm here."

"We're already on our way, okay? I'm going to do as much as I can to help you over the phone. Do you know how to do CPR?"

"Yes, my dad's a doctor. Please hurry."

"We're right around the corner. You're doing great, Rose. I want you to start compressions, two fingers at the tip of the breastbone, and I want you to place the heel of your other hand right above your fingers okay?"

"I know. Just please hurry," I beg. I lace my fingers the way my dad showed me and begin compressions, counting to thirty in my head. I breathe into his slackened mouth. "Come on, come on." I repeat this cycle over and over again. *Thirty, two, thirty, two.*

"That's it, Rose, you're doing great. You can probably hear the sirens by now."

"Yeah, I can hear them."

"Just keep performing CPR until they get there, okay?"

"Don't hang up," I say, panicked that those sirens aren't really for us and that I'll be left alone here.

"I won't hang up; I'll stay on the phone with you." The knock on the door startles me, and I cry out. I don't want to leave him. "Can you get to the door and unlock it for the ambulance officers, Rose?"

"I don't wanna leave him."

"I know, but he's in great hands, okay? You just need to let them in."

With salt on my cheeks, I stagger to my feet and run to the door, opening it wide. The paramedics ask me questions as they begin CPR. My brain seems to be on glue, and I can't answer their questions. Now that I'm not the one trying to save his life, I can't do anything but stare at his motionless body and beg him not to leave me.

I hover beside the paramedics and my best friend with my hands gripping my hair, waiting on tenterhooks until the team from the hospital communicates something, anything, to me that makes sense.

"We need to intubate," the female officer says to her partner. I feel sick to my stomach. My head swims. I'm forgotten. I don't know what's happening until they're shoving a tube down his throat and pumping air into his lungs with an Ambu bag.

"Is he breathing?"

"We need to get him to the hospital, ma'am."

"Is he breathing?" I grab her shoulder and force her to look at me.

"Please remove your hand," she says. She's like a robot, no feeling at all. And there isn't anything I can do but watch as they lift him onto a gurney and take him from me.

I feel as if I'm watching this happen to someone else and that it's not happening to me, not to him, not to us. I follow them downstairs, not even bothering to close the door to Harley's apartment, and I stand there completely oblivious to everyone and everything but the ambulance that takes Harley away with lights and sirens flashing.

Mom is opening the shop for me today, so it's no surprise that she's standing across the street wondering what the hell is going on and watching the ambulance drive away. She almost gets hit playing chicken with a car as she crosses the road toward me. "What happened?"

"He stopped breathing." At those words I stop breathing too, or at least it feels like it.

She cradles my face in her hands, forcing me to look at her. "Rose, look at me. He's going to be fine." Mom removes her coat and throws it around my shoulders. "Come on, let's get you dressed."

"No." I pull out of her grasp. "I need to be with him, I need …"

"Sweetheart, it's December. You're standing in the middle of the street shivering in your nightgown. Come and get dressed, get some shoes on your feet, and I'll drive you to the hospital myself."

"I'm scared, Mom. What if he leaves me?"

"Shh, we can't afford to think like that. Now come on, darling girl, pull yourself together. Come and get dressed."

I nod and let her lead me back up the stairs, but I feel panicked the second I set foot across the threshold. They'll be close to the hospital now. I should be there beside him.

I put on the clothes she gathers up for me, and I sit down heavily on the bed. I'm not sure I trust my legs to hold me up. My whole body shakes. I need to move. I need to go—we need to go. But I can't move. I can't think. I stare at the rumpled sheets and make a note to change them because even they smell like sickness and defeat.

"I can't lose him," I whisper.

"I know," she says, squeezing me tightly. Mom's phone rings, and from the end of the line I can make out Rochelle's panicked voice as Mom answers her questions as best she can.

With trembling hands, I attempt to tie my hair back from my face, but I keep dropping the elastic until Mom comes up behind me and takes over. She's no longer on the phone, and she ties my hair and leans down and kisses me on the forehead. "It's time to go, honey."

I nod and follow her down the stairs, remembering to shut the door behind me this time. In another fifteen minutes, we pull up to St. Luke's. I reach for the door handle; I'm shaking so hard it takes three goes before I can get out. I don't wait for Mom to park the car; I can't. I need to know what's happening with him. I need to be with him.

Harley's mom and dad are already here, and I feel a strange sense of guilt as Rochelle races over to me, pumping me for information. *I couldn't help him.* I don't have answers, I only have more questions and blurry memories of what happened. Dean continues demanding answers from the nurse in triage, but we're told to take a seat. The wait is agonizing.

My dad comes straight from his shift at a different hospital and waits with us. He's still wearing his white coat and garners several strange looks from the staff.

Hours later, Harley's doctor comes and tells us that he has a malignant pleural effusion, which my dad explains is a buildup of extra fluid between the lungs and the chest wall. He says they've performed a tube thoracostomy, and thank god Dad is here to explain all these terms in English because if he wasn't, I'd likely kick this doctor's ass ... not everyone went to med school. Dad says he's had a tube inserted into the chest to drain away the excess fluid. He's stable and breathing on his own, but only Rochelle and Dean can go see him.

"What about Rose?" Dean asks. "His girlfriend?"

"I'm sorry. Right now it's immediate family

only," the doctor replies.

I gasp like all the air just left my lungs, because we are family. We've always been family, and it isn't supposed to happen like this. It isn't supposed to be Rose and the parentals; it's supposed to be Harley and Rose. We're a family, he and I.

"Just go," I tell them, because even though it's killing me not to see him, I'd rather at least someone be in there with him instead of arguing out here.

Mom and Dad ply me with coffee and tea, snacks and water, but I want none of it. It has been two hours since Rochelle and Dean have gone into see him, and when they come through the doors from ICU I finally feel as if I can breathe again.

Rochelle puts her arms around me and says, "He's asking for you."

"He is?"

She nods. "First thing he said: 'Where's Rose?'"

Rochelle leads me through the doors into ICU, despite the icy glares the receptionist at the nurse's station throws us.

Harley is in an enclosed room with windows on all sides. I glance at him through the glass and burst into tears. His eyes are closed, his face is pale, and his jaw is slackened with sleep. He has an oxygen tube hooked up around his ears that rests beneath his nose, but at least he's not intubated like he was before. There is, however, a thick tube protruding from the wall of his chest, and fluid slowly drains from it into a collection bag. It's a lot of fluid.

"Maybe I should wait."

"No, honey, go on in," Rochelle says, stroking a hand over my hair.

I open the door and step into the room. The bright lights do nothing for Harley's ashen complexion, and the gauntness of his face frightens me. When I woke this morning he'd looked nothing like this. He'd been bright-eyed and literally standing at attention as we'd kissed good morning. Harley had wanted to make love; I wasn't sure that was a good idea, but it hadn't taken long for him to convince me otherwise. So as he'd complained of a little tightness in his chest, I'd climbed off the bed and gone to the bathroom to freshen up, and by the time I came back he wasn't breathing.

I enter the room as quietly as I can, attempting not to wake him as Rochelle shuffles in behind me. His eyes open just a crack, and his lips tip up in a half-smile.

"Hi," I say, knowing it probably hurts to talk after the intubation tube. "You really scared the shit outta me this morning." I take his hand in mine. He gives it a weak squeeze.

"I'll leave you alone for a bit," Rochelle says and smiles at us both. For the first time, I take a really good look at her face. It's haunted. Dark shadows form under her eyes, which are red and puffy. I know her son was just admitted to the ICU, but there's something she hasn't told me.

"Rochelle …"

"What is it, sweetheart?"

Without knowing what to say, I just narrow my eyes. "You're okay, right?"

"I'm fine, don't you worry about me." She leaves before I can ask any more questions. My stomach sinks. I don't want to think about all the things she's not saying. I don't think I can handle another blow today. I just want this time with Harley, so I hold his hand and I tell him stories of when we were younger, stories he knows by heart because he was there for every glorious second, and the thing that really breaks my heart is knowing that all the glorious seconds of the end will be cut short by about fifty years. He's leaving me. I know that now. And I'm too sad to hide how I feel. I'm raw and broken, beaten down by his illness, and I'm too weak to keep it from him so I drop my head into the palm of his hand and I cry freely.

"Love you … Wendy," he whispers.

"You too, Harley." I don't have the heart to call him by his nickname because I'm too old for fairytales.

"I thought you said you were taking me home," I mutter, as Dad pulls into their drive. I'm not angry. If anything, it's nice to be here in the comfort of my parents and the house I grew up in. I don't think I could stand to be alone tonight anyway. There will be plenty of time for that in my future.

Mom leads me into the house and to the kitchen where she sits me down and makes me tea and grilled cheese sandwiches the way she did when I was a kid. I eat a little, drink a little, and gulp down copious amounts of water to replace the fluids I lost today. There's been an awful lot of crying going on.

As she leads me up to my room, I'm hit with a million different memories of Harley climbing in my window, spooning me in my bed, throwing balls at the wall when I was trying to study, and the most recent memories of us making love before he left for Louisiana.

I climb into the bed I slept in as a kid, complete with the same duvet cover. Mom washes it weekly, even though I haven't slept at home since I moved out. She kisses me on the forehead and tucks me in, turning out the light, but I can't fall asleep because I close my eyes and something isn't right. I glance at the window, and even though I know it's been shut for years, that it's the dead of winter, and that Harley isn't coming through it any time soon because he's laid up in a hospital bed with a disease that's killing him, I pad softly over and open it. A gust of icy air hits me in the face, and I breathe deeply as I stare at his own closed window. I know it means nothing, because neither one of us have occupied these rooms for years, but seeing that window shut up tight is like a slap in the face.

I turn away and climb back into bed, listening to the sound of my parents moving quietly about their house, our house, and I fall asleep finally in the early hours of the morning to the sound of my city waking up.

Chapter Thirty-Seven

Rose

In the morning I go down to breakfast, and my mom falls all over herself to get to me and squeeze me tight. "My darling girl, Rochelle called. Harley's doing much better; there's still a lot of fluid around his lungs but he's sitting up and he's eating a little something. Isn't that wonderful?"

"Oh my god, why didn't you wake me? We have to go."

"No, they're not letting visitors in for another two hours. Sit, have some coffee and something to eat. I made your favorite pancakes with chocolate-chip smiley faces."

I shoot her an annoyed look. "Mom, I haven't eaten choc-chip pancakes since I was twelve."

"Well, you are today."

"I really just want to get to the hospital."

"And do what? Pace like a cat on a hot tin

roof for another two hours?"

"Mom, my boyfriend almost died yesterday. I don't need coffee. I don't need smiley-faced pancakes or a lecture, I just need to see him."

"Honey, there's nothing for you to do there. Besides, I'm driving you, and I want pancakes and coffee."

"I'll call an Uber."

She sighs. "You're not going to let up on this, are you?"

"No, I'm really not."

"Fine, let me get dressed and I'll drive you, but I'm wrapping some of these up to eat while we wait," she says, and shuffles about the kitchen at a snail's pace, gathering enough food to feed us on an expedition through the Congo for an entire year. Once she's filled the thermos and thrown a travel-sized coffee creamer into her purse along with several packets of sugar, she walks to the front door, grabbing her keys along the way.

I can't usher her out the door and into the car fast enough, and then of course she takes her time checking her lipstick in the rearview mirror before I lose all patience with her. "Mom!"

"I'm going, I'm going," she says, giving me a stern look as she puts the car in reverse.

When we make it to the hospital, the nurse tells us we're not permitted to see him because visiting hours don't start for another forty-five minutes. My mother rolls her eyes and shoots me an "I told you so" look. It's the longest period of my life.

When we're finally told we can go through, Rochelle is already in the room. I kiss Harley's cheek and throw my arms around him, mindful of the various tubes and wires attached to his body. "How are you feeling?"

He squeezes my hand. "Like I … went three rounds with … Mike Tyson. You?"

I hate that he's still so out of breath, and I worry that the tube they inserted in his chest wall isn't working, but the collectables bag attached to the line is almost full, so they must have done something right.

I don't want him to see my concern, so I lie through my teeth. "I'm perfect now."

"You've … always been …. perfect."

I chuckle. "And you've always driven me this nuts. Glad to have you back, Pan."

"The boy … who … never dies."

"Let's just keep it that way, okay?" I say, running my hands over his bald head. He nods and closes his eyes, and I don't know if he's just tired or enjoying my touch. "So when can he come home?" I ask this of Rochelle, so Harley won't be struggling for breath to speak.

"It will be at least a week or two, I imagine," Rochelle says, but just like yesterday I know there's something she's not telling me.

"What? What are you not saying?" I glance between them, and then over at my mom.

Rochelle takes a deep breath. "We've discussed it with Harley and his doctors and we've all decided that a hospice is the best choice for him from here."

I reel back as if she just slapped me. "A hospice? No! He's not going there. You go to a hospice to die."

"Rose, it's spread everywhere," Rochelle says quietly.

"So we'll do another round of chemo."

"He isn't going to get better, honey, I wish it were different—believe me I do. But Harley is dying. He knows this, we know this, but you—"

"I know the prognosis isn't good, but there are still things we haven't tried. Clinical trials, stem cell replacement therapy …"

"Rose … no," Harley says, squeezing my hand tightly.

Saltwater spills over my lashes, and I pull my hand from his. "You promised, remember? That day on the trampoline when you kissed me—you said we'd go together. You promised."

"We were … dumb kids," Harley says, and there are tears in his eyes now too. "If I … could … change it—"

"You can. You can choose to fight. Choose

me, Harley. Choose us."

"Honey," Mom says, gently squeezing my shoulder.

"I don't understand why none of you are fighting." I shrug off her embrace and turn on the both of them. "You sit there like it's all just said and done. Do none of you give a shit what happens to him?"

"Rose!" Mom shouts.

"What?" I snap back and see not only is Rochelle in tears, but my mom is too.

"Give us … a minute," Harley says, breathlessly. Rochelle nods, and my mother, who was already standing, takes hold of her arm and they leave the room. I glare at Harley whose soft smile undoes all the rage within me. "Come sit …" I close my eyes and shake my head. "Please."

I cave, pulling the chair closer to the bed so I don't disturb the wires and lines attached to his arm and finger, and the oxygen tube hooked beneath his nose.

He places his hand back on the bed, palm up, and I take it. "I'm not … getting better." I shake my head but he continues talking. "Listen … just listen. I'm not getting … out of here. It's here or a hospice, and I don't want to be … surrounded by doctors and wires. I want … I want the love of my life there when I go."

"Then come home," I beg.

"No … I won't do that… to you."

"Harley …"

"This is … what I want."

"What about what I want?" I search his gaze, seeking even the smallest glimmer of hope in them. There is none. "Don't I get a say?"

"Not … this time." He smiles, and even as tears spill over from his eyes he gives me that teasing grin I've seen a million times. "I'd stay … if I could. I'd stay forever … if I had a choice … just so you didn't have to … go through this."

"I can't do this without you. You're my best friend. How do I get through a single day without seeing you?"

"Done it … before. You'll … manage again."

"You dead is a lot different from living four states away," I snap. Harley flinches and I sob and squeeze his hand. "I'm sorry."

"It's okay … I get it, but you … have to let me go." He winces as he takes a shaky inhalation. "I told you I'd only … break your heart, didn't I?"

"Repeatedly," I agree on a sobbing cry.

"Because you wouldn't listen …" He laughs and I laugh too, but there's no humor in it, just a desperate, pathetic sound because the universe is cruel. God is cruel, and cancer is a fucking bitch.

It isn't time yet. It can't be. There's too many things we haven't done together, too much life we haven't lived—travel, marriage and babies. There's so many things we're yet to do, and time keeps tripping us at every turn. We aren't done yet. *We can't be done yet.* "Marry me?"

He slowly shakes his head. "No."

"Why?"

"Because you deserve more ... than to be widowed at thirty."

"It should be my choice, just like dying is yours."

Harley's face falls. He swallows hard. "Understand something. This is ... not a fucking choice. This is not my choice. I just know when to call it quits and you ... need to learn how to do the same." He squeezes my hand, but it's so weak. He winces, and I know even this tiny movement has caused him pain. "I'm not ever ... getting better, Rose. My organs are ... shutting down; there is no coming ... back ... from that. This is not ... my choice. My choice would be ... giving you the big ... fancy wedding ... you've always wanted."

His breath see-saws in and out of his lungs. I know it's hurting him and I want to tell him to stop, but I can't. It's selfish, I know. But I need to hear these words now in case I never get the chance again.

"I waited too fucking long and now ... there's no time left." Tears fall from his eyes and I lay my head on his palm, and stare up at the face of the man I love. "I squandered … every second I ever had with you because I believed … I was invincible. I believed we had forever … Cancer had other … ideas."

"Then give me what you have left. Please?" I beg on a ragged exhalation. "Please? All I ever wanted from the time I was five years old was to marry my best friend. You can still give me that."

"Rose, no. You deserve better."

"There is no better than that. If this is all the time I have left with you, that's what I want. We can do it right here. This afternoon. All I want is to be your wife, Harley Hamilton."

"You know … it was supposed to be me?"

My brow furrows in confusion. "What?"

"The one … who asked. It was … supposed to be me."

"Yeah, but you kinda suck at doing anything on time," I say. He laughs and then flicks the switch on his morphine drip so I know it's time to let him rest. "Harley, do you … do you think if we had more time that we'd have ever done this?"

"It was always you … I was … supposed to marry."

A choked laugh escapes me. "I thought that would make me feel better, but it doesn't. We both wasted so much time. The biggest mistake I ever made was walking away from you."

"Biggest mistake I ever made … was

watching you go."

"Better late than never … right?"

"Right … I love you, Rose. Even with one … testicle and dying … of cancer … I'm going to be the luckiest … son-of-a-bitch on the face of … the earth."

"Not as lucky as me." I'll be the luckiest woman on the planet until the cancer kills him, but every second I spend as his wife will be equal to a lifetime of happiness.

Chapter Thirty-Eight
Rose

I stand in an ivory taffeta, A-line silhouette vintage dress with three-quarter-length sleeves, button cuffs, and hidden pockets. I love pocket dresses. The dress had been my mother's and it had been hanging in her closet for as long as I could remember. It isn't my dream Vera Wang gown; my feet are not adorned with the beautiful Jimmy Choo *Viola 110* sandals with the white ostrich feather tassels; my hair isn't done up in a messy chignon the way I'd always imagined; and my bouquet isn't one of peonies, roses, and pink astilbe, but a bunch of wilted daisies from the hospital gift shop. It isn't an April wedding at the San Francisco Conservatory of Flowers, and I don't care.

Our parents have been all over this city collecting my dress and shoes, the rings and Harley's suit, which had to be altered by the moms with a pair of scissors from the nurse's station to accommodate for his thoracostomy tube. Dean had even bribed a Justice of the Peace he knew with tickets to the next Mariners game if he'd marry us in a hasty bedside ceremony.

"Rose, repeat after me," our new favorite Justice of the Peace began.

Harley's hand shoots out to grasp mine, and I snap my gaze toward him in surprise. "You don't … have to … do this."

I smile and nod. "I don't have to, but I want to."

The celebrant gives us a gentle smile and says, "Shall we proceed?"

I nod.

"With this ring, I thee wed."

"With this ring, I thee wed." I place the ring on Harley's finger and recite my vows after the preacher, then when it's time for him to do the same, he fumbles. He pushes the ring on my finger, and I try not to cry at how weak he is, how fragile those large, beautiful hands that used to hold me and bring me to the brink of pleasure with a few sure, steady strokes have become. I bite my lip; it's all I can do to keep from breaking in front of him, and I don't want that for today. I don't want that for him, and even though we're standing in a hospital room, I don't want my memories of this day to be tainted by how sick he is.

So I smile wide, and the tears fall anyway,

but I don't give them time for their grief. There'll be time for that in the days, months, and years to come, but not now. Not today.

"I now pronounce you husband and wife. You may kiss the bride," the JP says, and this Harley has strength for, even if his breath fails him before he can deepen the kiss and he has to pull away, abruptly sitting down on the edge of the bed.

"Harley," I say, concern twisting my voice.

"I'm okay, love." He squeezes my hand and tells me not to fuss.

"Congratulations, darlings." Mom comes forward and envelopes me in a hug as Dad and Harley's parents congratulate him, and I grin like an absolute fool because though I'm afraid of what's to come, I just married my best friend, the love of my life. It wasn't the wedding I'd always dreamt of, but it is the happiest day of my life, just like I knew it would be.

The nurse ushers everyone else out a few minutes after we say I do. She wants to check his vitals, and is worried the excitement was too much, but I think she knows our time is precious, and as much as I love our family, I want to soak up as much time as I can with my new husband.

Harley is in a private room now, out of the ICU, but the fluid on his pleural cavity seems to be increasing despite the nurses attempts to drain it with the thoracostomy tube. The nurses have wheeled another bed into his room so I can lie beside my husband on our wedding night. There will be no honeymoon for us, no consummation of our marriage, but it doesn't matter. All that matters are our joined hands and tender touches, and stolen kisses between ragged breaths. My tears finally come in a torrent, and his do too, because that's the way we've always been—when we're not driving one another mad, we are so crazy in love it hurts like hell.

Now, he wipes away the tears that fall thick and fast down my cheeks. "No more tears … for me, Rose … my beautiful … wife."

I smile at the sound of that. "Okay." I nod, but I think we both know I don't mean it.

"To die would be an awfully …"

"Don't," I plead, covering his lips with my hand.

He leans forward, kissing my forehead, and I close my eyes. "When I'm gone … I want you … to find someone else … to love."

I scowl at him. "What?"

"Not now. Give it … at least a month …

before you … take my … ring off your finger." He laughs, but it's a broken sound. "Find someone to love, Rose. Find someone … who'll give you the kind of life … I wish I could give you. Find someone who'll steal your heart … and not break it the way I have."

"You haven't—"

"Not yet, but I will. When I go it'll be as if … I've reached in … and pulled that beautiful heart … right out of your chest. I know it … you know it. But when … I'm gone, I want you to find a man … who'll put those pieces back together."

"I don't want to talk about this." I shake my head. "Please, I can't talk about this."

"Promise me."

"No."

"Rose … I need you to."

"Fine, I promise, but I won't ever love him the way I loved you."

He smiles then, not smug but sadly as he says, "I know. I wish I … could thank him, whoever that lucky bastard is. I kind of want to … punch him, too, for touching … my wife, but … I want to see you happy again and loved."

"I am happy."

"If you could … see your face right now … you'd know that's not true, but you will be one day. Whether it's five months … or five years from now, you will … be loved, Rose, and that lucky … son-of-a-bitch doesn't know … how much I hate him right now, but you tell him … Will you do that for me?"

"Harley?"

"Please? Tell him that I loved you first … and that he better take care … of you. He better take every opportunity … to love you right, because the man that would give anything for you … never got the chance. Tell him that if I could … I'd move … heaven and earth to be the one to … hold you every day. I'd go through a thousand cancers … for the chance to stay, but I can't. So … you tell that lucky son-of-a-bitch that … I loved you first, and that he better fucking treat you right … or I'm gonna preform … some poltergeist crap like he's never seen."

"I will. I'll tell him." I'm gasping for breath so hard that I can't breathe, I can't see through my tears.

Harley wipes his thumb across my cheek and smiles. "Don't cry … It's your … wedding day."

"Then stop making me," I say. He nods and tucks my head under his chin. He reaches for the dial on his morphine drip but misses, so I move it closer for him. He drifts in and out of sleep for a while, and I hold him as closely as I can without disrupting his rest or the oxygen tube over his face.

"Love you … Wendy," he whispers, when I

think he is asleep. "From now until … the end of forever."

"Forever is an awfully long time."

"Yes, it is."

Chapter Thirty-Nine

Rose

My husband, Harley Hamilton, died in his sleep at 3:23 a.m. We'd been married exactly twelve hours and they'd been the best and worst hours of my life. A flurry of medical staff entered the room, but their attempts to resuscitate him failed and the doctor called his time of death twelve minutes later. I climbed back into the bed beside him and lay there for some time, studying his face. I didn't see the way cancer had ravaged his body, but instead I saw the way he'd always been to me—beautiful, golden skin, high cheekbones, a stubborn jaw and lips that I wanted to kiss forever. Perfect in every way. He'd always been perfect. He was the love of my life, and now he is gone, and despite what I told him, I knew I lied. I won't tell any man those things he asked, because I'll never love any man enough to let him take the place of my husband.

I kiss his lips, lingering there, feeling how

soft and yet how cold they are already. I kiss his forehead, and every finger on his cancer-ravaged hands before I get up and I take my leave of him. I leave his body in the same hospital I'd married him in just twelve hours earlier.

I walk through the streets across town, disoriented, heartbroken, and completely shattered. I walk and walk until I make it back to his apartment. I let myself in, and I sink to the floor where I fall apart.

It's another hour or more before I crawl across the wooden floors and climb into his unmade bed. It smells so much like him still, though he hadn't been here for a week. Everything here smells like him, so I wrap myself in the sheets and pretend they're his arms, and I cry.

In one day, I've married and lost my best friend, the only man I've ever loved, the only man I'm likely to ever love. I lost everything, and I don't expect to ever be whole again.

Harley is dead, and I plan to spend the rest of my life here in this bed, *his* bed. I don't need anything else because everything I loved is gone, and this is the closest I'll ever get to him again. The boy who stole my heart as surely as the real Peter Pan had stolen Wendy's; the boy who was my salvation and my savior, my torment and my hero in every sense of the word, is gone.

Pan finally grew up, and the world is a

lonelier place because of it.

Chapter Forty
Rose

Three months on

The weight of losing my best friend still crushes me every day. I haven't left his apartment to sleep in my own because there isn't anything of him in there, and there is so much of him here. Too much, but I can't bring myself to get rid of a single thing. Neither can Rochelle and Dean, so while it probably isn't the healthiest option, we all go on living as though Harley were just out of town on a job.

The episode of My Wedding Affair aired last month and mom wanted to host a 'Darling Buds TV Debut' party, but I couldn't bring myself to watch. I knew I wouldn't cope seeing him alive and healthy, smiling that perfect Pan grin as I jumped into his arms—I was barely hanging on as it was. Instead, I put on his favorite sweater, got blind drunk and fell asleep in his closet, surrounded by clothing that still smells like him.

Mail addressed to Harley arrives every few days, and I don't think much of it. Except for the thick, heavy envelope that I hold in my hand. It's marked confidential, and has no return to sender. I don't know if I am supposed to open my husband's mail after he's deceased or not, but I often do to fix up certain accounts he has with his landscaping business or letters from his tax agent. I figure the police can come arrest me if they need to, but I'll be damned if they are cutting off my cable. *Say Yes to the Dress* is in its fourteenth and best season, after all.

Picking up the letter opener I'd bought Harley for Christmas one year, I jam it in the side of the envelope and jimmy it open. I stare at the letterhead and frown. I don't understand it, and my gaze darts across the page, swallowing up words that don't sink in until my third read through.

Dear Harley,

We are writing to inform you that the sperm deposit we have frozen and stored in our facility is almost due for re-entry into our systems. Please advise us if you wish to continue to rent space in our freezers within fourteen days of the issue date of this letter. Failure to do so will see the specimen destroyed.

Kind Regards,

San Francisco Bay Fertility Clinic.

My hands shake as I read the letter over and over again, and I sit down hard on the bed. Then I read it once more and just stare at the page with tears streaming down my face. He never mentioned anything to me about this, but I suppose he made the deposit before he began chemotherapy. And that hurts. God does that hurt, because I had always dreamed one day of having babies with that man, but not like this. I don't want them like this, so forgetting how late it is, I pick up the phone and dial the number on the letterhead.

Three rings later, it switches over to an automated message telling me to leave my name and number and that they'll return my call during business hours. I don't bother to leave a message. Instead, I throw my phone on the bed and stare at the now crumpled piece of paper in my hand. Then I tear it into a million pieces and sink onto the floor beside the bed. The hollow ache in my gut returns, the one I've tried so hard to ignore for so many weeks now. It's back, and it is as real as it was the day he died. I am as raw, as exposed as I had been the day he left this Earth, and I hate him for it all over again.

"Why did you leave me?" I cry to the empty room, but as usual, as expected, I get no response. He isn't here with me the way everyone always says the dead will be. That "I'll stay with you forever; I'll always be with you in spirit" is bullshit. He isn't here, he is gone, and nothing will ever bring him back. The hole in my stomach will never heal because I am empty. I am incomplete. Hell, without Harley I'm not even a real person. Just a drone. A shell. The empty husk of a woman who lost the will to do anything the day her husband died. And even worse is that I'm okay with this. That's the truly heartbreaking part of it all—that it wasn't just Harley who died that day. I died right alongside him.

Chapter Forty-One

Rose

Two days later, I'm at the shop getting ready to close up when the bell above the door rings. I sigh and come out of the cool room to find a bike messenger standing, waiting impatiently for me to serve him. "Can I help you?"

"Yeah, you Rose Perry?"

"It's Hamilton, now, but yes, my maiden name is Perry."

"Delivery."

I shake my head. "I didn't order anything."

"Look, lady, I don't ask who does or doesn't order the shit I deliver. All I know is I've got to get up Market Street before six p.m. So if you're Rose Perry, sign the goddamn form."

"Fine," I say, making a grabby gesture for his pen-pad thingy. "I know you're just delivering the packages, but it wouldn't kill you to be nice."

He raises a brow and pops his chewing gum

at me as if he were a bored teenager. "Have a nice day."

I roll my eyes and follow him to the door, slamming it closed and flipping the lock to ensure no one else comes in. I turn the open sign to closed and pull down the small blind over the door. Then I tear into the package. There's no note, but when I reach into the small satchel I pull out a clear DVD case. I stare at the blank disc and hope I didn't wind up the unlucky recipient of the video from *The Ring* as I climb the stairs to my apartment.

I work downstairs every day, but it feels like forever since I've been here, as evidenced by the thick layer of dust on the TV cabinet. I pop the disk in the DVD player, locate the remote, and stand in front of the TV, waiting for something to happen.

The screen flickers a few times, and then I'm met with Harley's face. A guttural cry escapes me, and I cover my mouth and sink to my knees, crawling closer to the screen. He looks good, full faced and not with the gaunt gray complexion he had the last month before he passed.

"Hey, Rose," he says, giving me a smile and a small wave. "So, if you're watching this it means I'm no longer there to torment you. Sorry about that. I told you blue balls would eventually kill me." He laughs at his own terrible joke. Tears stream down over my hands that are pressed so tightly to my face I can't breathe.

"So here's the deal. Right now you're likely filming your episode of *My Wedding Affair*, and me? Well, I'm currently in a hospital room about to have a testicle removed. I gotta say, I kind of wish you were here to hold my hand, but I didn't know how to tell you, and I didn't want to take away from your big day, so here we are, you at the shop and me in a hospital gown that shows my bare ass to the world. I may or may not have mooned my nurse." He waggles his eyebrows and chuckles. I clutch a hand to my chest because that simple gesture hurts so much.

Harley exhales a long, drawn-out breath. "Anyway, I don't know what happens after this. I don't know if I'll come clean or if I'll keep this to myself and hold out as long as I can—all I know is that I love you. I've loved you since we were five years old, and you pushed me over in the sandpit. Last night was … it was everything. It always has been everything when I'm with you." He wets his lips and glances down at his hands in his lap. I've seen him do this a million times, and yet I watch with rapt fascination as if it's the first.

"I've made a lot of mistakes along the way, but loving you was never one of them. So, if you're watching this and I did in fact die, I'm so sorry, love." He tears up, and mine spill over as I press my hand against the screen to stroke his face. "The good news is that a little earlier today I jerked off into a cup, they wanted to make sure I had a backup plan for populating the earth with teeny tiny little baby Harleys in case the problem arose and I didn't get my swimmers back after chemo, so ... San Francisco Bay Fertility Clinic are holding my sperm hostage until you decide if you want a couple of rug-rats with me." He scratches at his stubble.

"Fuck, I didn't think this would be so hard. I know this is crazy—believe me, I'm not even sure you'll talk to me again after the way I'm about to shut you out, but you have to know I didn't do it to hurt you. I did it to free you of me. Because I can't stand the thought of you being alone for the rest of your life if I don't make it through this. So there it is, my sperm are waiting for you to rescue them." He laughs. "Jesus, that sounds sick, doesn't it? If I had it my way we'd do this the old-fashioned way and you never would have seen this video at all, but I don't know if I'll get my way." He shakes his head and glances down at his hands that rest in his lap. "Maybe it's selfish, a last-ditch effort to immortalize myself in your life forever, a way to tie you to me for good, but either way, it's there, even if I'm not."

He huffs out a deep breath and clears his throat. "Well, I gotta go. Some asshole's about to bust one of my nuts, and I wish I could say I wasn't shaking in my fucking boots, but I am." His brow creases, his eyes brim with tears, and he wipes them away with the back of his hand. "Just know that I love you, I have always loved you, and I always will. And if you do end up watching this and I am in fact dead, I'll be waiting, Wendy. Second star to the right. I'll be waiting."

The screen goes black and I stare at it for entirely too long, and then I grab the remote and play it again, just so I can see his face and hear his voice. It isn't the same as having him here, far from it, but I spend the night lying on the floor beside the TV replaying the disc over and over, and I imagine he's here with me, until finally, with his words in my ears and my heart as ruined and raw as it'd been the day he'd died, I climb into my bed alone.

In the morning, with a clear head and a heavy heart, I make a decision that will change my life forever, but there really isn't another choice to make. My friends and family may see it as not moving forward with my life, but for me it is a gigantic step forward—it isn't wallowing in the past, stagnant and unchanging, but a step toward the life I've always wanted with Harley, only with one crucial element missing: him.

Epilogue
Rose

Six years later

"Peter, watch out for the little girl," I shout across a busy park.

"Jane, be careful," a voice says as the kids collide in the sandpit and go down in a heap of tears and flailing limbs. Peter gets to his feet and offers the little girl a hand. She takes it and he pulls her up, only when she's standing, and her pale pink dress is all smoothed out by her chubby little fingers, she turns on him.

"You douche canoe!" she shouts, and shoves my son back. He lands on his ass and I catch my breath, because instead of arguing or shouting back at her, he smiles, and for a second my heart stops. He's so much like his daddy that for a moment I'm struck dumb.

For a beat too long, I'm glued to the spot, and then I find myself running toward them, just as a man on the other side of the sculpture shouts, "Jane, no!"

I bend over and help Peter to his feet. I

brush the sand from off his arms and give him a onceover. "Are you okay, honey?"

"I'm so sorry," the man says from behind me, and I still because I know that voice. "Rose?"

Heat claws at my cheeks because I'm bent double, my ass is up in the air and I'm really hoping that this is not how he recognized me. Slowly, I straighten and turn around to face him. "Dermot, what are you doing here?"

There's a little more gray in his hair now, a few fine lines around his eyes, but he's still as handsome as ever as he gives me that charming smile. "We were just killing a few hours in the park."

"I see that. And who is this?" I ask, gesturing to the little girl holding tightly to his jeans.

"This is Jane. My niece." He gives her a tap on the shoulder and a stern look. I remember being on the receiving end of that expression a time or two, and it still manages to pull a thrill from me. He prompts, "Who is very sorry she pushed your boy over."

"Sorry," Jane says, sounding anything but.

"That's okay," Peter says, and I run my fingers through his soft, sandy blond curls.

"And who is this?" Dermot asks.

"This is Peter, my son."

His smile dims just a little. "I didn't know

you were married now."

I nod again. "Going on six years."

"He's a lucky man," Dermot says. My face crumples, and I swallow back the sting of tears as they prick my eyes. Six years later and it still doesn't get any easier.

"He was, and I was an even luckier woman," I whisper, more to myself than to him. Dermot's brow furrows and his eyes search mine. He opens his mouth, but I shake my head and silently plead with him not to say it. He glances at Peter and nods, and I give him a tight smile. "Well, we better get going."

"Of course," Dermot says, resting his hands on his niece's little shoulders. "It was really great to see you, Rose."

I smile. "You too."

I take my little boy's hand and lead him from the park. He walks along the sidewalk and hums to himself, and I wrap my sweater around me to ward away the January chill surrounding this city.

Peter stops walking and glances up at me. "Mom?"

"Yeah, honey?"

"Was that man my daddy?"

I stop and look at my son, getting jostled from behind as pedestrians shuffle past us. "No, sweetheart. Harley is your daddy."

He chews his bottom lip and stares at his feet with a troubled expression. "I know, but you looked at him the way you sometimes do with Daddy's pictures."

I let out a nervous laugh. "Dermot's an old friend."

"Are you gonna marry him?"

"No, Peter."

He grabs my hand and squeezes. "It'd be okay if you did. Get married, I mean. I don't want you to be alone."

"I'm not alone, silly. I have you."

"Yeah," he agrees. "I bet you were real lonely before I came along."

I wince, because he's right, I was, but I'm not any longer. I take a deep breath and swallow back my sadness.

"I was; my heart was broken." I crouch down and cup his face in my hands. "But you, little man, you fixed it." He places his chubby little fingers over my own and smiles. It's heartbreakingly familiar, and I'm teleported back in time thirty years to a different playground in this city, when a boy first grinned at me in that very same way and it took me but a second to fall in love with him.

I lean forward and kiss Peter's hair, and I take his hand and begin walking home through the streets of the city I love. A city that is filled to bursting with memories of a tawny-haired boy with aquamarine eyes and the girl next door who loved him. "Now come on or we'll be late. Grammy Evelyn's cooking dinner, and Grammy Rochelle is making that chocolate dessert you like."

"Mom," Peter says. "I kind of liked her hair."

"Whose?" I stare down at him in confusion. "Grandmas?"

"No, Jane's. She had princess hair. Maybe I can sneak into her window like Pan and steal her away to Neverland."

"Well," I say with a quiet laugh. "It would be an awfully big adventure."

Acknowledgements

To my darling non-husband Ben, you are my EVERYTHING! Thanks for being my confidante, my soul mate, my sounding board, my "Pan". You see a side of me that not everyone else gets to see. When I'm stressed and broken, deliriously tired and cackling like a crazy person or sobbing so hard I can barely breathe because of what my characters are putting me through, you are there through all of it. You remind me to laugh, and breathe and you kick my bum when I feel like I can't keep going, and I'm forever grateful. Seriously though, read my damn books already!

Ava Rose and Ari Danger, I love you more than the sun, and more than the stars, and more than the moon, and more than mars, and WAY MORE THAN ... CHICKENS!

To my gorgeous family both blood and extended, I LOVE YOU!

To my beautiful beta readers Ali Hymer, Kristine Barakat, and Kristina Zolnar. You girls rock my freaking world! Each of you are so valuable to my beta process and I'm honored to have your eyes viewing my words before the rest of the world. Thank you for being so patient with me, and for your willingness to drop whatever you were doing and read more chapters. I cannot thank you enough. I'm sorry I made you all cry … okay, not really. Mwhahahaha, I made you cry! ;)

Lauren McKellar from McStellar Editing, thank you for pushing me to give a little more, I couldn't be happier with how this book turned out and a huge part of that is thanks to you and your thorough editing eye.

To the ridiculously talented Hang Le, this cover! This cover is LOVE! I can't even with how creative you are. This is by far my favorite book cover. It's a joy to work with you, and I'm so glad I can finally hold this beauty in my hands, place it on my shelf and stare at it all day long. Don't ever leave me … because I will find you. ;)

Heartfelt thanks to Be Designs for the awesome formatting. You, sir, are a superstar. Here's to many more beautiful interiors together.

To my Sugar Junkies, who give me so much love and support and who constantly promote my work without ever having to be asked. THANK YOU! You girls are the reason I continue to write, and I can't tell you what it means to read your reviews and kind words and know that someone out there loved something I created.

To the lovely ladies of The Rock Stars of Romance, thank you for hosting the Harley & Rose blog tour. You girls have supported me from my debut novel right through to the tenth, and I'm so honored to be one of your rock stars.

And finally a huge, heartfelt THANK YOU to the readers, bloggers and fellow authors who read, support, pimp, review, and who follow me faithfully no matter which genre I write or how much I make you cry. Without you the stories in my head would just be tales I tell myself that would likely have me committed.

Books by Carmen Jenner

Welcome to Sugartown (Sugartown Series #1)
Enjoy Your Stay (Sugartown Series #2)
Greetings from Sugartown (Sugartown Series #3)
Now Leaving Sugartown (Sugartown Series #4)
KICK (Savage Saints MC #1)
TANK (Savage Saints MC #2)
REVELRY (Taint #1)
Finding North
Toward the Sound of Chaos

Coming Soon

The Way Back Home
The Trouble With Us
CLOSER (Taint #2)
HURT (Taint #3)
JETT (Savage Saints MC #3)
GRIM (Savage Saints MC #4)
KILLER (Savage Saints MC #5)

About the Author

Carmen Jenner is a thirty-something, *USA Today* and international bestselling author.

Her dark romance, KICK (Savage Saints MC #1), won Best Dark Romance Read in the Reader's Choice Awards at RWDU, 2015.

A tattoo enthusiast, hardcore makeup addict and zombie fangirl, Carmen lives on the sunny North Coast of New South Wales, Australia, where she spends her time indoors wrangling her two wildling children, a dog named Pikelet, and her very own man-child.

A romantic at heart, Carmen strives to give her characters the HEA they deserve, but not before ruining their lives completely first … because what's a happily ever after without a little torture?

www.carmenjenner.com
www.facebook.com/CarmenJennerAuthor
www.twitter.com/CarmenJAuthor
www.goodreads.com/CarmenJennerAuthor
www.amazon.com/author/carmenjenner

CPSIA information can be obtained
at www.ICGtesting.com
Printed in the USA
LVOW08s1947081116
512148LV00015B/784/P